CAN'T FIGHT THE FEELING

CAN'T FIGHT THE FEELING

Nashville Dreams
Book Three

Sandy James

**FOREVER
YOURS**

New York   Boston

Copyright © 2018 by Sandy James
Excerpt from *Can't Walk Away* copyright © 2017 by Sandy James

Cover design by Brian Lemus
Cover image © Shutterstock
Cover copyright © 2018 by Hachette Book Group, Inc.

Forever Yours
Hachette Book Group
1290 Avenue of the Americas, New York, NY 10104
forever-romance.com
twitter.com/foreverromance

First published as an ebook and as a print on demand: May 2018

Forever Yours is an imprint of Grand Central Publishing. The Forever Yours name and logo are trademarks of Hachette Book Group, Inc.

The publisher is not responsible for websites (or their content) that are not owned by the publisher.

The Hachette Speakers Bureau provides a wide range of authors for speaking events. To find out more, go to www.hachettespeakersbureau.com or call (866) 376-6591.

ISBNs: 978-1-4555-9564-8 (ebook), 978-1-4555-9565-5 (print on demand)

Lexi Smail, my editor, got me back into the swing of writing after all the changes in my life. This one's for you, Lexi.

ACKNOWLEDGMENTS

This book was very special to me because of the topic of Alzheimer's disease. My father suffered from Alzheimer's, and I'll never be able to thank my sister, Susan, enough for all she did in the last years of Dad's life. She is an amazing sister, a fantastic nurse, and someone I am blessed to share my life with.

My critique partners can never receive enough praise for the great job they do for me. Thanks, Cheryl Brooks, Nan Reinhardt, and Leanna Kay. Love you ladies to the moon and back.

My agent, Danielle Egan-Miller, and her assistant, Clancey D'Isa, do so much to keep my writing moving forward. Thanks, ladies!

The last three years of my life have been, to put it politely, hell. If not for the love and support of the faculty and students at Greenwood High School, I would have struggled to make it through the days. Thanks to all of you for the kind words, the nice messages, and the daily pats on the back.

CHAPTER ONE

The last place in the world Russell Green wanted was to find himself was here.

He hated the smell of hospitals. Disinfectant and misery. It didn't help that there was nobody there for him to bitch at about his dilemma. The restaurant's evening shift manager, Ellie Foster, had made sure he was checked in at the emergency room before she'd hightailed it out of there to get back to Words & Music, too busy to wait around long enough for Russ to see a doctor.

Since his bleeding had all but stopped, he didn't want to stay a minute longer. Unfortunately, a nurse had already taken his vitals, had a good look at the gash in his forehead, and led him back to a treatment room. He figured he might as well get the treatment, because the hospital was going to charge him now anyway.

He dutifully sat on the gurney despite the nearly overwhelming desire to flee. Before the nurse had left, she'd taken the dirty wad of tissues he'd used to stanch the bleeding and handed him gauze to keep pressure on the wound.

"I'm fine now. Really," Russ insisted when the nurse peeled off her gloves, tossed them in the trash, and headed back to the sliding door.

She frowned at him. "You're definitely gonna need stitches, Mr. Green. You want that wound to heal well, don't you?" Instead of waiting for his answer, she said, "Be sure to keep a little pressure on that until the doctor gets in here."

"I could just superglue it," he insisted. God knew he'd done that before. More than once.

"The wound's too large for that to work." A knowing smile blossomed on her face. "The doctor will give you lidocaine, so you don't have to be afraid of stitches."

Russ had to resist the urge to growl at her incorrect assumption. "I just need to get back to work." A lie. Jorge, the head bouncer who was on duty, could handle the Saturday-night crowd at Words & Music without him, and he didn't want the nurse to think he was some kind of coward.

"We're busy tonight," the blonde assured him. "But it won't be much longer." She looked deeply into his eyes. "Still no dizziness?"

"I don't have a concussion," he insisted. "I barely got winged by that bottle."

"You had a blow to the head. I'd expect a concussion screening at the very least. Better to be on the safe side."

"It wasn't a *blow*. Just grazed me."

The phone in her pocket started ringing. A quick check of the screen brought a frown to the nurse's face as she answered, "Francie. ER." After a litany of "yes" responses, she ended the call and shoved the phone back into her pocket. "Hang tight. Someone will be in shortly." She pointed to a white remote resting on the patient table. "You can watch TV if you'd like." Then she skirted around the curtain, opened the sliding door, and pulled it closed behind her.

Russ scowled at the empty room.

His head throbbed, but pain never fazed him much. A couple of aspirin would take care of that, maybe with an added shot of Jack Daniel's. If his blood hadn't been pouring so freely from the wound, he wouldn't have bothered to come to the hospital. Ellie had taken one look at his bloody face and freaked. The only way he'd been able to get her to stop worrying was to agree to let her bring him to the ER.

The emergency room? For a small gash on his forehead?

He was made of tougher stuff than that. Shit, he'd broken his nose on the football field. Twice. And both times, a trainer only popped it back into place and let Russ get right back in the game.

The door opened, and when the curtain was swept aside, he was surprised to find a familiar and very pretty face.

He grinned. "Well, what a surprise. How you doin', Josie?"

* * *

Joslynn Wright took one look at Russell Green and frowned. The name was familiar, but until she'd seen his face, she hadn't made the connection. This man was a partner in Words & Music with her best friend Savannah's husband, Brad Maxwell.

She'd only met Russ twice—at Savannah and Brad's wedding rehearsal and at the wedding itself. Three times if she counted that he'd seen her finishing a swim workout the day of the rehearsal. When Savannah had introduced them, he'd immediately given her the nickname Josie, something she found a bit endearing. Most people called her Jos or stuck with Joslynn.

"I'm doing well, Mr. Green." She pulled two purple gloves from the box on the wall and snapped them on. Then she gently removed the soiled gauze to see what brought him in. She'd read Francie's notes and knew he'd been hit in the head with a beer bottle. No surprise to find that the man had a rather nasty gash running along his hairline. "It would seem you're not quite as well."

Russ shrugged before he grinned. "It's only a flesh wound."

In all her years as first a nurse and now a nurse practitioner, she'd heard that Monty Python quote more times than she could count. It normally irritated her.

So why did she find it so cute coming from him?

The dimple. That was the difference. The man had the most delectable dimple on his left cheek. In fact, the whole package was rather attractive, something she'd noticed the first time she'd seen him. His body was no stranger to a gym, judging from the definition in his arms, the lean hips, and the firm thighs. She loved that he wore his blond hair in a short buzz cut. It suited him—and it would, of course, make closing the wound easier.

That thought made Joslynn stop gazing at Russ like some girl looking for a date to the prom, something very unlike her. She had a job to do. He'd come here for help, and she needed to remember that she was a professional. "Since we're acquainted, I could get another person to treat you."

He stared at her. "Why would you do that?"

"Some people find it uncomfortable to be treated by a person they know."

Russ scoffed. "Savannah said you're the best nurse she knows. Why would I want someone else?"

"Nurse practitioner," she couldn't help but say.

"Not the same thing?"

She shook her head, resisting the urge to set him straight on how hard she'd had to work to become an NP. The guy didn't deserve a lecture simply because he'd pushed one of her buttons.

"What's the difference?"

Since he'd asked with a tone of curiosity rather than condescension, she answered. "I'm not a doctor, but I do have a lot of the same privileges. I can see patients pretty much the same way, and I can write scripts." She opened some fresh gauze, gently pressed it against his cut, and offered him a smile. "And I can stitch up wounds."

He took over holding the gauze in place. "Thanks for taking care of this, Josie."

With a nod, she said, "Let me get a few supplies and we'll get you patched up." She peeled off her gloves and dropped them in the trash. Then she pumped a bit of hand sanitizer from the wall dispenser and rubbed her hands together. "I'll be right back."

Sweeping aside the curtain, she left through the sliding door.

* * *

Russ let out a sigh of relief. After all of Savannah's lush praise, Josie was sure to do a good job patching him up.

The door slid open with a whispered swish, and she strode

back in, arms full of packages. She set them on a silver tray and moved it closer to his bed. Then she handed him a folded light blue garment. "Instead of having you change into a gown, I figured you might like a scrub shirt."

"Thanks. That's very considerate." He pulled the bandage away, looking for where to put it.

"Let me take that." Josie grabbed it and tossed it in a biohazard container. Then she began to assemble the supplies into some order that probably made sense to her. One of the packages she opened first had tan gloves, which she put on with more care than she had the purple pair.

Russ carefully removed his stained polo, donned the scrub shirt, and then sat back on the gurney.

As soft as a breeze, she touched the wound. "Are you sure you don't want a plastic surgeon to take a look? It's a fairly big gash, and a plastic surgeon will probably leave less of a scar."

"Can't you just staple the stupid thing shut?" He glanced up at her.

How had he not noticed those chocolate-brown eyes before? Or her scent? Something floral and terribly enticing.

"Staples would leave a nasty scar," she replied. "If you don't want a plastic surgeon..." She cocked an eyebrow.

"Nope."

"Then let me see if I can do better with some tiny stitches. Just relax. I'll have you put back together in a jiffy."

With practiced ease, she went about getting everything ready. After she injected the area with lidocaine, something he hadn't wanted but she assured him would make him more comfortable, she started working on him.

Zoning out so he didn't have to think about what she was doing, Russ focused on the woman who was so close to him that her breasts kept bumping against his arm. Although he was aware that she was Savannah's best friend, he knew little else about Joslynn Wright. His fault, because he'd all but avoided going anyplace with Brad and Savannah when he knew Josie was going to be there too. That had stemmed from Savannah constantly trying to play matchmaker, always chatting Josie up and telling Russ what a great couple the two of them would make.

Hell with that.

The last thing he needed in his fucked-up life was a girlfriend, especially one who was so close to his partner's wife.

But in a moment of honesty, he acknowledged that he very clearly remembered the first time he'd seen her. The afternoon before the Maxwells' wedding rehearsal, he'd been striding across the pool deck, aiming for the tiki bar. A woman had been slowly ascending the elaborate pool's marble staircase. The sunlight had hit her perfectly, and damn if she hadn't looked like a goddess emerging from a forest pond.

As he'd taken in her toned body, his mouth had gone dry. High, firm breasts. Slim waist. Just enough muscle to look athletic yet still utterly feminine. She'd been dressed in a red bikini that was tasteful as well as enticing, and she sported a small tattoo of an orange butterfly on her left breast—it peeked out of the bikini top just enough to see it—over her heart.

He'd made up his mind to try to get to know her better—up until the moment Savannah had introduced her and Russ realized this was the woman she'd been trying to push on him.

Gorgeous or not, trying to date her hadn't seemed worth the aggravation.

Now he wasn't so sure.

The navy blue scrubs and white lab coat she wore hid that delectable shape, which helped him get a grip on his rampant imagination. Just because Josie was appealing to him didn't make the situation any less perilous. He had no business becoming infatuated with this woman. With *any* woman...

Not with the dismal future he had in store.

She looked down at him, brows knit. "You doing okay? Awfully quiet there."

"Just patch me up, okay?" Russ snapped. He was immediately contrite. His fascination with her bothered him, but that didn't entitle him to take his irritation out on her.

The way she narrowed her dark eyes told him she'd caught his tone. "Alrighty, then..."

He had to hand it to her. Josie was efficient. She'd thoroughly cleaned and then stitched the wound up quickly. "Done," she announced.

Probably a good thing for Russ, because the more time he spent with her, the more he started to wonder if Savannah had been right all along—that this woman might be worth getting to know.

He needed to get out of there before he did something stupid like ask her for a date.

Then he remembered the manners his mom had beaten into his thick head. "Thanks, Josie."

* * *

"My pleasure." Joslynn started to gather up the discarded wrappers and used supplies. She'd lost track of how many stitches she'd put in place, because she'd done her damnedest to keep them small and even.

A good job, if she did say so herself.

"When do I get them pulled?" Russ asked, jumping off the gurney.

"You don't," she replied. "These will absorb. I also sealed them with skin adhesive. Just don't pick at it. It'll peel off when it's ready."

"So I can shower?"

She nodded and then pointed to the gurney. "Have a seat. You might as well make yourself comfortable because you need the nurse to come and give you discharge instructions, and I think a quick concussion screening might—"

"Nope. Don't have time for that."

"You're already here. You might as well—"

"I have to get back to work." He picked up the blood-stained polo and tossed it into the trash.

Getting angry at his crappy attitude, she didn't press the point about a possible concussion. It wasn't as though someone had smashed a chair over his head. A screening wasn't absolutely necessary. "There are discharge instructions and—"

"I've had enough stitches to know what to do." The scars she'd seen before he'd put on the scrubs added weight to his claim but didn't excuse his rude dismissal. "Besides, you just told me how to take care of them."

She hadn't meant to stare when he'd taken off his bloody shirt. But as he'd changed into the scrubs, she'd gotten a healthy view of his torso. Scars. So many scars. His chest. His back. Right shoulder surgery—probably more than one.

Sweet Lord, what kind of hell had Russell Green been through?

It wasn't at all like her to notice a guy's body in any way except clinically, but she hadn't been able to stop from staring at his arms. His biceps were well developed, straining the sleeves of the scrub shirt. She found herself wondering what kind of sports he played. Football? Soccer? He had what she called a "rugby body"—muscular, sturdy, and exactly what she liked.

With a shake of her head, Joslynn resisted the urge to wag her finger at him as if she were scolding a naughty child. "At the very least, you have to sign the release paperwork." To give him something to do, she popped up the mirror that was built into the patient table. "Want a peek?"

Russ actually came over to see the stitches. After a good, long look, he grinned. "Nice job, Doc."

"I'm not a doctor."

"You did better than most probably could." To her great surprise, he kissed her on the cheek. "See you later, Josie."

And he was gone before she could regain enough of her wits to stop him.

Francie came strolling through the open door. "I guess he was in a hurry, huh?" she asked, watching him jog out the double doors to the waiting area. Then she shifted her gaze to Joslynn. "You okay, Jos?"

Her hand fell away from her cheek. She hadn't even realized she'd been touching the spot he'd kissed. "Fine. And yes, he was obviously ready to leave our exceptional hospitality."

Francie chuckled. "They always hate waiting on the paper-work." She shuffled through the yellow discharge papers. "Want me to mail them?"

Joslynn's first response would have been to do just that, but she couldn't get past Russ's rude exit.

A better idea popped into her mind, and a slow smile bloomed. "You know what? Please put them in an envelope. I'm going to make sure Mr. Green receives them. In person. He needs a lesson in manners."

CHAPTER TWO

The next morning, Joslynn was surprised to find her friend Savannah and Savannah's daughter, Caroline, in the park. Once her ER shift ended at six in the morning, Joslynn always unwound from the stress with a nice, long run. Even though it was barely nine now, this June day was already growing warm and muggy, one of many reasons getting out early suited her just fine. While it wasn't unusual to see other people in the park at this hour—dedicated runners, dog walkers—it was odd to find anyone on the playground.

Savannah waved, and Joslynn jogged over to her best friend. Putting her foot on the bench, she went through her post-run stretches, knowing Savannah would understand how much Joslynn needed to stick to her routine.

"Look at you," Savannah said. "So disciplined. Out running at the butt crack of dawn."

"Look at you," Joslynn countered with a wink. "Out in public and not getting hounded by your fans."

"Hence the early hour." Inclining her head toward the playground, Savannah smiled. Caroline and a tawny-haired boy were taking turns hurtling down the twisting slide. "Caroline is an early bird anyway, so here we are."

"Is that Ellie's boy?" Joslynn asked as she continued her stretches.

"Yeah, that's Sam. He spent the night last night. He and Caroline are really close. If they were a little older, I might worry." A light chuckle was followed by a gasp. "Caroline Marie, don't you dare try to jump from there!"

A quick glance at the kids made Joslynn smile. They were both looking penitent as they backed away from trying to work their way over a metal bar that protected them from a steep drop. "That's my goddaughter."

Still sternly glaring at the kids, Savannah said, "That girl will be the death of me."

"I've heard that more than a few times." The truth, considering Caroline had a penchant for getting into sticky situations exactly like her godmother. Still working the kinks out of her legs, Joslynn tried to sound nonchalant as she went fishing for information. "So...what's the story with Russ Green?"

Sitting up with rapt attention, Savannah asked, "Story? What do you mean?"

A health-care professional had to walk a fine line where patient privacy was concerned, making Joslynn choose her words carefully. "He just seems...unusual."

"You've only seen the man at our wedding."

Wishing she'd left well enough alone, Joslynn waved off the subject. "Forget I said anything."

"Wait…Have you seen him other times?" Eyes wide, Savannah said, "Did he end up at the ER again?"

Again? Not a shock considering the man's myriad scars and rather reckless attitude.

"Never mind," Savannah said with a flip of her wrist. "You couldn't tell me even if you did treat him, but I can tell from your face that you did. I'll just look for new stitches or a fresh cast." She let out a weary sigh. "Russ is getting a little…out of control."

Stretching routine completed, Joslynn finally sat next to her friend. "Out of control?"

"You know he's a partner at Words and Music, right?" Savannah asked.

"He owns it with Brad and Ethan. You told me."

"Well, the last month or so, Russ has been coming in on what should be his days off to act as bouncer."

"He throws people out of the restaurant?" Joslynn asked.

"Not the restaurant per se, but the bar can get a bit rowdy." Brows gathered, Savannah kept her eyes on her daughter. "It's not like we have to toss people out often. Usually the bouncers break up fights or call cabs for people who shouldn't drive. But Russ is getting a bit…*handsy* with some troublemakers lately. Brad and Ethan were talking about it the other day, wondering what they should do to get him to chill."

"Don't you guys have other bouncers?"

Savannah nodded. "We have several. That's why we're worried about Russ. He doesn't need to be there, and he sure doesn't need to be playing bouncer. It's almost like he enjoys getting rough with people, like he misses his quarterback days."

"And you want to set me up with a guy who's acting like a goon?"

"Russ isn't a goon," Savannah said with a shake of her head. "I'm sorry if I gave you that impression. He's just...stressed, and we can't figure out exactly why. But he's such a sweetheart. You should see him with Caroline. She adores him. I wouldn't try to get you two together if I didn't think he was a good person."

"How well do you know him?" Joslynn tried to keep her tone a bit bored, not wanting Savannah to start telling her what a great couple they'd make, as she'd done several times in the past. So far, what Jos had heard and her own interactions with Russ made her hesitate to spend more time with him.

But something about him called to her, something she couldn't quite put her finger on...

"He and Brad have been friends just about forever," Savannah said. "I've spent a lot of time with him, and I know that deep down he's a great person, someone you can rely on. He's always willing to pitch in when Brad or I need a hand with something."

"I remember...At the wedding, he was the one who helped out when the photographer snuck in. Got the guy out of there before he could get pictures of the wedding guests." Russ had put an arm around the photographer's shoulder and escorted him to the exit without much fuss—obviously a different approach from the way he was now handling rowdy customers at Words & Music.

Something had changed.

But what?

"He was a quarterback?" Since Joslynn didn't really follow

sports, with the exception of catching the Olympics when they were on, she had no idea if Russ was a famous athlete.

"Played in college—Kentucky, I think. And he was with the NFL for a few seasons, although I think he was a backup quarterback."

"So he was good?"

"Brad says he was. Doesn't play now because he hurt his shoulder."

That explained the extensive scarring on his right shoulder. Probably a rotator cuff tear, which was agony to come back from and usually ended an athletic career. "Poor guy."

An easy smile filled Savannah's face. They'd known each other for enough years to easily figure out what the other was feeling. "You like him."

"I don't know exactly *how* I feel about him," Joslynn admitted. She was still smarting from the way he'd fled the ER and planned to let him know how disrespectful he'd been. "Right now I just want to know how you think he'd respond to a little…constructive criticism."

"Tell me what you have in mind…"

* * *

Russ took a good look around, watching the subdued crowd. The people in the restaurant seemed to be enjoying themselves, and the bar was serving only a dozen or so customers. Pretty typical Sunday since it was one of the two nights per week Words & Music had no live entertainment scheduled.

He leaned his elbows back against the end of the bar and

watched the crowd. Some were eating. Some were dancing to the canned music over the sound system. One guy was trying to teach his lady a line dance, and she was clearly having trouble learning the steps. But the man never seemed to lose his cool.

Patience—a virtue Russ sure didn't possess.

Brad Maxwell came over to lean against the bar at Russ's side. "How's the head?"

All Russ did was shrug. As injuries went, it was petty.

"You're supposed to be off tonight," Brad scolded. "I mean, you did notice that I'm standing right here next to you, didn't you?"

"You're kinda hard to miss," Russ drawled.

"I can manage this place just fine on my own."

"Go home to your wife," Russ offered. "I can take care of things here through close."

"See that's the thing…I'm not sure you can."

Turning his face to scowl at his partner, Russ furrowed his forehead. "What the hell is that supposed to mean?"

Brad drew his lips into a grim line. "Ethan and I were going to talk to you tomorrow. But here you are tonight, doing exactly what we wanted to talk to you about."

Pushing away from the bar, Russ faced his friend and folded his arms over his chest. "Spit it out, then."

"This is the thirty-fifth day in a row you've been here. I checked."

Not that Russ doubted Brad, but he really didn't give a shit how many days he worked. This restaurant was his life, all he really had. Why was Brad criticizing him for being dedicated? "So what?"

"So…you're setting yourself up for a heart attack." Brad's ironic smile did little to lower Russ's temper. "See, you can't die on me. I don't want to have to deal with Ethan alone." How like Brad to try to diffuse a tense situation with humor.

"I'm healthy as a horse," Russ insisted. At least for now. He had years before he had to worry about… "I'm fine," he said, brushing away the unpleasant thoughts that always nagged him.

"Those stitches say otherwise." Pushing away from the bar, Brad came to stand in front of Russ. "Are you gonna tell me what's really bugging you, or do you even know?"

"There's not a damn thing 'bugging me'"—he stabbed air quotes to stress Brad's words—"and I'd appreciate it if you'd stop trying to psychoanalyze me."

A bar patron sitting near them—a stereotypical I-wish-I-were-a-real-cowboy type—let out a rather loud snort. "Couple of pussies," he muttered before taking a long pull on his beer.

Anger that had already begun brewing—did it ever truly stop?—turned to molten lava at the rude interruption. Fisting his hands, Russ invaded the guy's personal space, all but pushing him off the stool. "You got a problem, buddy?"

The man didn't even turn his head. "Yeah. I got you two standin' there, talkin' like a couple of fuckin' women. You're annoyin' me."

"You know what annoys *me*?" Russ asked. "People who stick their noses into other people's conversations."

The guy pushed his stool back hard enough that it tipped over. "Back the fuck off if you know what's good for you."

Russ knew he was losing control, but lately it seemed as if he couldn't stop himself from always doing the wrong damn thing.

"Your mama clearly didn't teach you any manners, so I might just have to beat some into you."

The wanna-be cowboy narrowed his bloodshot eyes. "I'd like to see you try."

* * *

Joslynn picked up on the hostility in the place the moment her eyes found Russ. His legs were braced apart, hands in tight fists, as he hovered over some fat guy in a weathered cowboy hat.

A fight was brewing.

Intent upon not having to stitch Russ up again and add any more scars to that incredible body, she set her purse on the end of the bar and hurried to intervene.

Working the night shift in the emergency room had helped her hone skills she'd never expected to need. How many potential brawls had she managed to squelch? How many belligerent patients had she talked down? How many drunks had she patched up?

Too many to count.

When she reached the men, Joslynn used Russ's obvious surprise at seeing her to her advantage. As he stared at her, she wrapped her hand around his biceps. "Russ, I need your help." With a gentle tug, she tried to lead him away.

She sent an entreating look to the other man in the red Words & Music polo and only then realized it was Brad Maxwell. Hoping he'd see what she was trying to do and help with the other combatant, she gave him a quick nod. Judging from the way the chubby cowboy was swaying on his feet, he was inebriated, or at least well on his way to getting there. Someone needed to call him a cab and get him out of there.

Russ's eyes widened as the fierce frown on his face eased. "What are you doing here, Josie?"

"I came to talk to you." She pulled a little more insistently on his arm. "Now, if you please." When he tried to turn his head to look back at the guy at the bar, she put her palm against his cheek to keep him focused on her. "Come with me, Russ."

As though in tune with her thoughts, Brad took the drunk guy by the shoulders and guided him in the other direction.

Russ tried to look away one more time, but since she kept a firm hand against his face, he gave up. "What do you need?"

"Is there someplace we can talk in private?" she asked, keeping her tone soft.

"Sure." He took the hand she had around his biceps and lifted it away. Then he laced his fingers through hers. "Let's go to the office."

As he led her toward the far side of the restaurant, Joslynn glanced back and offered a smile to Brad.

He gave her a nod and grabbed his phone, hopefully calling the drunk a ride.

After walking down a long hallway, Russ opened a door and swept his hand in invitation.

Although she normally disliked having a man hold a door for her, thinking it was an archaic and rather condescending action, Joslynn stepped into the room. The place looked a bit like a tornado had recently swept through. Since she liked to keep things in her home neat as a pin, the office bugged her. A lot.

Papers were strewn across the desk. A ratty old sofa rested

against one wall. There were boxes—opened and unopened—scattered around. An electronic keyboard took up most of the desk, and she wondered if that was Brad's. He was, after all, a composer in addition to owning Words & Music.

Russ plopped on the sofa and stared at her expectantly. "So what can I help you with? After the way you patched me up last night, I owe you."

With the anger he'd shown back at the bar, Joslynn didn't think now was the proper time to pull out his discharge papers and scold him for his rather rude exit the night before. So she scrambled to think of something else she could use as a reason for seeking him out. "Um…I…need…"

He cocked his head and smiled.

That damn dimple made her train of thought derail. She couldn't come up with a reason, even a ridiculous one, for being in that office with him.

"Josie?"

Since all she could think about was spending time with him, she latched on to that thought and improvised. "Last night. At the ER. I noticed you were a bit…um…stressed. Yes, you were stressed." She was babbling like a moron.

All he did was stare at her with those hypnotic blue eyes.

"I thought you might want my help to…you know…deal with that." As she always did when she was nervous, she tucked the stray hairs that had slipped from her messy bun behind her ear.

"But you told me *you* needed *my* help," Russ said.

"I did say that, didn't I?"

He grinned and nodded.

His smile was going to be the death of her. At the moment, it was making her brain go blank. "It was an excuse," she admitted, figuring a little embarrassment wouldn't kill her. She simply couldn't think of anything else to do except admit her feelings.

"An excuse?"

Her cheeks were scorching hot. "To see you again."

When Russ chuckled, Joslynn relaxed. He clearly wasn't offended, and she wasn't truly lying—she *had* wanted to get to know him better. She'd just refrain from telling him that she'd actually come to scold him and give him a lesson in what not to do when leaving an emergency room. If she was honest with herself, it might've been a flimsy excuse to see him again.

"Have you eaten?" he asked, rising from the sofa.

She shook her head.

As he came to stand by her side, she couldn't help but react to his size. Back on that gurney, she'd judged him as tall, but she'd underestimated. He towered over her, and she wasn't short by any means. The top of her head barely reached his chin.

"Since you went to all the trouble to track me down, how about I buy you a nice meal?" he asked, staring down into her eyes.

"How tall are you?" God, she sounded like an idiot. It was a wonder Russ wasn't telling her to take a hike. The way she'd acted from the moment she'd interrupted his altercation had to scream "crazy lady." And now she was staring up at him as though he were the Jolly Green Giant.

"Six six." At least he was still grinning. "Want my weight, too?" he teased.

His calm acceptance of her nervousness helped her relax. "No, thanks. But I will take you up on dinner."

"Well, then…" Russ picked up her hand and led her out of the office. "Let's go."

CHAPTER THREE

Still perplexed why Josie had so brazenly told him that she wanted to spend time with him, Russ stared at her across the table. Accustomed to being the pursuer rather than the prey, he could only marvel at how open she'd been. Not many women were that honest, and he couldn't help but admire her directness.

Instead of staying to eat at Words & Music, she'd told him about a mom-and-pop Italian place not far away that she loved and asked if they could go there instead. Although he normally hated new restaurants, he would've done whatever she asked, no doubt because he was still flattered by her attention. She'd offered to drive, but he'd taken one look at her boxy little car and feared the electric-blue Kia would be too confining to his tall frame. They took his SUV instead.

After ordering from a waiter who seemed familiar with Josie, Russ figured he should make polite conversation. Despite Savannah's attempts to hook him up with this woman, and even with

Josie's aggressive pursuit, he still wasn't sure getting into any kind of relationship was a smart move on his part. Yet the overwhelming pull to her was making it next to impossible for him to resist thinking about.

At the very least, he could offer her a pleasant date. "So you obviously eat a lot of pasta."

"How would you know that?"

He let out a chuckle. "The hostess and the waiter knew your name."

"Yeah, I love the food here—especially when I'm carb-loading," she replied with a smile.

They spoke the same language. "You sound like me from the weekends I had big games. Are you a runner?"

She nodded again. "Almost my whole life."

"Marathons?"

"Two, and I'm hoping to complete at least one again this year."

"Boston?"

With a shake of her head, she said, "That's on my bucket list, though."

"You're too young to have a bucket list," he commented.

Then the irony of the statement hit him. Since his father's diagnosis, Russ had made his own bucket list. Josie appeared to be about the same age as him, but there was no compelling reason for her to contemplate her mortality—not a reason like he had anyway.

"No one's too young to have a bucket list," she said, a weight of seriousness in her tone. "So, do you still work out?"

Since it was clear she was trying to get away from talking about bucket lists, he obliged her. Maybe when they got to know each other better, they could share more personal topics like that. Tonight was obviously too soon. "When I have time."

"Put in a lot of hours at Words and Music?"

"When a guy co-owns a restaurant, he's gotta give it the time it needs. I imagine a nurse practitioner feels the same about her job. Ever feel like you *own* that ER of yours?"

He loved her soft, husky laugh. It went straight to his groin. How long had it been since he'd felt that kind of attraction to a woman? The chemistry was definitely there. Now he just needed to figure out what, if anything, he was going to do about it.

"All the time," Josie said. "And when I'm not there, I'm thinking about what I should be doing when I get back there."

"Like you shouldn't ever leave?" Russ asked. "Right?"

She nodded.

"I know the feeling well. Wanna hear something stupid? My partners are pissed at me because of it."

A dark eyebrow arched. "Why would they be pissed that you're dedicated to your business?"

"My question exactly. Before you got there, Brad was—" He'd almost forgotten that this woman was Savannah Maxwell's best friend. The last thing in the world he needed to be doing was gossiping about the man married to Josie's best friend.

"Brad was what?" she asked.

To hell with it. Brad had been a jerk. Why shouldn't Russ go ahead and tell Josie so?

"He was scolding me because I was there on my day off."

Her smile hit him like a shot of twenty-year-old bourbon. "Good thing I dragged you away from there, then. I hate when the people I work with tell me to either go home or just go ahead and move all my stuff to the hospital since I live there." Her smile fell. "Working too much isn't good for a person, though. You don't want to burn out, do you?"

Russ shook his head.

"It's healthy to get away from work and leave it behind for a while."

Suddenly feeling tongue-tied, he scrambled for something to say, not wanting to look like some meathead who had plenty of substance to his muscles but not much to his brain. "You…um…mentioned…stress. Back at Words and Music. Something about you knowing I'm stressed out?"

* * *

Joslynn's heart started hammering at his question. How was she supposed to come up with some reason she had brilliant insight into Russ's stress level when in truth she'd been talking with Savannah about him, fishing for information?

"I…I…" She could feel the heat of embarrassment spreading up her neck.

"Figured it was something you guys all look for in the ER," he said. "Like rashes and such."

As good a theory as any…

Except she'd never been able to lie with a straight face. Not once. So, despite knowing she'd be humiliated, she went with the truth. "We do, and I'd noticed the changes in your blood pressure from the other visits you've had there. Mostly, though, I asked Savannah about you."

The smug smile on his face didn't come as a surprise, and she accepted it as her due. "I'm flattered, Josie. Not only did you have the guts to come and find me, but you also talked to Savannah to learn more about me." His smile morphed as he glanced at the table, showing her a bit of vulnerability that touched her heart. "I've kinda been thinking about you, too."

"You have?"

Russ nodded, giving her a smile so filled with emotion that her stomach fluttered in response. "I almost talked to Savannah. About you. But"—he shrugged—"I guess I was worried about asking you for a date."

"Why would you be worried?"

He shrugged again, emphasizing those broad shoulders she couldn't get enough of. "Worried that you'd refuse me—that we're both good friends with Brad and Savannah. I mean, if we did date and things didn't work out…"

Following his train of thought was easy. "It would make things really awkward, right?"

"Exactly. So, I guess I should ask…Is this a *real* date?"

The million-dollar question, one Joslynn knew would take a lot of courage to answer.

Ah, well. Fortune did, as the proverb claimed, favor the brave.

She offered Russ a smile. "Why not? I mean, worst-case scenario, we don't hit it off. Then we can just glare at each other whenever we're with the Maxwells until we grow old enough to laugh about how we went on that one date way back when."

* * *

Their salads arrived, and around bites of food, he tried to keep up their conversation. It dawned on him just how little he knew about her. Since she didn't have the same Tennessee drawl that he was accustomed to hearing, he asked, "Always lived in Nashville?"

She shook her head. "Grew up in a small town in Michigan. St. Ignace."

"Can't say I've heard of it," he admitted.

Her chuckle made him smile. "Not many people have. I was really glad when Mom took a new job and moved us here when I was in middle school. Nashville just felt like home to me. I even went to college here. How about you?"

"Born and bred here. I did head to UK for college, though."

Her brows gathered. "You mean University of Kentucky?"

Russ let out a laugh. "Guilty. I'm a Wildcat through and through. Had a football scholarship and then got drafted by the Indianapolis Colts."

"Savannah told me that you played professional football."

"Yes, ma'am." He rolled his bad shoulder, which he did habitually whenever he thought about what had brought his mediocre career to a swift end. "Ripped my shoulder apart and had no choice but to hang up my pads. I was lucky Brad and Ethan let me throw in with them when they set up Words and Music."

After setting her salad bowl aside, Josie dabbed her mouth with her napkin and then laid it across her lap again. "What do you do for fun?"

"I play my guitar."

"You do?"

"Don't look so surprised," Russ said at her incredulous expression. "I'm from Nashville. Everyone here wants to be a star."

"Have you ever sung at the bar?" she asked.

He couldn't contain his amusement as he pictured the protests his partners would launch should Russ ever attempt to perform at Words & Music.

She cocked her head.

"Sorry," he said. "It's just…Ethan and Brad might let me *play*, but there's no way they'd let me *sing*."

"Why not?"

"Because I'm horrible."

"Horrible?" A chuckle slipped out. "You can't be *that* bad, Russ."

Thankfully, the waiter brought their entrées, which saved Russ from explaining that "horrible" might be an understatement. Brad had compared Russ's singing to nails being scraped down a chalkboard.

* * *

As always, the food had been wonderful. Joslynn finally had to set her fork down. She'd enjoyed Russ's company as they'd talked throughout dinner, but she kept getting stuck on one point.

"I have to say," she commented, "that I think you're telling me a fib."

"A fib?"

She nodded. "Your speaking voice is so…smooth. I can't believe you can't sing well. Admit it. You have stage fright, right?"

His laughter echoed through the now almost deserted

restaurant, a sound she found infectious. "I'm not about to prove it."

"Why not?"

"Because I'd like to go on a second date with you."

"And you think if I heard you sing I'd refuse?" she asked.

"Absolutely." He leaned back, suddenly looking a bit nervous. "So what do you say, Josie? Want to go on a second date with me?"

"I would love to."

Russ grabbed the check the moment the waiter tried to set it on the table.

"Hey," Joslynn protested. "At least let me pay my part!"

"It's on me," he insisted. "I guess we can go ahead and tell our grandkids this was our first official date."

"Moving a little quick there, aren't you, Mr. Green?" she teased. "Grandkids when we haven't even had a second date?"

"Just kidding," he replied. "But I am a quick kind of guy. Ran the forty in under five seconds."

That comment brought the conversation back to one of her favorite topics. "Do you still run?"

"Nah. I'm too lazy." After taking the change from the waiter, Russ left a generous tip—something she always found classy, having waited tables while putting herself through college.

He came around to pull out her chair.

"If you want to handle that stress problem and get your blood pressure back in check, I could design a running program for you," she offered. "Or better yet, yoga. It's amazing to help keep stress down."

When he took her hand and led her out of the restaurant,

she got the most delicious shiver. There was no way she could deny the physical pull toward the man, which made her happy the evening had turned out as well as it had. Her original intent was to give him a setdown for his rude behavior. Instead, they'd shared a wonderful date that revealed a rare compatibility.

Russ snorted. "I'm too big and bulky for yoga." He reached to open the passenger door for her.

Joslynn brushed his hand away, wanting to set her rules from the get-go. "Nice gesture, but too old-fashioned for me. If you don't mind…"

"Just trying to be a gentleman."

"You are, but you're out with a liberated lady."

At least the comment drew a smile. "Well, okay then. We'll do it your way."

"Thanks, Russ." After she opened the door, she slid inside and buckled her seat belt, waiting for him to slide into the driver's seat. Warming to the idea of teaching him yoga, she smiled as he fastened his seat belt. "Back to yoga, you'd be amazed at the people in my classes. All shapes and sizes. I have an eighty-two-year-old great-grandmother and a former Titan linebacker."

After firing up the engine, he eased the SUV from the parking lot into the flow of traffic. "Your classes?"

"I teach a few times a week at the Brown Sports Complex."

"I love that place. Great weight room."

This time she was the one who snorted. "Weight room? You mean weight *field house*."

She loved his chuckle. So warm and growly and downright masculine. "It's amazing," he said. "Any kind of workout you'd want."

"I'd be happy to show you some moves," she said before realizing how dirty that might have sounded.

His hand reached over to hold the one she had resting on her lap, but he didn't say a word. Instead, he chuckled again.

Her radar went up, and she tried to gently tug her hand back, wondering why the thought that he might be laughing at her bothered her so much.

He gave her a quick glance. "Josie? What's wrong?"

"Nothing." She stopped trying to pull away. *Just unusually sensitive.*

"As much as the idea of me falling on my face when I try to learn that yoga stuff seems embarrassing, I might give it a try."

A glance at the passing street made Joslynn ask, "Are we heading back to Words and Music?"

Russ nodded. "Figured it was getting late and you'd want to be heading home."

Having no idea what time it was, she dragged her purse up from where it rested between her feet and set it on her lap. Then she started searching for her cell phone. She normally watched the time like a hawk, and it came as a bit of a shock to realize she'd been having such a good time in Russ's company that she hadn't bothered to check once.

When she finally found her phone in the bottom of the purse, she jerked it free. An envelope spilled out—the envelope with his discharge papers. The damn thing landed on the console between them.

Joslynn snatched it up and shoved it back in her purse.

"What was that?" he asked.

"Just some papers."

"That envelope had my name on it."

In big red letters, thanks to Francie.

There really wasn't any need to hide it, since he had no idea why she'd brought it along. "They're your discharge papers."

He fired a skeptical look her direction. "Why didn't you give them to me earlier?"

The way he asked the question left her with a dilemma. Tell him the truth about her plans or fib and claim she simply brought them along?

"Josie?" He kept stealing glances at her, concern in his eyes.

The growing silence stretched between them.

Joslynn heaved a sigh. "I was going to…lecture you."

"Lecture me?"

Another sigh escaped as she realized her penchant for being truthful would probably bring a screeching halt to the tentative momentum they'd begun. But lying not only went against her grain; it was a terrible way to establish a friendship.

"I was peeved," she admitted. "You ran out of the ER like you were on fire. You didn't even wait for discharge instructions."

"So?"

"I figured I could find you to scold you and…Oh, never mind."

Brow furrowed, Russ pulled the SUV up next to her car. He killed the engine, turned to her, and held out his hand.

She picked up the envelope and gave it to him. "It's really no big deal. In retrospect."

He took a quick peek at the papers and then tossed the envelope in the backseat, where several empty sports drink bottles and a few wadded-up fast-food bags rested. "In retrospect?" There was an irritated thread to that normally pleasing voice.

"You know, before…" Joslynn couldn't spit out the words. Opening up had never been easy for her. Being a private person, she couldn't help but feel the need to close herself off now, before she became too vulnerable.

"Josie…" The thread of irritation was now clearly anger.

"Before…we connected," she admitted. "Before tonight. Before this date."

Russ sat there for moment, a frown on his face and his hands clenched. Then he opened his door and started to come around to her side.

She beat him to the punch since he was probably too pissed to remember to let her handle her own door. She met him behind the SUV. "I'm sorry, Russ."

Folding his arms over his chest, he leaned back against his red Escape. There was a tick in his left cheek.

When he finally made eye contact with her, she was surprised to find no anger. If she read him correctly, he was feeling hurt, probably because she'd wanted to reprimand him.

Joslynn slid her hands into her jeans pockets. "Look, I was being stupid, okay? It was adolescent of me to think I could march up to you and scold you like a child because you stitched-and-ditched."

Was that a hint of a smile on his lips? "Stitched-and-ditched?"

"Yeah, our ER lingo. You'd be amazed how many people want to get the heck away from us when their treatment is complete." She shrugged. "I figured if I let you know how much you'd pissed me off…maybe I'd teach you a lesson on hospital etiquette."

"So you lied about why you came to me?"

"I did. And I'm sorry."

"Did you lie about anything else?" The question came out nearly a whisper.

She shook her head. "I had a great time tonight. Please don't let something this petty ruin it."

"I guess it all depends on one thing."

"What one thing?"

Russ unfolded his arms and stood to his full height. *"This."*

For a big man, he moved surprisingly fast. In one fluid motion, he'd snaked his arm around her waist, turned her back to his SUV, and put his lips on hers.

Joslynn's eyes widened for a moment, and then she closed them in surrender. His lips were soft and warm, and she slowly put her arms around his neck.

Heart pounding, Russ couldn't keep the kiss he gave Joslynn gentle. This wasn't a first-date kiss. Instead, he pulled her closer and physically expressed all that he wasn't able to say.

He couldn't seem to hold back. He didn't wait for her to open her lips for him. Instead, he thrust his tongue into her mouth, needing to know that what he'd felt tonight was real, that the connection wasn't something he'd imagined.

Her tongue was every bit as insistent as it rubbed across his, and he growled deep in his throat. The sound must have emboldened her, because she continued the deep kiss as she pressed her breasts against his chest.

Russ had never been like Brad and Ethan in their earlier days. He hadn't needed to date a bunch of women, and he sure as hell had never slept with one on a first date. Yet he wanted Josie so badly that he was considering asking her to come home with him right now.

Knowing he was close to losing all control, he forced himself to end the kiss. His ego loved that she cupped his face in her hands and pulled him down as she rose on tiptoes to put her lips against his again. A short and very sweet kiss that made him smile.

She was smiling too as they slowly separated. "Does that mean you forgive me?"

He nodded, still grinning as he put his hands in his pockets so he wouldn't grab her again.

"Then give me a call when you want to go out again." She went to the passenger side and yanked her purse out of his car. "I should go."

"Yeah, it's getting late." He pulled out his cell phone. "Can I have your number?"

She gave it to him and said, "I usually work nights, so don't be surprised if I don't return any calls or texts until late afternoon."

"Got it."

Russ followed her to her car. After she opened the door and got in the driver's seat, he blocked the door with his body, unable to resist another quick kiss.

She was beaming when he closed the door and walked away.

* * *

Joslynn was still trembling when she pulled out of the parking lot.

How could one kiss—well, three, actually—have thrown her into such a state? Her breath was still choppy, and her core felt as though it were on fire. No man had ever been able to arouse her as quickly, and she wasn't sure if she loved that Russ could get to her so strongly or hate that he had that kind of power over her.

She eased into traffic, trying to regain her composure.

Only one thing was for sure—she wanted to spend more time with him, to get to know him and see if the connection they'd felt had a chance to grow.

But first she needed to get rid of her boyfriend.

CHAPTER FOUR

Boyfriend" wasn't exactly the correct term for Matthew Tomb, MD.

"Guy that I casually sleep with" fit much better.

Joslynn had first met Matthew when he'd been hired at the hospital right after his internship. She'd done a lot of his training over the year they'd known each other, and he seemed to enjoy her attention as they grew closer. Although her true motive had been to ensure there was a doctor working in her ER who wasn't constantly asking for help with things he should be able to handle himself, she'd been a bit flattered by his obvious infatuation.

She had to admit he was cute, but not nearly as appealing as Russ. Where Russ was muscular, Matthew was svelte—built more like a distance runner instead of having Russ's bodybuilding physique. Russ was blond; Matthew had dark brown hair. Should the men stand side by side, Russ would tower over barely-six-foot-tall Matthew.

And Matthew didn't have that delectable dimple…

She'd agreed to a date with Matthew, and it had been an un-mitigated disaster. A late-autumn tornado had rumbled through the Nashville area, and the movie theater they were at had forced all the patrons out of the theaters and into the hallways. He'd thought it was romantic when the lights went out. She'd been pissed that a really good comedy had been interrupted.

But there'd been a bit of chemistry when he'd kissed her, so after a few dates, she'd slept with him. Chemistry had been her favorite subject in high school and college. She understood it. She believed in it. And she trusted it. Why approach her love life any differently?

Joslynn had made it clear to him, as she had with the other men she'd slept with over the years, that their connection was nothing more than a "friends with benefits" arrangement. Not once had she allowed a guy to spend the night at her house; nor had she stayed at any of theirs. Sleeping equaled defenselessness, and she wasn't about to be that vulnerable.

Her life was her own, and she'd never wanted to share it entirely with anyone. Yet in the back of her mind, she'd always wondered if the right guy might come along one day. But Mr. Right still hadn't made an appearance, and she saw no reason to deny herself physical pleasure if there was a good friend who was willing to satisfy her and allow her to satisfy him.

She was content.

At least she had been until tonight. The pull toward Russ had been so overpowering, she was willing to think about him differently than she did men like Matthew—she was even considering something deeper than her usual involvement with guys.

When Russ had kissed her, the chemistry had been explosive,

which made it a surprise that she hadn't felt any physical pull toward him back in Georgia at Savannah and Brad's wedding. Then again, they'd barely met, let alone had time to get to know each other. She'd been busy being Savannah's maid of honor. There was only one thing that had made an impression, and it wasn't his exaggerated height. She'd clearly forgotten that.

No, his smile was what she'd remembered. That incredible smile.

Thankfully, he hadn't gone off in a huff over her plan to scold him for not signing his discharge papers. A shock, because it seemed he was so strung out from stress that she'd braced for an exaggerated overreaction, especially in wake of Savannah's concerns about him being a bit out of control.

One of her philosophies—honed from her rough childhood—was that a person came into someone's life when there was a true need. Perhaps Russ needed something from her.

But what did the universe think she needed from him?

Good question...

After a quick stop at the grocery store to pick up a few things, Joslynn finally pulled into the driveway of her small house—the one Savannah always called "the Cottage." Though she was happy to be home, her mood changed considerably when she looked around.

Matthew was sitting in his car, which was parked across the street.

He was frowning as he got out of his Accord and strode toward her while she fished the two grocery bags out of her Kia.

He tried to take one of the bags. "Where were you?" he snapped.

Joslynn narrowed her eyes, then glared at him for a moment. There was no way she'd let him believe he had any right to know where she'd been. That had never been a part of their little dance. When she'd told him no emotional ties, he'd agreed.

His shoulders slumped. "Sorry. I was just…upset. I came by to see if you wanted to go to a late show. There's a new indie film at the Art House and…" He shrugged.

"I thought you had a shift tonight." She shut the car door with her hip. Not that she kept track of when he worked. The doctors currently assigned to the ER were all pretty decent at their jobs, Matthew included. That meant she never had to shuffle her schedule around to be sure she wasn't stuck on the night shift with doctors who couldn't pull their weight and needed her to pick up their slack.

Instead of inviting him inside, which she might normally do, she turned to scowl at him and let him know this kind of popping up unannounced was out-of-bounds. "Why are you here?"

He rubbed the back of his neck. "I just missed you."

The last few times they'd been together, Joslynn had been a bit concerned that Matthew's feelings had grown beyond their physical attraction. Even before the date with Russ, she'd been easing into ending her arrangement with Matthew. Subtle was evidently wasted on him, so she'd have to be more deliberate in letting him know they were done. There was no guilt at going on a date with Russ, because she and Matthew had never agreed to be exclusive anywhere except the bedroom.

Now he was getting territorial, something for which she had no tolerance. "Why don't I come in for a while?" he suggested, which he typically said when he wanted to have sex.

With her mind full of Russell Green, she didn't think being with another man was a good idea. "Matthew, I really think we should talk…"

He let out a groan.

"It's just…Look, it's time we went back to being just colleagues."

"You're breaking up with me?"

"There's nothing to break up," she insisted. "Not really. We both agreed—"

"But we've been together nine months, Joslynn. Of course there's something to break up."

Had it been that long? Then it was past time to end things, especially if Matthew felt as if they were a true couple now. "I told you all along that this was just sex, Matthew."

"Can we go inside?" he asked. "I'm not in the mood to blab our love life to the whole neighborhood."

She owed him an explanation, so she nodded. "Come on in. I'll get us some wine, and we can talk."

* * *

Joslynn took a sip of merlot as she looked at Matthew over the rim of her glass. They'd been talking in circles for long enough that she was about to lose her temper. "We both agreed to keep things casual," she said yet again.

"Things changed," he said, still frowning at her.

Perhaps by pointing out a few facts, he'd stop insisting they were a romantic couple. "I know you've been on other dates, Matthew. You went out with Maggie a couple of times. And didn't you bring Pam to that 5K in May?"

"Well, yeah, but…"

She put her glass down and leaned forward, putting her elbows on her thighs and folding her hands together. "There's no 'but' here, okay?"

"But I think I love you, Jos."

Fuck a duck. That was the last thing she wanted or needed to hear. *Love?* Who had time for that kind of nonsense?

Love was an illusion. In her life, she'd learned the hard way that there was passion, there was pity, and there was loyalty—those three covered everything. She'd yet to meet a man who could change her opinion on the subject.

"You don't love me, Matthew. You're just comfortable with me. That's all."

"You don't understand."

"No, *you* don't understand. I told you the first time we were together that I'm not the kind of woman who ever wants to be tied down. It's not my nature." She took a deep breath and tried to spin things in a positive direction. "You're a great guy. Someone out there is gonna be lucky to catch you."

"I want *you* to catch me," he said, giving her puppy-dog eyes.

They didn't work. She couldn't help but feel manipulated, and she decided to draw a firm line. Adopting the stern voice she used with patients who were unruly, she leveled a hard stare at him. "Listen to me now, because I don't want to have to say it again. Are you listening?"

With a heavy frown on his face, he nodded curtly.

"I like working with you. You're a great doctor. I enjoy talking to you while we're at the hospital. But from now on, please don't come to my house. Please don't call or text unless you really need to talk to me about work. Okay?"

His emotions played across his face, and he bowed his head for a bit. "Joslynn…"

"I mean it. There's nothing between us except friendship. Got it?"

Then he looked up, still frowning. "Fine."

A sigh of relief slipped out. She was glad Matthew seemed to see things through her eyes, although she knew there'd probably be a few more times she'd have to remind him of their new status before it finally sank in. "So we can just be friends? You won't keep showing up when I run or when I teach yoga?"

"Do I have to give up the yoga?" He gave her a lopsided smile. "There are some cute girls in your class."

Joslynn let a hint of a smile bloom. "Fine. You can come to yoga."

* * *

It felt odd to be heading home before the restaurant closed. How long had it been since Russ wasn't the one to lock the doors on his way out?

Thirty-some days, according to Brad.

Russ pulled into his garage, turned off the engine, and just sat there. He checked his phone, hoping Josie had texted.

You idiot. She saw you less than an hour ago.

He forced himself out of the SUV and into his home, not sure what to do with himself. Maybe he could catch up on the laundry that had piled up. He tended to collapse on the couch as soon as he got home. There were a lot of chores he could do since his house badly needed cleaning. The place was a mess, and if Joslynn came to visit…

Now he was getting the cart in front of the horse. He had no business even going out with her again. She was a nice woman who deserved better than the likes of him.

Well, maybe not so nice. She had, after all, come to Words & Music to tear him a new one. He hadn't realized it was that big a thing to not hang around for stupid stuff like paperwork. From now on he'd try to be a little more patient and a little less rude.

"Try" being the key word.

Everything about his life now seemed frantic, frenzied, and he didn't have a clue how to slow things down. Ever since his father's diagnosis, everything in Russ's life was different. Urgency seeped from every pore. While he might always have been a bit manic, now he felt out of control, like he had to do everything at once and right fucking now.

Before it was too late for Russ to enjoy his life.

His phone rang—John Lennon's "Mother" revealing the caller.

"Hey, Mom. How was today?"

"A good day," she replied, and he could hear the smile in her voice. "He was himself."

"Glad to hear it. So what's up?"

"I wanted to see if you were still going to be able to stay with him Tuesday. I promise not to be gone long, but my hair's a mess."

"I'll be there," Russ promised. "And take your time. You don't get out enough."

His mother snorted. "Like I can stay away for long."

"We'll be fine for however long it takes you to get a haircut. I wish you'd go to a movie or something, too. You know, just get out of the house for a bit."

"I get out plenty," she insisted.

This time he snorted at her. "Is the cleaning service going to be there Tuesday while I'm there?"

"No. They're on Mondays now. I'll never be able to thank you enough for them. I don't think I've had a better gift in my whole life."

"You've got enough on your hands with Dad," Russ said. "The least I could do is get some people to clean your house for you."

"Thanks, honey. You're my favorite kid."

"I'm your *only* kid," he said, as always, with a grin on his face.

His father's voice bellowed in the background, and Russ caught a profanity, something that never would've slipped from Baron Green's lips before.

"Uh-oh," she said. "Dad needs me."

"Everything okay? He sounds agitated."

"We're fine, Russell. I've got this." Her typical admonition whenever Russ offered to help. "Love you." With that, she was gone.

Setting his phone aside, he tried to relax. It wasn't easy, because the worry for his parents was always there. Like background noise that grew steadily louder, adding to the frenetic intensity of his life.

It wasn't as though he needed psychoanalysis to figure out his problem. He was utterly terrified that his days were numbered—at least his *normal* days. The days as Russell Green, a man who knew who he was, held tight to the memories of his past, and was in control of his own life.

Alzheimer's disease was slowly stealing all those things away from his father—and at the horribly early age of fifty-eight.

At first Russ and his mother had thought Baron was just getting forgetful. He constantly lost things, but everyone at work had joked about it. Sometimes when he tried to talk, he couldn't seem to find the right words, like he was tongue-tied. Then his work began to suffer—forgetting shifts, not completing his duties—until his boss at the security firm finally had no choice but to fire him.

When the diagnosis had finally come, it had been devastating—early-onset Alzheimer's disease, something that had no cure. The meds that did exist only offered hope of slowing the progress of the damage.

Russ couldn't help but admire his mother—Yvonne Green was a saint among women. She approached Baron's diagnosis the way she approached everything else in life. She met the challenge head-on and did everything she could to help her husband. After putting in her early retirement papers with the police department where she'd been a dispatcher, she'd taken on her husband's care, constantly searching for things that would help Baron cope with the cognitive changes.

Thankfully, money wasn't an issue. Russ had never been an NFL star, but his agent had done one brilliant thing—he'd practically forced Russ to take out injury insurance. Three years into his unexceptional NFL career, Russ had destroyed his right shoulder. At least the payout that came when he had to resign from the Indianapolis Colts after three seasons softened the blow. He'd been a decent player, but it wasn't as though the team truly missed their backup quarterback, especially when they already had a franchise player leading the team.

He'd used some of the windfall to become partners with Brad and Ethan in Words & Music and never looked back. Now he did everything he could to help his parents, from hiring a physical therapist to being sure his mother had the help she would need as her husband continued to deteriorate. Russ's Christmas present to his mother was to hire a housekeeping duo to come clean once a week so she no longer had to worry about those tedious chores.

He tossed his wallet on the kitchen bar, then set his phone beside it. He toed off his boots, leaving them on the rug as he went to the refrigerator. He wanted a beer, but he couldn't remember if he had any.

Couldn't remember? Damn. Wasn't that a symptom of Alzheimer's?

"Stop it," he grumbled to himself. He couldn't live whatever was left of his life terrified that he'd be a victim. Just like his father.

But that was exactly what he was—terrified. Absolutely, utterly terrified of losing himself.

The moment he opened the fridge's door, he saw the longnecks and remembered buying them a couple days ago. Sure, he might develop the fucking disease someday.

But not today.

After opening the bottle, leaving the cap on the island with other stuff he'd discarded, and taking a long swig of the beer, Russ took a seat on one of the bar stools and started shuffling through the mail. Nothing but junk, which he shoved aside before taking another pull of the brew, hoping it would relax him.

His shoulders felt tight, especially his bum one. The damn thing ached, which meant there was probably rain in the forecast.

In fact, his whole body hurt. Pretty sucky that he was thirty-four and had enough arthritis in his battered body to predict the weather.

When his cell phone signaled a text message, he was grateful for the reprieve from his troubling thoughts. Then he smiled when he saw it was from Joslynn.

Want to run with me tomorrow? Good for your stress level.

He'd never seen a runner emoji before, and it made him smile a little broader.

Running had never been his thing, but if it gave him a chance to see her…He quickly typed out his response before he could talk himself out of it.

Why not? Sounds like fun.

Her reply was swift.

Modine Park. 6am. Shelter B. See you there.

"Six?" he squeaked.

Oh, yeah, running at six in the morning sounded like *loads* of fun.

CHAPTER FIVE

Good morning," Joslynn called as she watched Russ walking across the dewy grass, yawning all the way.

He was dressed as if she'd invited him to a touch football game—T-shirt with the sleeves ripped off and long nylon shorts. His shoes were more suited for basketball than running.

Had the man ever run for distance before?

"No such thing," he grumbled as he sat down next to her on one of the shelter's picnic tables and retied one of his shoes. Then he let out another exaggerated yawn.

"Not a morning person?" she teased as she double-knotted her Asics.

"Not even close." He looked at her feet. "Those are the ugliest shoes I've ever seen."

"Ugly?" She glanced down at them. The soles and laces were a neon turquoise, and the fabric was covered in graphic art that resembled comic book action balloons such as "pow" and "bam."

The moment she'd seen them, she'd fallen in love, and they were probably the best running shoes she owned.

Leaning back against the picnic table, he shook his head. "Yeah, ugly. *Über*ugly."

"I think they're cute." She shrugged. "Really doesn't matter. They're comfortable and do a great job supporting my arches."

"By all means, then—wear your ugly shoes."

She loved his teasing. "I intend to. And they're not ugly."

Russ flashed her one of his heart-stopping smiles. "How about we skip the run and grab some coffee and a muffin?"

So that was how it was going to be—he was one of those runners who had to be practically forced into starting. Hopefully, he'd be fine once she got him moving.

Hopping up, Joslynn took his hands and tugged him to his feet. "We'll just do a light mile to warm up, and then we'll stretch before we settle in for a good run. Okay?"

His eyes widened. "A mile warm-up? How far do you usually run?"

"It's a short day," she replied as she stretched her arm over her head. "Only five miles or so. I like to watch time per mile instead of total distance." She switched arms.

"What's your pace?" His voice squeaked.

"For a short day, only ten minutes a mile or so." After his eyes widened, she said, "We could go eleven. Even twelve if you need a snail's pace."

Russ looked utterly panicked. "Ten minutes? Each mile? Are you insane?" The squeak had been replaced with disbelief, and the grin was long gone.

"Just on slow days."

"How far did you say you run again?"

Evidently, he was finding a schedule she saw as routine as daunting. "Five miles or so. Eight to ten on long days."

Since those times and distances were pretty average for serious runners, she couldn't understand why...

Duh, Joslynn.

Russ *wasn't* a serious runner. Football players were sprinters. Distance running was seldom on their agenda.

She'd have to taper the workout to his level. She could always supplement their run with one of her own when he was ready to call it a day. Or she'd give in to the fatigue that had been dogging her lately. "We can go slower and not as far until you get in better shape. The most important thing is that you're here and moving. How about we just jog easy for a while and see how things go?"

With a brisk nod, he got to his feet. "I still think coffee and a muffin would be a helluva lot more fun."

"They might taste good, but they won't help your stress level." Smiling, Joslynn swept her arm in invitation. "After you."

* * *

Russ's body was screaming at him the same way it always had the first days of summer training camp. He hadn't realized how little he'd exercised since his last game. He was sadly out of shape. If he didn't stop soon, he was going to be sore by evening. But he'd be damned if he'd show Joslynn any weakness. His pride was already smarting from seeing how effortless this pace was for her.

One foot in front of the other.

His heart hammered and his lungs burned, and the stitch in his side was becoming so painful he couldn't straighten up. He finally acknowledged that no matter how humiliating it might be, surrender was the only option he had left. That, or collapse on the ground and die of cardiac arrest.

"Josie," he said between gulps of air. "Uncle!"

Glancing over her shoulder, she smiled. "Just a little farther?"

Damn if the woman didn't even sound winded.

"Not unless…you want me…to die." The words came out in bursts of air.

Russ gave up, fell to his knees, and then flopped to his back. Sure, it might've been a bit melodramatic. At least he made her chuckle. His back was wet, but he couldn't tell if that was because he was sweating or because the grass was still sticky with dew.

All he wanted was a huge cup of coffee, a handful of ibuprofen, and a couple of blueberry muffins.

He kept gulping air as she stood over him, jogging in place. Then alarm registered on her face and she stopped to stare down at him. "I'm sorry. I pushed too hard."

While his vanity wanted to tell her he was fine, his heaving chest said otherwise. "Maybe…a…little."

"I'm sorry, Russ." Joslynn crouched next to him, pressing two fingers to his neck and staring at her watch.

He brushed her hand away and sat up. "I'm fine."

"You're sure?"

With a curt nod, he took a look around. "Is there a water fountain close?"

"The fountains here have rusty water." She tilted her head toward her electric-blue car. "But I keep bottles in my car. Need some help up?" She stood and offered her hand.

Russ let her assist him to his feet and then walked with her back toward their starting point, where her car was waiting next to his SUV. "How about that cup of coffee now?"

"I was going to get some rest. I've got a couple days off, but I'm still on 'night schedule.'"

Since there was a note of hesitation in her voice, he took heart. "If you're lucky, I'll throw in a doughnut or two."

A smile blossomed on her face. "How about we go to a juice bar I know instead? You could use some potassium so you don't cramp up."

"Juice bar? Ugh." The last thing in the world he wanted was some blended fruit or vegetable concoction.

"Don't sweat it. They've got coffee and baked goods, too," Joslynn said, fishing her car remote from where it had been tucked inside her waistband. The lights on the car responded when she clicked open the door. She grabbed two bottles of water from a small cooler in the trunk.

The water was cold enough Russ had to remind himself not to chug the whole bottle. Despite his need for hydration, he wasn't about to give himself brain freeze.

"I adore their banana bread. It's made with Greek yogurt, so loads of protein, too," she added.

"That sounds a lot more promising than juice," Russ said. "You win. We'll head there. Your car or mine?"

"Yours." She walked around to the passenger side of his Escape. "You can drop me off back here after so I can finish my run."

"Way to rub it in, Josie." He popped open the locks as he slid into the driver's seat.

She was buckling her seat belt when she said, "Keep working with me, and we'll have you running as far as I do in no time."

* * *

Mackenzie Boles, the owner of Shamballa and a student in one of Joslynn's yoga classes, smiled at them when she and Russ strolled up to the counter. "The usual, Joslynn?"

Joslynn smiled in return. "Sounds like heaven."

"What's your usual?" Russ asked.

Mackenzie was the one to answer him. "Mango, banana, pineapple, some frozen yogurt, with a scoop of whey protein. And for you, sir?"

"Coffee. Black. Large."

"A man after my heart," Mackenzie said with a lopsided smile. "Anything to eat?"

"Oh, yeah," he replied. "What do you have?"

Pointing at the glass case, Joslynn said, "I'm sure there's something there that'll look good to you."

While he busied himself with perusing the bakery items, Mackenzie went about getting Joslynn's breakfast mixed.

"That looks interesting," he said.

She went to see what had intrigued him. "The banana bread?"

"No, the zucchini muffins."

"They're really good."

"Want one?"

Although the smoothie was usually filling enough, she nodded. She could nibble at it now, then take the rest home to snack on after she slept.

Mackenzie set the finished smoothie down and picked up a porcelain plate from a tall stack next to the bakery case. "Did you decide?"

"Two of those zucchini muffins," Russ replied.

While Mackenzie retrieved the food, Joslynn plucked a straw from the dispenser and then stabbed it into the thick liquid.

She brushed Russ's hand away when he tried to pay. There was no way she was going to let him think that what was happening between them was some kind of stereotypical "relationship." She wasn't about to give him the upper hand by establishing himself as the payer every time they ate together when she still had no idea what she wanted from him. "My turn," she insisted as she handed her debit card to Mackenzie.

"I wish you'd at least let me pay." He sounded pouty enough to make Jos quirk an eyebrow his direction. "My ego is shot to hell."

"Why?"

"Because you literally ran circles around me."

"You did great for a first workout."

He picked up the plate, swiped a few napkins from the aluminum dispenser, and followed her to a small table in the front of the store, where they made themselves comfortable. After peeling the wrapper off one of the muffins, he took a big bite. A smile formed on his lips as he chewed.

"Told you the stuff here was good," she said as she stirred her smoothie. The sounds he was making as he enjoyed the treat seemed far too erotic, so she forced herself to glance out the front window of the store and watch people wander past. Her fascination with Russ was unnerving.

Her attraction to him was stronger than she'd ever experienced, making her wonder if there might be more than simple chemistry involved. Everything about him appealed to her—from his looks to his masculine scent. Even his rather off-beat sense of humor. Although they barely knew each other, she found herself thinking about Russ constantly, planning when she could see him again.

And that thoroughly appalled her.

Her whole life had been about independence, about doing what she had to do to make it through whatever fate shoved in her path without needing anyone else. Joslynn had learned early that only she could see herself through any challenge. That lesson had come when her mother had always been too busy to be there when Joslynn needed her. Now Joslynn prided herself on her independence. She'd never even had a roommate. Why would she need to be anchored down by a relationship?

Yet something inside her was already softening toward Russ, making her wonder if he would finally be a person she could cling to when the going got tough.

The idea that she might someday need this man almost made her jump up and run out the door.

A warm hand covered hers. "What's wrong?"

Pasting a smile on her face, Joslynn faced him again. "Nothing. Just thinking."

"About?"

"About how we need to get you stretched out so you don't get too sore."

"That was an awfully fierce frown for something as simple as stretching."

She flipped her hand, hoping to dismiss the topic. "You ate that muffin at world-record speed."

With a skeptical eye, Russ finally took the bait and followed the new topic. "Not bad for a muffin made of vegetables."

"She uses healthy ingredients. No white sugar. No white flour. Applesauce instead of oil."

"Hard to believe it tasted as good as it did." His gaze dropped to her muffin, which he eyed with unmistakable appetite.

Joslynn smiled. "Want mine?"

"You don't want it?" he asked, sounding hopeful.

Stirring her drink again, she gave him what he clearly wanted. "Take the muffin. This is more than enough for me."

The dimple was back when he smiled. He picked up the muffin and held it between them. "I'll tell you what. I'll make you a deal."

"Deal?"

"You give me this muffin, and I'll show you the fun way that *I* exercise."

"That sounds…intriguing."

"I hope so. Are you working Wednesday?"

She shook her head.

"Then how about we meet at Words and Music around seven?"

"In the morning?" She winked.

"As if…"

CHAPTER SIX

Even though Russ had already paid the Uber driver's fee, Joslynn still tried to give the man a tip.

The driver waved her off. "Already taken care of."

"Are you sure?" Her gratuities tended to be a little higher than most, and this guy had a clean car and had been very polite.

"Whoever paid already overtipped," he replied with a smile.

"Okay, then." She got out of the backseat and shut the door. "Thanks," she said through the open driver's window.

The Words & Music parking lot had quite a few cars, a surprise considering it was a Wednesday night. Russ had told her the crowds tended to be smaller in the middle of the week. The delicious aroma reminded her why there were so many people there on a weeknight—the food was always amazing.

She stepped through the front door, which had been held open by one of the two hostesses. When the second twentysomething girl asked how many in her party, Joslynn didn't even have a chance to answer.

"She's with me, Amanda," Russ said, striding up to the hostess station.

Joslynn knew she was staring, but...*damn*. The man looked as delectable as strawberry cheesecake. His denim shirt hugged his broad shoulders, and he'd rolled the sleeves up to his elbows, showing off strong forearms that were lightly dusted with hair. The top few buttons opened just enough to reveal a bit of chest hair. The tight jeans accentuated his slim hips and firm backside. He'd worn a weathered cowboy hat, and his black boots were scuffed up enough she could see that he really wore them instead of donning them for show.

When he held out his hand and offered her a smile, she swallowed hard, wondering if she was in over her head. Her whole body had already flushed warm. Just seeing him looking so ruggedly handsome was enough to make her want to drag him right out of Words & Music and take him to her cottage. She'd never wanted a man as much as she did Russ at that moment, to the point she could only helplessly follow him as he led her to the dance floor and then took her into his arms.

She found security there, in his embrace. His arms were strong, his manner steady. Simply being held by Russ gave her a comfort she'd never known before.

"You look amazing tonight," he whispered in her ear, his warm breath brushing against her skin.

"So do you." Her heart was slamming against her rib cage, and for a moment she was light-headed. Thankfully, the song echoing through the place was slow paced and gave her a chance to catch her breath. She tried to hide her reaction to him, giving him a smile, albeit a weak one, when he stared down at her face.

"You okay, Josie?"

"Of course."

"You're a little flushed."

Probably because I want you so badly.

"I'm fine. Really." She let the smile become more natural as she teased him. "I'm a nurse practitioner. I should know."

He surprised her by brushing a quick kiss on her mouth. "Just want to be sure you're in good enough shape to exercise *my* way."

The bantering helped her regain some control. "And what exactly is *your* way?"

As though on cue, the music ended and the crowd that was already on the dance floor turned to face the stage.

"I thought there wasn't live entertainment tonight," she commented.

He gave her an enigmatic smile. "There isn't. But…" He led her toward the front of the dance floor, closer to the stage, while people filtered from the tables to take different spots. "There's line dancing. That's *my* exercise."

Whistles and applause rose in response to the Chelsea Wright song that began to echo through Words & Music, and people began to dance in unison.

Now she understood the crowd. Although its heyday might have passed, line dancing was still popular in Nashville, probably always would be. It was no wonder Words & Music was turning a good Wednesday-night profit.

"This one's the Slipknot Double Slide," he said. "Ever tried line dancing before?"

She shook her head. "But I'm willing to learn."

"Then let's get to it." He pulled her to stand beside him. "Just do what I do."

"I'll try."

"That's all I can ask, darlin.'"

After showing her a few steps, he had her try them with him. Then he added a few new steps. And then a few more.

So far, so good. She managed the steps without tripping over her own feet, and she hoped the rest of the Slipknot Double Slide was as easy.

After a few repeats of the steps he'd taught her, Russ said, "Now we add the cowboy boogie."

She laughed at the name and at how much she was enjoying learning the dance. "Show me!"

And Russ did, making it look effortless.

Counting with the beat, Joslynn thought she was doing well. Her mistake was glancing up to see how the rest of the dancers were doing. Missing a couple of steps, she stumbled against Russ, stopping herself from an embarrassing fall by grabbing his arm and holding tight.

That arm was as solid as steel, and the dimpled smile he gave her in response made her grin in return. "Sorry," she murmured.

"No worries. You'll get the hang of it."

The song changed, and Joslynn was proud to hear her friend Savannah's distinct alto fill the cavernous club.

At least Joslynn wasn't feeling too awkward, because it took only a couple repetitions of the steps to dance without mistakes. Just when she thought she was getting good, Russ upped the ante.

"Time to add the slipknot." He launched into a series of steps where his feet kept switching from crossing over to crossing behind so many times that she lost track.

Once again, she stumbled into him.

Russ put his hands on her hips and turned her to face him. "Watch me." He whirled so that his back was to her and then took a couple steps forward.

Eyes glued to his feet, Joslynn found it much easier to duplicate his moves. Her athleticism kicked in, and she discovered the intricate steps weren't as difficult as she'd feared.

She tried to focus on the task at hand, but Russ was making it damned difficult. He moved with such grace, which came as a bit of a surprise. She'd always considered football players to be a bit big and awkward.

She'd been wrong.

He'd shake that ass of his and all of her concentration would vanish. She lost her footing multiple times.

"And now…" Russ flashed her a heart-stopping smile as he pushed back the brim of his hat with his knuckle. "Time to add the double slide!"

The music switched to another up-tempo song, this time sang by a guy Jos didn't recognize, but she loved his Tennessee twang.

When she forced herself to stop staring at Russ's ass, she found herself truly enjoying the dance. She loved how he was constantly glancing over his shoulder to check on her, and when he finally had her join him at his side, she felt as if she belonged there.

It was so much fun to be a part of a group of people who were all dancing together—the same steps, the same rhythm—and she realized that she was actually getting a workout. It wasn't as tough as running, but line dancing was definitely raising her heart rate and using muscles she didn't normally use.

When Russ finally ended the dance, he chuckled and gave her a big hug.

She was so anxious to touch him that she tripped into his arms.

"Having a little trouble there, Josie?"

"A little. Sorry about catching your heels so many times."

"I'll live. So I taught my dance. Now we can do whatever you want. Wanna keep dancing? Or we could get a bite to eat..."

"I vote for the latter," she replied. "The smell of the food is making my stomach growl." Which was the truth but not even remotely responsible for her brain turning to mush. No, that was solely Russ's doing, and the man wasn't even trying.

He took her hand and led her to an empty table close to the dance floor. Then he gave a quick signal to one of the servers in the red T-shirts and black shorts, who nodded in return.

"Want a drink?" he asked Joslynn as he pulled out a chair for her.

She didn't scold him for the gesture and had to admit to herself that she loved the courtesy he gave her when they were together. "Sure. How about some white wine?"

Russ whispered a few things to the waitress after she came over. She nodded, hurried away, and then he took his own seat. "I'm guessing this dancing thing was a bust for you."

"Not at all," she insisted. "I really got into it once I learned the steps."

"Seemed like you had trouble with your footing."

"Nah, I was just having some trouble concentrating."

"Why?"

Because you're so damn sexy. "Tough shift last night. Didn't sleep well after. I'm a little punchy, I guess."

The waitress came back with a glass of white wine and a beer in a frosted mug. She set them down and then cocked an expectant eyebrow at Russ. "The usual, boss?"

"What's the usual?" Joslynn asked.

"Fried pickles to start," he replied. "Might not be as healthy as what you're used to, but they're one of our signature foods. Sound okay to you?"

"Sounds yummy. I'm in."

Russ nodded at the waitress. "Thanks, Tara."

"My pleasure." She turned to Joslynn. "Would you like a menu?"

"Sure. Thanks."

After retreating to give Joslynn a few minutes to look over the menu, Tara returned. Joslynn ordered and Tara left them and logged on to one of the computer terminals near the bar.

"You guys have a lot of computers," Joslynn commented.

"Brad's big on making our jobs as easy as possible," Russ replied as he nodded at one of the computers. "When the waitstaff logs orders, that info not only goes to the kitchen, but it heads directly into a spreadsheet that helps us with ordering supplies. Then we tailor the menu to what's selling versus what's stagnant. The waitstaff said the orders coming from the kitchen aren't wrong nearly as often as when they had handwritten tickets."

"Sounds like Brad found something that works for you guys. When we first went to all electronic at the hospital, some of the nurses were annoyed."

"Why? I'd think it would make their jobs easier." He leaned forward and folded his hands together, as though he were truly interested instead of simply being polite.

She obliged him with an explanation. "Most of them were used to making quick notes along the way and then charting at the end of shift or during downtimes. They hated taking the time to enter all the information as they went along." She chuckled. "Although they were thrilled at the end of their shifts when they didn't have to spend another hour or more charting."

"What about you?"

"I embraced the change. It's second nature now." A frown formed. "So, have we reduced ourselves to talking about our jobs?"

Russ let out a warm chuckle. "I suppose we have."

Tara returned and set the fried pickles between them. "Careful," she cautioned. "They're hot."

Picking one up, Joslynn let out a gasp at the intense heat against her skin, immediately dropping the breaded pickle back in the basket and waving her fingers to cool them. "You ain't kiddin.'"

"Your meals should be out shortly," Tara said before shifting her attention to another table.

"I have a better conversation topic," Russ said, quickly transferring a couple of pickles to the small plate he'd placed in front of himself. "How did you meet Savannah?"

As always, when she told the story, Joslynn framed her words carefully. "We met at a childbirth class."

He'd been taking a swig of his beer and sputtered out some foam, exactly the reaction she'd wanted. "Gotta say that I didn't see that coming."

"Yeah, it makes a great story when anyone asks."

"So, you were at a childbirth class?" Leaning forward, he whispered, "Do you have a kid I don't know about?"

She loved catching him off guard. "I was *teaching* the class."

"Now, *that* makes sense."

"After the class, Savannah came up with a bazillion questions. We ended up going out for a cup of coffee and we just sort of hit it off. I was with her when Caroline was born since her dick of a boyfriend had abandoned her."

Russ nodded. "I remember Michael trying to cash in when Savannah's star started rising."

"Yeah, that was a bad time for her."

"She's lucky to have you," he said.

"From what she told me, she's lucky to have all of you guys and Chelsea around, too," Joslynn said.

After eating the pickles he'd put on his plate, he pushed the empty plate aside and tossed her the same kind of frown she'd given him earlier. "So, now we've gone from talking about work to being a mutual admiration society?" He winked. Then he stood and held out a hand to her. "How about we go dance again before dinner is served?"

* * *

Russ enjoyed line dancing almost as much as playing football, but when he was able to head back to the dance floor, standing beside Joslynn and dancing next to her was the last thing he had in mind.

No, he wanted to hold her.

Thankfully, by the time he and Josie had finished dinner, the line dancing was coming to an end. When people filtered back to the dance floor, they did so with a more subdued attitude as the lights were dimmed and the music switched to a slower tempo.

Great for dancing cheek to cheek instead of at each other's side.

Pulling her into his arms, he couldn't shake the feeling that holding her felt…different. Right.

Perfect.

Swaying to the music, he loved how she rested her cheek against his shoulder, a kind of intimacy that usually only came with time. Yet he understood, and it was comforting that she seemed to feel the same draw to him that he had toward her.

Joslynn just fit.

She glanced up at him. "This has been so much fun."

"Yeah," he drawled with a grin. "It has."

"So two dates down, and things are going well." There was an uncertainty in her dark eyes, something he wasn't accustomed to seeing in such a self-confident woman. "Right?"

Russ brushed a quick kiss against her lips. "Absolutely. Which means there'll be a third. And a fourth. And…"

Her smile washed over him, and she laid her cheek against his shoulder again.

They danced for quite a while, so long he lost track of time. He didn't mind. The night could go on forever so long as Josie was in his arms.

The music ended, a signal from stage manager Randy that the restaurant part of the club was winding down.

Josie eased back and glanced at her silver watch. "Are you still planning to take me home? It's getting kinda late."

"Yeah, we should probably get you back to your place."

"You'll get to see the Cottage."

"The what?"

Josie let out a pleasant chuckle as she followed him to the front doors. "That's what Savannah calls my house. The Cottage."

Opening one of the double doors while she pushed the other open, he said, "That sounds intriguing. Will you give me the grand tour?"

"Of course. But as the name implies, don't expect something big and grand."

Once Russ had her in his SUV, he hesitated with putting on his seat belt and starting the engine, not wanting the evening to end. "Did you have a good time, Josie?"

She reached over and took his hand, giving it a squeeze. "I did. A very good time."

He turned to face her, finding her smiling at him in a way that hit him viscerally. She hadn't fastened her seatbelt, either. The temptation to kiss her was too strong to deny. When he leaned closer, she beat him to the punch.

Each time his lips touched hers, he was surprised by the wave of heat that flashed through his body. She was the first to heighten the exchange, slipping her tongue between his lips.

Her taste was now familiar to him, and he drank her in. When she tore her lips away, she was panting for breath. He was every bit as breathless and wondering exactly where they should go from here. Despite cautioning himself that he wanted more from Josie than a roll in the sack, he couldn't slow his physical response to her. This woman filled him with desire almost too strong to fight.

"Can your seat go back any farther?" she asked, her husky voice washing over him.

Instead of answering her, he hit the button to push the seat back and smiled at her. If she wanted to neck in his car, he had no objections.

Smiling back, she moved closer until she could straddle his hips. As she lowered herself against him, he captured her mouth for another passionate kiss.

Russ tried to lace his fingers through her dark hair, but she'd tied it up in a ponytail. Fumbling with the fastener, he kept kissing her until he could cast the damn thing aside. Then he buried his hands in that luxurious, silky mass and growled his appreciation.

Joslynn had opened a few of the buttons on his shirt, and now she stroked his chest, playing with his chest hair as she sucked on his tongue.

His hard cock pressed painfully against the front of his jeans, and he wanted nothing more than to feel her slender fingers wrapped around it. At this rate, they'd be naked in his restaurant's parking lot in the next five minutes. But he just couldn't make himself stop kissing her long enough to ask if she wanted to go to a more private location.

Easing her lips away from his, she tickled his neck with her tongue. "I want you, Russ. Let's go to my place. Now." She followed that order with a stinging bite and then a soothing lick.

"My place is closer," he said, breathless and near desperate to be skin to skin with her.

"Then your place it is."

CHAPTER SEVEN

Russ fumbled with his keys, finally getting the door open and pushing it wide.

The look Josie flashed him was so full of desire that he sucked in a quick breath. She took his hand and led him into his house. Then she took off his hat, tossed it aside, and smoothed her hands through his hair. "Your hair's so soft."

What did a guy say to something like that? "Thank you."

She nuzzled his neck. "And you smell so good." Kissing and licking her way to his ear, she ran her tongue around the shell as her fingers began to open the buttons on his shirt. "So sweet," she murmured.

He tried to catch his breath, to take a moment to think about what was about to happen and decide whether they should take this huge step. His body was ready.

Yet there was something holding him back.

After she finished with the buttons, she tugged his shirttail out of his jeans and spread the shirt wide. He shrugged out of the garment and cast it aside while she rubbed her nose against the patch of hair on his chest.

When her hands went to work on his belt, Russ felt as if he were caught in the middle of a tornado, swept up in the intensity to the point where he had no control.

He grabbed her wrists. "Let's slow down, darlin.'"

Joslynn cocked her head but didn't let go. "Slow down? Why?" She leaned in and kissed him again.

He tried to relax and surrender to her kiss.

But his thoughts suddenly clouded with doubt.

Before he could sort out exactly what was bothering him, she had his belt unbuckled and was almost done unbuttoning his jeans.

Something just wasn't right—something he needed to work through before he opened up to her so personally.

Then suddenly he knew exactly why he couldn't make love to her yet. Yes, there was a part of him that wanted to revel in the sexual storm. But he knew there was a much larger prize at stake.

There was something about her, something that told Russ he might have found someone who was worth taking a risk despite his possibly scary future.

Maybe it was the intelligence that radiated from her, or her quick, witty humor. Maybe it was the gentle way she'd cared for him in the hospital. Maybe it was how easy it was to just *be* with her, to talk to her, to share himself in a way he'd never wanted to with another woman.

Josie made him want to learn everything about her. Which meant he wanted to get to know her before they traded what could one day be a lasting relationship for a roll in the sheets.

He seized her wrists again when she tried to slide his jeans over his hips. "Wait. Please. We need to talk."

Her hands smoothed over his bare chest. "Talking is the *last* thing I want to do." Her gaze found his. "Oh, are you out of condoms?"

"No. I've got condoms, but—"

Bending down, she licked his nipple, making him groan and drop his head back. Her fingers trailed down his chest, over his abdomen, and under the waistband of his briefs.

He forced himself to take a step back. "Wait. Please, Josie."

Joslynn frowned at him. "What's wrong?"

"We're moving so fast..."

Her frown deepened. "Don't you want me?"

"God, yes."

With a stern glare, she folded her arms under her breasts. "And I want you. We're consenting adults; we have privacy and condoms. So what's the hang-up?"

He rubbed the back of his neck. "I need to tell you something."

She dropped her arms and took a step toward him; he took one in retreat.

"Russ..."

"Can we sit and talk?"

"You really want to *talk*? Now?"

"Yeah, you know. Get to know each other a little better."

A confused sulk formed on her face as her arms dropped to her sides. "I don't understand. I mean, you're a guy."

He had no idea what she was talking about. "What?"

"You're a guy," she said. "Guys never want to stop and talk."

"*This* guy does."

She shot him an incredulous frown before she sighed. "Fine. Let's sit and talk."

Russ buttoned his pants and picked up his shirt. After thrusting his arms in the sleeves, he pulled it closed and fastened a couple buttons.

Joslynn had turned on the lamp and was taking a good look around his mess of an apartment.

"Sorry," he immediately said out of habit. "I'm not here much, and cleaning isn't my thing."

She didn't comment, just picked up the clothes he'd left draped over the sofa and set them aside before taking a seat.

He was having difficulty reading her, partly because he still wanted her so desperately he was having a hard time holding on to his resolve that they should wait. What they could share as a couple—the future they might have together—gave him strength...and a thin thread of patience.

How odd. He was going to fight for a relationship, something he'd all but vowed never to do after his father's diagnosis, not wanting to burden a significant other with that sharp sword perpetually hanging over his head.

Yet the more time he spent with Joslynn, the more determined he became that they could—no, *would*—share something more than a bed. If Russ had his way, it would grow and evolve into the kind of love his parents shared, one that went beyond the here and now and embraced the future—even if his future might include a horrible illness.

That thought gave him pause. Was he setting her up for the prospect of watching him deteriorate?

For the first time since his father's diagnosis, Russ wondered if his own future wasn't necessarily written in stone. Was he truly doomed to be reduced to what his father was slowly and agonizingly becoming?

He found that he didn't have the courage to find out for sure. His father's doctor had offered genetic testing, but Russ had declined. For now he simply preferred to stay in a state of denial rather than discover that he was doomed.

Nothing in life was certain. *Nothing.*

Joslynn inspired him to take a chance. She was worth the gamble. Even if there might one day be a genetic storm coming their way.

Why throw his future away, especially if the odds might not be stacked against him—against them? Why not try to discover if the connection he felt to Josie could be more than a few tumbles between the sheets and an awkward parting?

"Well?" Josie had drawn her lips into a tight line. "You wanted to talk. Let's talk."

He hadn't realized he'd lost himself so deeply in thought. "I think we should take things slow. Physically, I mean."

"Are you saying you don't want me?"

That statement made him laugh. "Of course I want you. I want you badly."

She cocked her head. "Then I don't understand, Russ."

"I think we should take a little more time before we…get too physical."

"Because…?"

He answered with honesty. "Because I think we might have something special here, and I don't want to mess it up."

"Special? You mean like boyfriend and girlfriend? No. No way." She shook her head.

Russ blinked a few times, unsure why the tone of her voice was so adamant. "Why not?"

"I'm not looking to tie myself down," Josie replied. "I've never been one for having a boyfriend." She gave him a sharp frown as she again crossed her arms under her breasts as though hugging herself. Her gaze drifted away until she was staring at the wall.

It wasn't what she said as much as how she said it. Adding the shakiness of her words to her body language, Russ realized there was a reason she was so resistant to the idea.

Joslynn was afraid.

But of what?

As always, he dove in headfirst. "What's got you so scared?"

Her head whipped around, and she frowned at him. "Scared? I'm not scared."

"Horse shit."

"I'm *not.*"

"You're terrified of getting involved with me."

"I *am* involved with you." She let out an inelegant little snort. "At least I was *trying* to be involved with you."

He shook his head. "You're talking about wanting sex. I want more."

"More?" Her tone was incredulous. "What *more* could you want?"

"Honestly?"

"Of course."

"I want the whole damn thing. I want our own happily-ever-after."

* * *

Joslynn let out a rueful laugh, not at all surprised when he glared at her in response. "There's no such thing as a happily-ever-after, Russ. Those don't exist."

Russ cocked his head. "You really believe that?"

She shot him a curt nod, hoping he'd stop saying stupid things.

Life had shown her that all connections were fleeting. People might say they were in love, but what they truly meant was that they were in lust. The going got tough, and someone always left.

Fuck happily-ever-after.

Without another word, he strode over to a set of shelves next to his television. One of the tiers was full of picture frames, something she'd been too preoccupied to notice when they'd come inside. After picking up one of the frames, he came to sit next to her on the sofa. He set it on her lap. "Tell these two that."

The picture was clearly old, a black-and-white image. Two smiling faces from long ago stared back at her—a beaming bride and groom, looking ready to take on the whole world.

"Who are they?" she asked, her voice only a whisper.

"My grandparents. Their happily-ever-after lasted sixty-one years."

While Joslynn was inclined to shrug that story away, she didn't. Not only would it hurt Russ's feelings, but she wouldn't negate what these two people had achieved.

Yet the idea of a couple staying together sixty-plus years was hard to grasp. There had to be something different about them, something that made their connection last when myriad others had broken apart.

Perhaps they were older when they said their vows, which meant their marriage was a commitment made between two mature people who'd had a chance to live and were ready to be tied down. She'd heard of those kinds of couples staying together. "When did they marry? In their late twenties? Early thirties?"

He chuckled. "Hardly. They tied the knot right out of high school. Grandma was barely eighteen," he replied, lightly touching the photograph of the woman's face. "Grandpa was close to twenty."

Joslynn shrugged and set the frame on the coffee table. "I guess they were lucky."

"My parents have been married thirty-eight years."

She simply shrugged again.

"I like you, Josie. A lot." The serious tone of his voice felt like a punch to the gut.

"I like you too, but liking doesn't mean we'll be successful in a relationship like your parents or your grandparents. They aren't the usual. Not in this day and age. Couples don't stay together anymore. Getting married is just the first step toward getting divorced. Relationships are nothing but heartache waiting to happen."

He stared at her, frowning. "Are you divorced?"

The man was fishing for personal information, which was enough to make her squirm. "No."

"Your parents are, though, right?"

She'd have to distract him from his inquisition. The last thing she'd wanted tonight was to start sharing her life's story. Blabbing about her father's betrayal, her mother's emotional distance? Discussing how her own childhood trials had been what cost her parents any chance of happiness? Those were cards she had no intention of showing anyone, not even someone as special as Russ.

The sexual heat still flaring inside her made her want to show him that there were better things they could be doing. She put her hand on his thigh and inched up the thick muscle, hoping to give him something more pleasurable to think about. "Look, Russ…Can't we forget this happily-ever-after stuff for now? There are ways we can spend our time that are a helluva lot more fun."

His hand covered hers. "Is that really all you want? Just a roll in the hay?"

How was she supposed to answer that?

No man had ever been worth more than a "roll in the hay" to her. Except…

No, she wasn't taking that trip down memory lane. Once upon a time, when she'd been young and stupid, she'd opened her heart and let someone in.

Her reward for that love and trust?

Her heart had been shredded and tossed right back to her.

Then there was her "beloved" father…

Another trip down wretched memory lane better left untraveled.

Yet Russ had her so confused, she wasn't sure how to respond to his question. Yes, of course she wanted to sleep with him, to see how great they'd be together in bed. The desire for him racing through her was deeper than she'd ever felt for any man, and the chemistry was undeniable.

But could that mean she'd finally found someone she was willing to open up to, to take a chance again? Someone with whom she could share something other than passion?

Fairy tales. Love was only for fairy tales, not for real life. "Relationships are doomed to fail, Russ. That might've worked for your grandparents, even for your parents, but people don't stay together anymore."

"What about Savannah and Brad?"

"They're great together, but…" She shrugged. "Time will tell."

"And the same for Chelsea and Ethan?"

"They're all grown-ups. They've lived enough to know what they want."

"Aren't we grown-ups, too?"

All she did was shrug again, but his arguments were wearing her down, much to her astonishment.

Can he be right? "Maybe…But…"

He cocked an eyebrow. "So you're not willing to give us a try? You're not even going to give me a chance to prove you wrong?" He surprised her when he brushed his mouth over hers. A quick kiss that was over and done in the blink of an eye. "There's something here, Josie. You know it as well as I do. There's something that might just be that *more* that people are always searching for, and I want to know if we can have something special. I want to know that we are at least willing to try."

* * *

Josie had been hurt. That much was plain. But when? By whom?

She wasn't going to make things easy for him. This was going to be a prize Russ would have to wage war to win.

And deep down, his gut was telling him that was exactly what he should do. Fight for her.

He stood, pulling her up with him. Then he wrapped his arms around her, holding her close as she lay her cheek against his shoulder. "I like you, Josie. A lot. And I want you. But for the first time in a long, long time, I want to see if I might have finally found a woman I can share everything with." He nudged her chin up so he could see her eyes. "You might not believe two people can stay together, but won't you give me the chance to try to prove you wrong?"

Emotions played across her beautiful face, but Russ couldn't read them. He was pretty sure there was no anger, but was she showing him fear?

"Tell me what you're thinking," he said. "I can't read your mind."

"I like you too," she said.

He dropped a kiss on her forehead. "I know a lot of other guys would shut the hell up and just take you to bed. But if we take that step now, too quickly, you and I both know we're probably killing any chance of having something more long-term."

"You really believe that, don't you?"

He nodded.

Her lips pulled into a tight line. "I've never seen a relationship that works."

"Never?" He wasn't sure how to respond. "What about your parents?"

"Dad left the moment I got—he left before I really even knew him."

"Grandparents?"

"My mother never knew her father. He died in Vietnam a few

months before she was born. I've never had any contact with anyone from my sperm donor's family."

Sperm donor? No wonder the woman had commitment issues. "I'm sorry."

She shook her head. "Don't be."

There was clearly more to the story, but she'd opened up a lot for one night. The rest would come with time and trust.

Russ kissed her, a slow, deep kiss. When he pulled back, Josie followed him, putting her lips against his again. Then she eased back and let out a small sigh.

"Okay," she said with a brusque nod.

"Okay what?"

"Okay...you win. We do this the old-fashioned way. I can't promise you anything..."

"I only want one promise," he insisted. "Just be honest with me. That's all I can ask."

"Honesty, huh?" Her coy smile made his heart skip a beat. "Then I can honestly tell you that you'd better take me home now, or I'm gonna change my mind and jump you instead of letting us get to know each other."

Sweeping his arm toward the door, he said, "Your chariot awaits, m'lady."

CHAPTER EIGHT

The next day, Joslynn wasn't surprised to find Russ waiting when she got to the park for her morning run. She was quickly discovering his tenacity, a trait she couldn't help but admire. He was sitting on the same bench she usually stretched against, his arms draped casually over the back, his legs extended in front of him and crossed at the ankles.

At least he'd come ready to run, dressed in a Kentucky Wildcats T-shirt, dark shorts, and what looked to be brand-new Nikes that were suitable for jogging. The grin on his handsome face made her smile in return.

"You're here," she said when she reached him.

"I am."

"Not too sore to try it again?"

"Oh, I'm plenty sore," he said with a chuckle. "But I know the best thing to do is work through it. So tell me about this running program you've developed for me."

Casting a glance back to her car, she frowned. "I need to get my tablet. I've got the whole thing programmed into an app and—"

Russ shook his head. "No need. Just give me the CliffsNotes version."

"But I could get my tablet and show you—"

Coming to stand in front of her, he set his hands on her shoulders. "It's fine, Josie. I'm not that picky about things."

But I am! she wanted to shout.

The admission wasn't easy. Keeping a tight rein on things was an enormous part of her personality, but it wasn't until he'd thrown out the term that she realized exactly how much of a control freak she'd become. At that moment, she was fighting the nearly irresistible need to show him the running program she'd spent hours designing for him.

"Can't we just…run?" he asked.

She shrugged. "I guess…"

His lips touched hers. Then he tossed her a smile that chased the frown from her face. "Let's get to it." Turning, he started jogging away from her.

Despite the urge to call him back to look at the tablet, she followed, happy to see no hitch in his gait that might show that his last run had caused any real harm.

Thankfully, the rhythm of the run and her desire to help him improve quickly distracted her. Before long, she was offering him suggestions and tips as they worked their way around the park.

She decided to forget the damn tablet.

* * *

Russ wasn't about to turn into a big baby again. While Josie might've surprised him last time they ran together, he'd awakened that morning with the same mind-set he'd always had on the football field.

Show no pain.

The added benefit of their agreement from the night before was that he could concentrate on plans for things to do with her as a couple instead of focusing on the way his calves were screaming at him.

By mile three, he was getting close to admitting defeat. Before he could call a halt, she veered to a shelter with a picnic table. "I need to stop for a second," she announced. Putting the front of her feet on the slab, she dropped her heels before rising on tiptoes. "My calves are tight."

How did she know the exact thing he needed? He joined her on the slab, giving his own calves a much-needed stretch.

Eyes on his lower legs, she kept alternating between lowering her heels and then rising to her toes. "You might want to get some inserts. They'll help those Achilles." With a nod to his shoes, Josie said, "Those shoes look fine, but some good inserts will help you."

"Want to go help me find some after we run?"

To his disappointment, she shook her head. "Much as I'd like to, I'd better catch some sleep. Got a shift tonight." Straightening, she gave him a smile. "Ready to get back at it, or are you crying 'uncle' again?"

He returned the smile, catching his second wind. "Let's see exactly how far you can push me." On that, he sprinted toward the running trail, enjoying her laughter as she quickly caught up with him.

Before he was entirely out of breath again, he said, "When do you have time off again?"

"I've got a three-in-a-row; then I'll have two days off."

"Wanna go catch dinner and a movie after your three days on?"

"Sure thing." Pitching him a wink, she sprinted ahead of him. "If you can catch me."

* * *

Later that evening, while on a break, Joslynn filled her Styrofoam cup with hazelnut coffee. Taking a seat at one of the tables by the window, she kept an eye on the cafeteria entrance.

Savannah had called, wanting to talk to her while she was on a break. Not a surprise since Jos had reached out to her friend in a bit of a panic after Russ had taken her home the night before. Even now, waiting for Savannah to show up, she felt as though she were on pins and needles.

Why? Because Russ had used the one word that could send her anxiety soaring.

"Relationship."

He had turned down what had promised to be hot sex because he wanted to give the two of them time to get to know each other better. How old-fashioned was that?

Yet his logic stuck in her mind, twirling in her thoughts. She'd had a few "friends with benefits" over the years, and once the sex began, that was the focus of all of their time together. There weren't any leisurely dinners where they talked about themselves. There weren't any dates that included things like holding hands or exchanging sweet kisses. There was only the ultimate goal of physical satisfaction.

Joslynn's pairing with Matthew had lasted nine months, the longest of any of her other…

Her other *what*? Relationships? Sex partners? Fuck buddies?

And in all that time, she and Matthew had shared practically no intimacy beyond the physical. She wasn't even sure where he'd grown up or if his parents were still in the picture.

Maybe Russ was right. If they really wanted to get to know each other, it was probably better to keep their clothes on for a while.

Thankfully, she glanced up to see Savannah waving from the cafeteria entrance. Bypassing the food and drinks, she made her way to Joslynn. After taking a seat, she gave one of her typical smiles—the content type she'd worn since she and Brad had become a couple. "Long time no see."

"Yeah," Jos replied. "How's Caroline? Brad?"

"They're great. But I think we've got other things to talk about." Savannah set her phone aside and folded her hands on the table. "So, are you ready to explain those rather…freaked-out messages?"

Joslynn shifted the cup between her hands. "Yeah, sorry about those. I guess they were a little intense. I was just—as you said—freaked out."

"Well, since all I got from them was that there was something up with Russ, I have to admit that I'm dying of curiosity. Especially when you mentioned that he wants to do something that you find…what was the word? Oh, yeah. 'Repulsive.'"

"I said that?" Jos asked.

"Sure did," Savannah replied. "That word lends itself to some rather vivid imaginings. So you'll see why I've been dying to find out what's going on."

"He wouldn't sleep with me," Joslynn blurted out. "Can you believe it?"

Eyes wide, Savannah kept quiet.

"I mean it," Joslynn said with a nod. "We went back to his place, and he turned me down flat."

"And that was 'repulsive'?"

"No. What's repulsive is what he *did* want to do."

With a flip of her hand, Savannah revealed her impatience. "If you don't tell me the whole story soon, I think I'm going to lose my mind."

Joslynn let out a sigh. "He thinks we should wait for sex, that we should have a...a...relationship."

Savannah's response was a broadened smile. "No wonder you're terrified. You're pretty accustomed to being alone."

Alone.

Seemed to Joslynn as if she'd always been on her own. Always.

Her sperm donor had heard the word "leukemia" and promptly bailed, and she'd refused to waste a minute of time thinking about him after that. They'd never been close anyway since he'd been a truck driver who had seldom been home. The memories she had of him had faded to a haze.

Her mother had at least *tried* to be there through the worst of Jos's illness, offering to hold her ten-year-old daughter's hand through her chemotherapy infusions. But then work interfered, and Joslynn had spent those long days with many different people—relatives, friends, anyone who could spare the time—listening to music or watching TV. They always acted so uncomfortable, finding reasons to leave the infusion area often.

Her mother hadn't had a choice except to work. There were

bills to be paid, and if she hadn't worked, there would've been no insurance to pay for the treatments. Jos didn't blame her. But if there was one thing childhood leukemia did for a person, it taught her that when everything was said and done, she was fighting the battle alone. Her body was her own enemy, and she'd learned to face each problem with stoicism—resigned to fate and yet still ready to do what needed to be done to survive.

And no one could save her unless she saved herself. It was her own spirit, her own fortitude that ultimately allowed her to survive leukemia and the horrible process of systematically poisoning her body to rid herself of the disease.

Once the battle ended, Joslynn had vowed to help other sick people. She'd been obsessed with any subject that allowed her to understand how to heal. Chemistry. Biology. Psychology. While medical school had seemed appealing, crippling debt hadn't. So she'd opted for nursing and had found her place in life—at least as far as a vocation was concerned. After a few years as a nurse, she'd decided to become a nurse practitioner since it allowed her to grow even more.

She'd specialized in emergency medicine because she enjoyed the frenetic pace, but when she could find the time, she visited the pediatric oncology ward, doing what she could to encourage the patients and their families, to give them hope for beating down the enemy within.

Her personal life had been every bit as deliberate. She wasn't about to let the life she'd fought so hard to keep be defined by some man's opinion of her, especially after watching the agony her mom had gone through when her husband left. No way. Jos had already fought one war; she wasn't going to invite another one into her life. Besides, the one time she'd tried a normal relationship had only reaffirmed her belief that independence was the better route.

"Earth to Jos," Savannah said, laying a gentle hand over Joslynn's.

"Sorry. Got a little lost in thought."

"You were looking pretty fierce there, so I'm guessing you're not thinking too kindly about Russ."

Russ. Joslynn was right back where she started. What was she going to do about him?

Savannah pulled her hand back. "You know, I think you're going about this with a little too much worry."

"Meaning?"

"Meaning you shouldn't keep acting like he asked you to make some kind of lifetime commitment. Instead of angsting over whether you two are going to have a long-term relationship, why not just go on a few dates? See if you two click?"

Joslynn couldn't stop a smile. "Oh, we 'click' just fine."

A knowing grin blossomed on Savannah's face. "So it's like that, is it? Good for you two."

"But we're back to the original problem. He wants to wait."

"A couple of dates, Jos. Give the guy a couple of dates. It doesn't work out, what's the worst that could happen?"

He could break my heart.

That thought almost made her gasp. Since when was her *heart* involved?

"Look," Savannah said. "If things don't work out, you guys don't see each other that much anyway, right? You're working night shifts, which means you don't come to a lot of our Friday barbecues. And it's not like you spend a ton of time at the restaurant."

"Yeah, we really don't bump into each other often." *Pretty much never.*

"So, I ask again, what do you have to lose?"

"Are you happy, Savannah? I mean, you went through hell with Caroline's father…"

"I did, but Brad is the best thing that ever happened to me. And to Caroline. I'm very happy."

Somehow, Joslynn didn't see Brad running out on his adopted daughter should she get sick. "Brad's a good guy."

"I think Russ is a good guy, too. If I were you, I'd give him a chance to prove it."

* * *

It was only a few minutes before midnight when Russ realized he hadn't gone into Words & Music at all that day. Brad and Ethan would be thrilled that he'd found something better to do with his days off.

What had he been doing instead of knocking heads at the bar? He'd sat down with his guitar and worked on the song he'd been writing.

He'd first picked up a guitar in middle school, wanting to impress some girl he'd had a crush on. He'd found out pretty quickly that he had a talent for it, so he'd convinced his parents to let him take lessons. Not that he wanted to be a country music star or anything. All he had to do was open his mouth and try to sing and it became quite clear that he was never meant to perform.

His father had always joked that the dogs in the neighborhood would start howling whenever Russ tried to sing, which wasn't far from the truth.

But he kept up the guitar, finding that it was soothing to play it on game days when he often got too wound up. A few songs and he could focus better. The Colts used to have a sing-along as part of their pregame ritual. Russ played; they sang.

It was only in the last year that he'd thought about writing a tune. The hobby was relaxing, which meant he should probably do it more often. His temper seemed to be getting the better of him lately. Time with his guitar, plucking out a new tune, helped him keep a good grip on things.

The song he was currently working on had been so much easier than any of his others. The melody was nearly done, and it was a tune that was soothing to the ears. But the nascent songwriter had not a clue as to what lyrics to match to it.

Was it a love song? A funny tune? Kitsch?

All of the above?

Depended on the tempo.

It's Josie's song, Russ suddenly realized.

That was when he understood Brad on a deeper level. When Brad had a dry spell, being unable or unwilling to write songs, it was Savannah who had inspired him to compose again—the same way the words to this new song were coming straight from Russ's budding feelings for Joslynn.

So he'd sat down and fiddled with the words, trying to match them to the music, and lost all track of time. He thought about Josie for a minute, wondering how her shift was going. By midnight, she was probably just getting warmed up.

He scribbled a few more words down before a yawn slipped out. How could Josie handle being up—not only awake but working—so late and still face another six or so hours of seeing patients? Not only was she incredibly strong, but her body had to be on a different rhythm from the rest of the world.

Why did each new thought of her bring around a few more words to the song?

Finally setting his pen and his guitar aside, Russ picked up his phone to text her.

Hope you're having a good night. Running in the morning?

The reply wasn't long in coming.

Of course. See you there?

Absolutely.

CHAPTER NINE

Russ put his hand against the small of Joslynn's back as he guided her into the pancake house. It wasn't often he went on a breakfast date, mostly because he liked sleeping late, but if getting up early allowed him to spend time with her, he'd meet her anywhere and anytime.

She had dark smudges under her eyes, and she'd covered a yawn more than once. He couldn't imagine how hard it was to rush around a busy emergency room for fourteen straight hours three days in a row. That she hadn't wanted to run this morning was enough to tell him how exhausted she was.

"I want some eggs and some sleep," she said as she slid into her side of the booth. "I'm dead tired."

"You'll get both," Russ promised as he turned his inverted coffee cup over to alert the waitress he needed some caffeine. When Josie didn't mimic his action, he asked, "No coffee?"

She shook her head. "It'll keep me awake."

"Ah. Makes sense."

Instead of picking up the menu, she unwrapped the napkin holding her silverware.

"Know what you want?" he asked.

"My usual."

"So you come here a lot?"

"Yep. Some of us come over here after our shift. Huge portions and the waitresses are awesome."

As though to prove her point, a fortysomething waitress brought a coffeepot over to fill Russ's cup. "Good morning."

Before he could even take a sip, his cell rang, and he checked the ID. "Mom?"

"I need your help!" his mother said, her voice frantic.

Adrenaline rushed through his body. "What?"

"Please come home!"

Heart pounding, Russ asked, "What's wrong?"

"Just come home. We need your help."

"Did you call 911?"

There was no response. A quick check of his phone showed she'd ended the call.

He anxiously tried calling back, but his attempt went right to voicemail. "Damn it."

"What's wrong?" Josie asked.

"I'm not sure. Mom begged me to come home right away. Said she needed my help," he replied, debating whether to call 911. Since he had no idea exactly what was going on, he didn't know what to tell a dispatcher. Did they need the police? Firefighters? An ambulance?

His parents' home was only a brief drive away, and he figured he'd go there first to get the facts. "I'm sorry, Josie. I've gotta go."

She was on her feet as well, tossing some money on the table. "I'm going with you."

Russ hadn't told her anything about his father's illness, and he wasn't sure this was the best way for her to find out. "It's okay. I can handle this." Then his brain kicked in.

She's a nurse. They might need medical help.

"I want to go with you," she insisted. "You can fill me in on the way there."

With a hard swallow, he nodded. Her tagging along meant that the time had come to share with her exactly what was wrong with his father. He only hoped that she wouldn't come to the conclusion that her boyfriend might be a ticking time bomb and decide a relationship simply wasn't worth the effort.

She grabbed her purse and slung it over her shoulder. "Let's go."

* * *

"How far?" Joslynn asked as she buckled her seat belt.

"Only about five miles," Russ replied, firing up the engine. The tires squealed as he sped out of the parking lot.

"Please tell me what's going on." He'd sounded so worried on his phone call, but she knew little of why they were rushing away from the restaurant.

After taking a corner so quickly that she was forced to brace herself against the door, he finally said, "I'm not sure, but I imagine it has to do with my dad."

"Your dad?"

"I wasn't quite ready to tell you yet, but he has Alzheimer's."

She placed her hand on his thigh and gave him an affectionate squeeze. "Oh, Russ. I'm so sorry."

What else was she supposed to say? Alzheimer's was one of the most insidiously tragic things that could happen to a person—to a family. Her first thought was that Russ's father had to be too young for that kind of diagnosis, but then again, the disease could hit at any age.

"Yeah," he said, his mouth bowing to a fierce frown. "So am I."

"What was the call about?"

"All she said was to come home right away."

Joslynn was surprised when Russ pulled his SUV into a driveway. Seemed as though they'd just left the restaurant. They scrambled out of the vehicle as a middle-aged woman with disheveled wet hair came hurrying down the front porch steps in her stocking feet.

"What's wrong? Where's Dad?" Russ asked, jerking his phone from his belt. "Tell me what happened so I can call 911. Did he fall? Is he hurt?"

The woman—one who Jos recognized as a former ER patient—shook her head and went hurrying back up the stairs. "He ran away."

"He what?"

"He's gone, Russell." She waved them into the house, and Russ and Jos obediently followed.

"I took a quick shower, and when I came out of the bathroom, he wouldn't answer me. I've been looking everywhere." The woman shoved her feet into her shoes and then bent over to tie the laces. "He must've gone outside. We need to search for him."

Joslynn took a good look around, trying to assess the situation.

Her gaze fell to the front door. The rug that touched the threshold had a distinct border, which was something in their favor. "Was the door open?"

"Mom," Russ said, "this is Josie. Josie, this is my mom, Yvonne Green."

After a quick look of pleading directed at Jos, Yvonne shook her head again. "We need to start in the garage. Then we can check the shed out back."

Since Yvonne clearly didn't want Russ to know they'd already met, Joslynn focused on the problem at hand. "Was the front door open?" she asked again.

"No. None of the doors were open, but…"

"I don't think he went outside." Jos pointed to the floor by the front door. "That rug has a visual boundary. He probably wouldn't cross it."

Russ cocked his head. "What do you mean?"

Pointing to the rug again, she replied, "Alzheimer's patients normally won't cross a thick line like the border of that rug. Most Alzheimer units have carpet borders put all around the perimeter of any room the patients congregate in. It keeps them from wandering."

"I have a rug exactly like that by the back door," Yvonne said. "You really think he didn't leave?"

Joslynn nodded. "Have you searched the house?"

"Not well," Yvonne replied, combing her fingers through her damp hair. "I hurried to get dressed so we could start searching."

"Then we should start in the house. If we don't find him here, we'll call 911 and get some help for a larger search." Jos shifted her gaze to Russ. "Why don't you start upstairs? That's where the bedrooms are, right?"

He nodded.

"Closets to hide in," she said. "Look everywhere. Under beds, anyplace a body could fit."

"I'll check this floor," Yvonne said. "Would you mind looking in the basement, Josie?"

"I'd be happy to."

As Russ ran up the stairs, Yvonne led Joslynn to another stairway. "Down there."

"We'll find him," Jos said, placing her hand on Yvonne's arm.

Wiping away a tear, Yvonne nodded. Then she hurried off as Joslynn headed down the stairs.

The lights were on when she entered the basement. The first cavernous room held a pool table and a vintage pinball machine. Old-fashioned paneling lined the walls, and the floor was covered with rust-colored carpet that had to be older than she was.

A door leading from the room was open and the naked lightbulb hanging in the center of the ceiling was illuminated, which made her think she might be on the right track. After a quick check under the pool table and pinball machine, she headed to the next room. This was a utility area with a water heater, the furnace, and a washer and dryer. Instead of being finished, the room had a concrete floor and the walls were open to the studs. She searched behind anything where a man could fit and found nothing. There was one more door, again open, and she walked through it.

A masculine chuckle made her let out the breath she hadn't realized she'd been holding. Fumbling against the wall for a switch, she turned on the lights to find a storage room full of shelving units. Resting on those metal surfaces was everything from board games to large boxes marked with myriad descriptors from "Christmas" to "baby clothes."

She didn't know Russ's father's name, so out of habit, she called, "Sir? Are you in here?"

Another chuckle helped her focus on the direction of the sound. She started walking between the shelving units.

"Sir?"

"You found me!" A man stepped out from between two of the sets of shelves to her left. "I thought I had a good hiding place!"

"You did. It took us a long time to find you," Joslynn said.

"Sharon?" When he tilted his head, she saw clearly the resemblance between father and son. All Russ had to do was look at his father to see himself in another twenty-five years. The same face shape, bright eyes, and short light hair, albeit his father had a peppering of gray at his temples.

"My name is Joslynn. Would you like to go upstairs to see Yvonne and Russ?"

"I was hiding from Yvonne. I thought she wanted to play. She loves to have fun."

Holding out her hand, Jos nodded. "She'll be glad I found you."

He took her hand. "I'm glad to see you, Sharon."

"I'm Joslynn," She led him out of the storage room and then the utility room, turning off the lights and shutting the doors behind her.

Dragging his feet, he pointed at the rack of pool cues. "Do you wanna play a game of pool?"

"No, thank you. Yvonne is worried. We should go see her."

With a pouty lip, he followed her up the stairs.

"I found him!" Joslynn called. "Russ? Yvonne?"

Heavy footfalls sounded upstairs, and as she led him toward the family room, Russ came bounding down the stairs. "Dad!"

Yvonne hurried in from the back of the house. "Baron! I was so worried."

Baron Green dropped Jos's hand and wrapped his arms around Yvonne when she threw herself against him.

"Where was he?" Russ asked, coming to stand next to Joslynn.

"He was in the basement storage room, playing hide-and-seek."

Easing back, Yvonne frowned at her husband. "Hide-and-seek?"

"You like playing games," Baron announced.

"When I know I'm playing them," Yvonne scolded.

"You hid, so I did too." He pointed at Joslynn. "Sharon knew."

"Who's Sharon?" Jos asked.

"His baby sister," Russ replied. "She lives in Arizona."

Yvonne let out a heavy sigh. "You do look a lot like her when she was younger." Then she swatted Baron's chest. "Don't you ever scare me like that again!"

Having spent some time working geriatrics, Joslynn immediately wanted to rattle off ideas on how the Greens could make a few changes. Helpful supplies like special locks. Places where they could connect with other Alzheimer's families to share ideas on coping. Workers that would help keep an eye on the patient when his caregiver had other activities.

Why hadn't Yvonne told her that her husband had Alzheimer's when she'd visited the ER? Joslynn remembered stitching up a cut on Yvonne's arm, and they'd chatted amicably during the procedure. Most people who were caregivers for a chronically ill spouse wanted to talk at length about their situation. Yvonne hadn't said a word, so Joslynn had never had a chance to make suggestions about his care.

Baron wasn't her patient, and Jos had no business telling him what to do. She could, however, offer help. "There's a really great social worker at my hospital who specializes in helping families with Alzheimer's and dementia patients."

Pushing away from her husband, Yvonne flashed Joslynn a rather fierce frown. "We don't need a social worker. I can handle things fine by myself."

Ah. So that's the way of it.

Yvonne's pride was keeping her from asking for the help she clearly needed—a problem that was common enough for Joslynn to understand and sympathize with. Jos figured there wasn't a single thing she could recommend that Yvonne would accept since she was intent on caring for Baron all by herself.

* * *

Russ bristled at his mother's quick dismissal of Josie's suggestion that they get some help.

Ever since his father's diagnosis, his mother had been killing herself trying to show that she was capable of giving Baron everything he needed. It had taken a lot of heated arguing just to get her to agree to have the housekeepers come once a week.

"Maybe *I* can talk to the social worker," he offered, not surprised when his mother's frown was quickly focused on him. Her need to stand on her own two feet was admirable, but in this case not necessarily wise.

"You'll do no such thing," Yvonne insisted. Taking her husband's hand, she announced, "We should have breakfast now." A glance back. "Would you two like some oatmeal?"

Russ looked to Josie, who gave him a quick shake of her head. "No thanks, Mom. Josie is exhausted. She's a nurse and works nights. I should get her home so she can get some rest."

Instead of grilling him over the fact that he'd brought his new girlfriend here, Yvonne merely nodded and led Baron to the kitchen.

Once Russ and Josie were back in his SUV and leaving his parents' driveway, he figured he owed her an explanation. "Dad's only fifty-eight. He was diagnosed with early-onset Alzheimer's last year. Mom swears she doesn't want their lives to change because of it."

"I hate to say it, Russ, but that's a bit naïve."

He let out a sigh. "I know. But what am I supposed to do?"

"Your homework. The more you know about the illness, the more suggestions you'll be able to offer to help them. Would you like me to contact the social worker? Just because your mother doesn't want to talk to her doesn't mean that you can't learn how to help anyway."

Although conditioned childhood obedience wanted to kick in, he nodded. Josie was right—he needed to learn more about what his parents faced.

"There are a lot of simple things they could do that would prevent things like what happened today," she said. "Your mom just needs to be willing to let someone else give her a hand."

A snort slipped out. "Not likely, but I'll try."

Her palm covered his thigh. "I'll help any way I can."

"You mean learning this deep, dark secret isn't going to send you running for the exit?"

"It's not a deep, dark anything," she insisted.

It was hard to have this conversation when he was still driving because he wanted to see her eyes. Thankfully, they were close to the restaurant. "You're not worried about the genetic connection?" It was a deeper question than it seemed on the surface. They'd been a couple only a short time, and should she admit any concern about Russ one day being affected, she might also be admitting that she'd developed feelings for him.

"Genetics isn't everything," Josie replied. "Have you been tested to see if you have the gene?"

Russ shook his head. "Not sure I want to know…Maybe someday."

"From what I've learned, it's like a lock and a key," Josie said. "You need both. Genetics might give you the lock, but something in the environment is the key that opens that lock. You're not necessarily going to have the same fate as your father."

"So I can go ahead and have the six kids I was planning on?" he teased as he pulled up next to her car.

A glance to her face found a frown every bit as ferocious as the one his mother had given her earlier.

"What's wrong?"

"You want kids?"

"Well, yeah. Not six," he said with a chuckle. "But a couple might be nice."

Her frown didn't ease.

Russ picked up her hand. "Tell me what's got you so upset."

"I guess since you told me about your father, I should confess my own deep, dark secret."

"You have a secret?"

She let out a sigh before nodding. "Now that we're a couple, I have something I should probably tell you…I can't have children."

CHAPTER TEN

Joslynn hadn't meant to tell Russ that secret, to just blurt it out like that. But after what she'd learned about his father and the fact that he'd been so open with her about the battle his parents faced, she felt the need to be every bit as candid about her life.

"How do you know you can't have kids?" he asked.

"When I was ten, I started feeling really terrible. I was exhausted. I had no appetite. Every time something touched my skin, I got a bruise."

Pulling into the parking spot next to her car, Russ killed the engine and turned to stare at her. "Do you want to tell me this over breakfast since we missed it?"

She shook her head. "Let me spit it all out. Please."

He took her hand. "Okay. Tell me."

"Things only got worse. My gums would bleed for no reason. I had a bunch of nosebleeds. Then, out of nowhere, I had a grand mal seizure. When they took me to the hospital, they ran a bunch of tests. Turned out I had leukemia."

"Oh my God."

An ironic smile crossed her lips. "Yeah, that's exactly what my mom said."

"What happened?" he asked. "I mean, you obviously beat it." He squeezed her fingers. "You're sitting here with me now."

"Damn right I beat it. I got a tattoo to prove it. Did you see the butterfly—back at the pool in Georgia?"

He nodded.

"I got it when I turned eighteen to show I'd won."

He nodded again. "I can't imagine how horrible leukemia would be."

"Yeah, chemotherapy sucks, but sometimes it works." Saying chemo sucked was an understatement, but she wasn't about to whine about something that had ultimately saved her life. "What you have to remember is that it's also poison, for all intents and purposes. Sometimes there are side effects that have nothing to do with the cancer."

"So one of your side effects left you unable to be a mom?"

"It's not a hundred percent," Joslynn admitted. "I can't be entirely sure, but most girls who receive the chemotherapy regimen I went through end up sterile. I remember a doc telling me about it back when I was being treated, and when I became a nurse, I learned what chemo can do to a person's chances of being a parent."

"Then you don't know for sure."

"I don't know for sure, but my research shows I've got less than a ten percent chance of having kids. My cycles have been anything but regular. I've never been tested or anything."

"Kinda like me and the Alzheimer's gene," Russ said. "Not sure you want to know, right?"

"Yeah, kinda like that. I haven't had the nerve to be tested. Not yet." She shrugged. "I really don't want kids anyway."

"You don't?" Russ sounded shocked at the notion.

On this she knew she would never budge. "I really don't. I'm independent. I don't even have a pet. I like my life the way it is. Why would I want to tie myself down with an eighteen-year burden?"

The incredulous look he gave her made her wonder if she'd just stepped in a pile of shit. Then she realized since she truly didn't want to have children, he needed to accept that. If he was bound and determined to be a father, this relationship they were trying to establish was doomed from the start.

"Do you have any brothers or sisters?" Russ asked.

"Nope. Just me, and considering what I put my mom through, that was probably a good thing."

"Wanna tell me about your dad? I know he's a sore spot…"

Since she was telling the story, she figured she might as well confess all. "I think I told you that my dad left. The entire truth is that he took a hike right after my diagnosis—took his girlfriend with him. I guess he couldn't cope with the possibility of watching his kid die. I haven't laid eyes on him since."

* * *

Now Russ understood. No wonder she wanted nothing to do with a serious relationship. The most important one she'd seen in her formative years had been between her mother and a fucking cheating coward.

What kind of man left his daughter when she learned she had leukemia?

Selfish bastard.

He patted his lap. "Come here."

A confused frown bowed her lips. "Why?"

"I want to hold you."

Even though she still looked perplexed, she slid across the bench seat.

Russ turned her back toward him so he could wrap one arm around her shoulders while he slid his other hand under her knees. Then he lifted her onto his lap. Holding her against him, he gave her a quick kiss. "I'm sorry."

"Don't be." Josie shrugged before laying her head against his shoulder. "He didn't give a shit about me. Why should I give a shit about him?"

Although things weren't always that simple, all Russ did was nod. Her father was obviously a sore topic, and he didn't want to rub salt in the wound she denied she had. "You seem really healthy now."

"I intend to stay that way. That's why I run, do yoga, and eat healthy. I also try to keep stress to a minimum."

"Yeah, you're helping me with that, you know."

She smiled. "The running is doing the trick, is it?"

"It got Brad and Ethan off my back." He rubbed his neck. "There was a guy at the bar, a drunk, who I tossed out of the place. He threatened to sue us. Brad and Ethan said I need to get a grip." He let out a weary sigh. "They said they might have to buy me out if I don't get my act together. I need to stop losing my temper."

"So you're running with me. Are the workouts helping?"

He nodded. "So far, so good. I'm sleeping like a baby. I don't go to the restaurant all the time to look for someone to take my stress out on."

"Not beating on your patrons now?" she teased. "Good for you. Next thing we'll do is get you to one of my yoga classes."

Like *that* would ever happen. Because she was opening up, he decided to fire another question at her. "Since this boyfriend-girlfriend stuff is new to you, I take it you haven't been in other relationships." He held his breath, waiting for her to either bolt or scold him for being so nosy.

"One," she admitted. "In college."

After several moments passed without her adding anything, Russ had to resist the urge to heave another sigh. Nothing with this woman was easy, but getting her to talk about herself was the hardest thing he faced. "I almost got married once," he said, hoping to encourage her to tell him more.

She leaned back to look into his eyes. "Really?"

"Yes, ma'am. Lasted all of three months before we both decided twelve was a little young to make a commitment like that."

Her laughter was so sweet that he didn't even mind when she swatted his chest. "You're being silly."

"I take it your college romance didn't work out well."

Now she was the one to sigh, almost as though she'd resigned herself to his digging into her past. "Not well, no. Tim and I were like oil and water. There was only one place we were compatible."

"In bed?" he guessed.

"Yeah. We were young enough we thought sex was all that really mattered. It wasn't. Especially when I found out he was also very…*compatible* with other girls."

Sitting there in stunned silence, Russ wondered if he even had a chance with Josie. For shit's sake, the woman had basically been conditioned to never trust a man. How was he supposed to get past those walls she'd built around herself?

Time. Time and patience.

He'd always enjoyed a good challenge, and the way he felt just holding her in his arms told him that he'd been right about her—she was someone he could love. The power of their mutual physical attraction was only icing on the cake.

Putting his finger under Josie's chin, Russ lifted her face to his. Then he kissed her the way he wanted to, a hot, lingering kiss that showed her how much he wanted her. She returned his passion, pushing her tongue past his lips. He grasped it between his teeth, tugging gently.

Her arms went around his neck as she eased toward him, pressing her breasts against his chest. As she awkwardly tried to shift her position, her knee connected with his groin.

Stars shot through his vision as he let out a yelp and then sucked in a hissing breath.

"Oh, Russ," Joslynn said, carefully moving back to the seat. "I'm so sorry."

Hands shielding his stricken balls, he could only offer her a curt nod. Thankfully the pain began to ease, but the magic of the moment was broken.

"Are you okay?"

The humor threading through her voice made him frown. Through clenched teeth, he replied, "I'll live."

"Sorry." She kissed his cheek and smiled. "I guess this means we're not going back to my place for hot sex."

"Not tonight." After a few deep breaths, he felt enough relief to think about something else. "Do you work this Friday?"

"Nope!" she replied. "For once, I have a Friday and a Saturday off." She grinned. "At least until they call me to fill in for someone."

"Well, if they call for Friday, just tell them you can't make it."

"Any reason why I can't make it?"

"Because you're going to Brad's with me for one of our famous Friday cookouts."

"A chance to see Savannah and Caroline?" she asked. "Count me in."

* * *

Plate of cookies in hand, Joslynn walked up the porch steps to the Greens' house. Even though she'd been exhausted after she and Russ had finally finished breakfast, she'd had trouble sleeping. Things had been so tense when they'd searched for Baron, and she hated to think that Yvonne might still be angry at her.

Joslynn had caught a few hours of rest, but by late afternoon, she'd rolled herself out of bed, baked a batch of chocolate chip cookies, and printed out a slew of pamphlets meant to help families of Alzheimer's patients. Then she'd set out to see Russ's parents.

Her knock was answered by Yvonne, who opened the door with wide eyes. "What on earth are you doing here?"

Holding up cellophane-covered plate, Joslynn smiled. "I came to see how you and your husband are doing and to find out if we could start over."

After opening the door wide, Yvonne motioned for Joslynn to enter. "Come in."

Joslynn gave Yvonne the plate. "I made the two of you some chocolate chip cookies."

"How kind. Let's go to the kitchen. We'll have some tea." As they passed from the foyer to the family room, Yvonne inclined her head toward her husband, who was sound asleep in a reclining chair. "He likes a short nap before supper."

With a smile, Joslynn followed her into the kitchen. When Yvonne swept her hand toward the table, Joslynn took that as an invitation. Pulling out a chair, she put her purse on the floor and sat down.

Yvonne peeled the cellophane from the plate and set it in front of Joslynn. "Have a cookie while I pour us some tea."

"Thanks, but I ate plenty of the dough. I'm still full." A lie, but there was no need for her to launch into all the reasons she seldom ate sweets.

After pouring two glasses of iced tea, Yvonne set one of them in front of Joslynn. Then she pulled out a chair and sat as she sipped her own tea. "We really did get off on the wrong foot, didn't we? I'm sorry for that. I was just frantic over Baron."

"I totally understand. I see plenty of frantic people at work. You were actually quite calm." Taking a deep breath, Joslynn finally asked, "Why didn't you want Russ to know I treated you at the ER?"

Yvonne dropped her gaze.

"If I remember right, you only had a cut on your arm that I had to stitch up."

"I didn't want to tell Russell about that."

Suddenly, Joslynn understood. "Baron cut you, didn't he?"

Still staring at her tea, Yvonne nodded.

"You told me you broke a glass."

"Baron was the one who broke it by smashing it against a table when he was…confused. He cut me with the jagged edge because he thought I was someone else." Her worried gaze found Joslynn. "He thought he was back in grade school, that a bully was hurting him. He was only defending himself."

Things were worse than Joslynn had thought, and it was obvious Yvonne didn't want her son to know how badly the Alzheimer's was affecting Baron. "Your hand looks like it's healed well."

"It has. Thanks." Quiet settled as Joslynn watched Yvonne fiddling with the plastic container holding a few paper napkins, clearly thinking through something. Waiting patiently, Jos thought about the best way to share the information she'd brought along with her. If Yvonne wasn't ready to set her pride aside and admit that she needed help, there wasn't much Joslynn could do.

Yvonne finally spoke. "May I ask you a question? About Baron?"

"Of course."

"Do you…?" Yvonne swallowed hard. "Do you think there's any chance—any chance at all—that he'll get better?"

The hurt in her voice almost made Joslynn cry. She saw so much pain and loss at the hospital, and despite her best efforts to keep her distance, she often shared the emotional turmoil of her patients. In this case, Yvonne and Baron were Russ's parents, and they faced an uphill battle that simply couldn't be won. That thought brought an acute feeling of unfairness and a wave of sadness.

When she noticed the hand Yvonne now rested on the table was trembling, Joslynn reached over to offer a comforting touch. The moment her hand covered Yvonne's, the woman grabbed it, holding on tightly.

"Alzheimer's is degenerative," Joslynn said, keeping her voice soft, as though that would make breaking the bad news easier.

Staring at her glass of tea, Yvonne tugged on her bottom lip with her teeth.

"I don't know of anyone who has come back from it. I know that's hard to hear."

A curt nod.

"But that doesn't mean you can't enjoy a lot more years together," Joslynn said. "There are good meds that can slow the progress, and there are resources that will help you and Baron cope with your situation."

When Yvonne turned her head to look at Joslynn, there were tears welling in her eyes.

Joslynn gave her hand a squeeze. "I'd like to help you two."

"I shouldn't have lied to you earlier," Yvonne said, sniffling. She dropped Joslynn's hand to grab a paper napkin and dab her eyes. "I was just so worried…"

"Totally understandable." Joslynn picked up her purse. "You were worried about your husband." She pulled out the plastic bag full of information she'd assembled before her visit. "I have some resources for you, if you'd like to take a look at them. I can give you some phone numbers, too. There are people that can help you."

Yvonne offered a weak smile but didn't ask for any of those numbers. "I can't thank you enough for coming here."

Joslynn smiled. "And thank you for giving me a second chance." Checking her watch, she realized she needed to be on her way. "If you'll excuse me, I have a yoga class to teach soon."

"Yoga? Oh my, that sounds like fun."

"You'll have to join us sometime." Slinging her purse over her shoulder, Joslynn stood. "Thank you for the tea."

"Thank you for the cookies." Yvonne got to her feet. "I'll walk you to the door." In the foyer, she gave Joslynn a heartfelt hug. "Come again, honey. Promise you will."

"Hang on a second." Joslynn fished around in her purse, trying to find one of her business cards. After grabbing one, she found a pen and wrote her cell number on the back of the card before handing it to Yvonne. "I promise, but only if you promise to tell me if there's anything I can do to help. All you ever have to do is call."

Yvonne frowned. "Please don't tell Russell about the cut. I—I don't want to worry him."

"I won't tell him about the cut. But you should know that Russ wants to help any way he can."

CHAPTER ELEVEN

The next day, Joslynn grabbed her hoodie and then picked up the apple pie she'd baked. The spring evening was comfortable at the moment, but she always liked to be prepared for the cold. She'd baked the pie that afternoon, although Savannah had told her she didn't need to bring anything. Jos never liked to turn up as a guest without something to offer her hostess. Besides, according to Yvonne, apple pie was one of Russ's favorites.

She hadn't mentioned her trip back to the Greens' house, mostly because there wasn't anything new to tell him. If she told him, then she'd have to explain that his mother had been in the ER, and she'd promised Yvonne she'd keep that secret.

Besides, what was there to tell? All it would do would be to make him worry about his parents more, and he was under enough stress.

When he made no move to take either the garment or the dessert, Joslynn smiled to herself. He'd been so respectful of her wishes to be independent. She only hoped that whatever woman was next to enter his life would forgive her for conditioning him to forget his gentlemanly practices.

Why did the mere thought of Russ with another woman make her frown so fiercely?

Unwilling to explore her motivations, she headed toward the gate in the wrought-iron fence. Joslynn led the way to the enormous backyard. Russ closed the gate behind them and followed her to the three-tiered patio.

"Welcome!" Savannah said as she stepped through the open double doors. Setting a pitcher of lemonade on the glass table, she came over to hold out her hands.

Joslynn handed over the pie. "I brought some dessert."

"Looks yummy." Savannah's brows knit. "Eat a piece later, Jos. You're getting too skinny."

Joslynn knew she was a few pounds lighter, probably because she'd been running so much. "I will. Where's my goddaughter?"

"Spending the night with my parents," Savannah replied before grinning at Russ. "Gotta say I've always wanted to see you and Jos coming here together."

With a roll of his eyes, he said, "So you told me. A million times."

A sharp whistle made Joslynn shift her gaze to the backyard. Brad and Ethan were playing corn hole, and she wasn't at all surprised when Russ excused himself and went jogging over to join them. He spoke of them so often, she was beginning to realize how important his two friends were to him. Since she felt that way about Savannah—and was starting to view Chelsea Harris as a confidante—Jos understood the need to have the support of friends.

"Let's go inside," Savannah said. "I could use a glass of wine."

"That sounds heavenly." Joss fell in step behind her. After crossing the threshold into the kitchen, she saw Chelsea standing at the island cooktop, stirring something in a large pot. "How are you, *superstar*?" she teased.

The redhead glanced up from her task. "Hi, *Doc*. I'm doing fine. How about you?"

"Life is good," Joslynn replied. Then she picked up a carrot stick from the vegetable tray and took a bite.

Before they could start a conversation, a voice called from the open doors. "Knock, knock. Can I come in?" An African-American woman Joslynn didn't recognize was peeking into the kitchen.

"Come in, Leslie," Savannah said, motioning for her to enter.

The woman was a good foot taller than Savannah. While Joslynn was accustomed to being one of the tallest women in any room, Leslie had at least four inches of height on her.

Setting a covered bowl on the island, Leslie turned to talk to a man who'd followed her inside. "Ladies, this is my brother, Marc."

Probably in his early thirties, the guy wore his hair short and neat, the same as his tidily trimmed beard. He was dressed in a white polo shirt and gray shorts. His physique was sleek and strong, although his muscles weren't quite as well developed as Russ's.

Chelsea gave him a little wave and kept working on whatever was in the pot.

Since Marc wasn't staring at her in response, either he didn't know Chelsea was one of the biggest stars in country music, or he wasn't impressed by her celebrity.

"Glad you could make it, Marc," Savannah said. "Since I know the guys are anxious to talk to you, why don't I grab you a beer and you can go meet them outside? They probably want to conduct a little business before Brad puts the steaks on the grill." She opened the refrigerator door. "Is there a particular brand you prefer?"

"I'm not choosy," Marc replied. His gaze settled on Joslynn. A smile blooming on his face, he came to stand beside her. If his sister was tall, this man was a giant. "Pick one for me." His gaze swept her from head to toe, and his smile grew.

Before she met Russ, Joslynn might have responded to that inviting grin with a bit of flirtation. Marc was an attractive guy. Although she had no idea how he and Leslie knew the other people at the cookout, she recognized a welcoming face—and this man was definitely interested in her. Yet she felt not an ounce of pull toward him…

Odd.

He held out his hand. "Marc Guinan. And you are…?"

"Joslynn Wright." She shook his hand, not surprised at his firm handshake. "I'm a good friend of Savannah's."

Inclining his head at his sister, he said, "Leslie just got promoted to head chef at Words and Music. She said her bosses wanted to have a talk with me about their marketing plan since they knew that was my area of expertise."

No wonder they were at Brad's place. Jos couldn't imagine anyone more valuable to the three partners than the person who ran their kitchen. If her brother was in marketing, they'd want to see what he could do for Words & Music. "Nice to meet you, Leslie."

"Back at'cha," she said. Then she peeled the cellophane off the bowl she'd brought, revealing what looked to be a salad filled with large peach slices. "New recipe. Grilled peach salad with mustard vinaigrette. I'm anxious to see what everyone thinks."

Chelsea let out a chuckle. "Like you ever cook anything that isn't sinfully delicious."

"Best compliment I could get," Leslie said.

Clearly impatient, Savannah set the beer bottle aside, grabbed a fork, and scooped up some of the salad. Humming as she chewed, she nodded at Leslie. "Fabulous. Is it going on the menu?"

"Thanks," Leslie replied. "And hopefully. I'd love to have it available all summer, if the guys allow it."

"No way they'll refuse." After setting her fork in the sink, Savannah snatched up the beer and handed it to Marc. "The guys are playing corn hole, so be sure to grab some beanbags on your way out. They're sitting on the patio ledge."

"Corn hole?" He laughed. "What's corn hole?"

Dropping her jaw, Chelsea shot him an incredulous stare. "Are you serious? Corn hole is only the best game ever invented."

Savannah tapped his longneck with her finger. "Plus, the more you drink, the more fun it gets."

"Well, then…this I gotta see." Marc lifted the bottle in salute and then took a drink. "If you ladies will excuse me, it appears I need to receive a quick education in what exactly corn hole involves." He strode out of the kitchen, giving Joslynn a wink as he left.

"I should probably tag along with him," Leslie said, pausing at the door. "After all, the head chef might want some say in how we market the restaurant. Besides, that's my baby brother heading out to the lions' den. Those three can be intimidating when they're together." She jogged out of the kitchen, a wave of laughter in her wake.

"Damn," Chelsea said, tapping her spoon against the rim of the pot and then setting it aside. "That is one fine-looking man."

"Whoa there, girl," Savannah said, a teasing lilt in her voice. "What would Ethan say if he heard you talking about another guy?"

After putting a lid on the pot, Chelsea shrugged. "I might be in love with Ethan, but I've still got eyes in my head." She glanced to Joslynn. "Being tied down doesn't stop a girl from appreciating a nice ass."

"Amen to that, sister." Savannah held up her hand to invite a high five from Chelsea, who gave her palm a loud slap.

Funny, but Joslynn hadn't noticed the guy's backside. That was unusual since it was her favorite part of a man's body.

Well, at least my second *favorite . . .*

Maybe she hadn't checked out his butt because she was taking the relationship stuff more seriously than she'd realized. Savannah was married, and Chelsea was engaged. Yet they both took notice of Marc. What Joslynn had thought was that Russ was better looking.

Savannah broke into her reverie. "How are things going with Russ?"

"Fine. At least I *think* they're fine," Jos replied, feeling no hesitation in speaking freely in front of her friends. "We've had some nice dates. I'm . . . comfortable around him."

"That sounds promising," Chelsea said.

"Very promising," Savannah added. "Jos doesn't do relationships."

Chelsea's brows knit as she stared at Joslynn. "What's that mean?"

Joslynn shrugged. "I hate the idea of losing my independence."

"Aren't you lonely?"

With a shake of her head, Jos said, "I like being alone. Besides, a date every now and then is fine. I just don't want to be smothered by some guy."

"But Russ is different," Savannah said. "He might be 'the one.'"

"Don't get ahead of yourself," Joslynn cautioned. "We're dating. That's all. And we run together several times a week. I'm hoping it'll help him with his stress level."

"Thank God for that," Savannah said, sounding relieved. "The man has been driving Brad bat-shit crazy, like he's always looking for a fight. He's fine when he pulls his management shifts. But when he helps the bouncers...not so much."

The criticism made Joslynn bristle, which seemed odd considering she also thought he should get away from Words & Music more often. "He's just stressed."

"Of course he is, but so are Brad and Ethan. They both make sure they have other things in their lives to maintain some balance, and they sure don't enjoy tossing drunks out on their asses."

Chelsea plucked a bottle of wine from the refrigerator and refilled her almost empty wineglass. "Ethan says Russ has been a little...out of control. I mean, it seems like he looks for any hint of a fight so he can lay hands on some troublemaker."

"Think about it, Jos," Savannah added. "He pretty much appeared in your life by showing up at your ER to get stitches because he was grappling with some drunk."

The truth of their words was there, but Joslynn had an almost overwhelming need to defend Russ anyway. Where had her need to be brutally honest gone? Normally, she'd be jumping right into the fray, telling her friends that she'd been every bit as concerned about his behavior and was doing everything she could to help him. Instead, she just shook her head, refusing to criticize him.

Savannah, always in tune with Joslynn's moods, must have sensed the time had come for a change of topic. "I think we're ready to put on the steaks. How about we tell the guys to quit playing games and come get some work done?"

* * *

As Marc marched toward the house, his sister at his side, Russ turned back to his partners "I think we made the right choice hiring him."

Ethan nodded. "He knows his stuff. Once we start that new ad campaign, I think we'll see increased sales."

"I haven't been happy with Hallick and Associates for a while," Brad said. "I'm glad you guys were willing to give Marc a chance."

"Hell," Russ said, "I would've hired him just because he's Leslie's brother. She's the hardest worker I've ever known—including you bozos. He seems like he's adopted the same work ethic."

"Brad!"

Turning to see Savannah waving from the deck, Russ grinned. "Looks like it's time to put the steaks on the grill."

A moment later, eighties music filled the air, the typical soundtrack to the Friday-evening cookouts. As the partners headed back to the house, they were serenaded by REO Speedwagon.

Josie strode through the doors, carrying a large bowl. Before she could set it on the table, Marc jogged up to her and swept it from her hands before putting it down. The smile that had been on Russ's face dropped to a fierce frown as Marc took her hand, twirled her in a pirouette, and then pulled her into his arms and began to dance with her.

Feet now frozen to the grass, Russ clenched his fists at his sides. The feelings roiling through him made his stomach churn and his face flush hot. All he could do was stare as Marc danced with Josie, the two of them laughing and clearly enjoying themselves.

Anger? No, that wasn't what was eating at him. That was too light an emotion to describe his desire to march right up to them, jerk Josie out of Marc's arms, and drive his fist into the guy's nose.

A hand touched his shoulder, and Russ snorted out a breath, resisting the urge to forcefully shove away whoever was bothering him.

"If I didn't know better," Ethan said, "I'd guess you were thinking about punching someone's lights out."

"I'd have to agree," Brad added as he came to stand at Russ's side. "A little jealous there, partner?"

Jealous?

Oh, yes. Brad nailed exactly what was eating away at any self-control Russ had. "He's got his fucking hands all over her. I should break his arm."

"Yeah, about that…" Ethan drawled. "I don't think it's a good idea to assault the man we just hired to handle our marketing."

"Gotta agree with that," Brad added. "Plus I'd really hate to have to call the guys in blue to break the two of you up. Marc looks strong enough to give you a run for your money."

Ethan gave Russ a friendly cuff on the shoulder, which was greeted with the hottest glare Russ could fire at him. "Look, can I give you a little advice?"

Russ shrugged, although he felt as far from nonchalant as he could get.

His temper had been a problem his whole life. One of the reasons sports had been so important to him was that they'd given him a way to channel that negative part of his personality. After knocking a few heads on the field, he was able to get a tight rein on the rest of his life.

"If Chelsea taught me anything about women," Ethan said, "it's that they don't mind a little bit of jealousy. But if you head up there and pull Joslynn and Marc apart as though they're a couple of high school kids misbehaving at the prom, you're going to piss her off something royal."

"Again, I gotta agree," Brad said. "Savannah doesn't mind if I get a bit territorial. She says it shows I care. But I start doing the 'me, Tarzan; you, Jane' thing, she digs her heels in."

"A woman likes to know that you want her for yourself," Ethan added. "Just don't start acting like she's your property or something."

"How can my telling Marc to keep his hands to himself be seen as me saying that she's my property?" Russ asked. While he wasn't thrilled to be lectured by his friends, he had to admit that they were in successful relationships. He didn't have nearly as much experience with women as they did.

"Think about it from her point of view," Brad explained. "You're telling her who she can and can't dance with. From what I've seen of Jos, she's an independent person. I doubt she'd take kindly to being ordered around."

"Food for thought, my friend," Ethan said. "Food for thought."

Every bit of ground his friends had made in calming him down vanished when Russ saw Marc drop his head to whisper something in Josie's ear and then press a kiss to her cheek.

It was time to let Marc Guinan know the score.

* * *

Joslynn laughed as Marc spun her in another circle. "Enough. You're making me dizzy."

All he did was smile in response. A new song began, a slow number, and he wrapped his right arm around her waist and grasped her hand with his left, swaying their bodies in rhythm.

Drawing closer as though he had some secret to share, Marc whispered in her ear, "I'm really glad I came here tonight. I didn't expect to meet such a pretty lady." His lips brushed her cheek before he eased back.

She stopped dancing and was about to let Marc know that his flirting was wasted on her when she was startled by Russ, who was now standing right beside her. A quick glance in his direction revealed a face so red that he appeared to have a wicked sunburn. "Hey, Russ."

Instead of any kind of greeting, he glared at Marc. "Quit dancing with my girlfriend. *Now.*"

Marc seemed entirely unfazed by the threat in Russ's tone. Instead, he lowered a confused expression at Joslynn. "Girlfriend? You're his girlfriend?"

She nodded, a bit surprised by Marc's critical tone.

Marc took a rapid step back, his gaze shifting to Russ. He held up his palms in surrender. "I didn't know she belonged to you, man. Sorry about that."

Russ replied with a curt nod, and his rigid stance relaxed.

Eyes narrowing, Marc glared at her. "You introduced yourself as Savannah's friend. I wouldn't have... You never said you were here with anyone."

Feeling as though she were being accused of something untoward, Joslynn's anger rose. Marc's words still echoed in her ears.

"I didn't know she belonged to you."

Joslynn Wright didn't belong to anyone but herself. "What's your point, Marc?"

"I don't trespass. But you danced with me, so..."

She folded her arms under her breasts and began drumming her fingers on her arm. "So what?"

Everyone had gathered around the three of them, and she started feeling as though she were a sideshow attraction.

Rather than answer her, Marc extended his hand to Russ. "I really am sorry."

With another gruff nod, Russ shook Marc's hand.

"What exactly are you sorry about?" Joslynn demanded. "We danced. Is that illegal or something now?"

"You're my girlfriend," Russ announced, as though that statement were sufficient to explain the ridiculous exchange between the men.

"And what exactly does *that* mean?" she demanded.

"That means that you're mine."

"Are you saying that you own me, Russ? That because I happen to be your girlfriend I can't dance with someone else?" Temper in full flight, she was ready to stomp out of there simply to prove that no one told her what she could and couldn't do.

It was Savannah who broke the heightening tension by stepping up to offer Russ a plate full of raw steaks. "Why don't you help Brad and Ethan get the steaks on the grill?"

Although his face was still flushed, Russ nodded and accepted the plate. He fell in step with his partners as they headed to the far side of the patio, where the stainless-steel grill waited.

"Leslie?" Savannah glanced to the chef. "Could you and Marc please bring out the sides? I figured it's so nice tonight that we'd eat out here."

"Sure thing," Leslie replied. With a flip of her hand, she got her brother to follow her into the house.

Then Savannah turned to Joslynn. "How about you come have a quick talk with Chelsea and me?"

Why did Jos feel as if she were a naughty student being sent to the principal's office?

CHAPTER TWELVE

Joslynn followed Savannah and Chelsea into the house and then down the stairs into Brad's basement recording studio. Her thoughts were in turmoil as she tried to make sense of the feelings her exchange with Russ had inspired.

Part of her wanted to walk away from him—*run* away from him—and his antiquated and far-too-macho jealousy. How dare he embarrass her in front of everyone? So she'd danced with Marc. So what? It was only a dance. She hadn't even given the guy more than a moment of notice, and she'd been just about to tell him that she was Russ's girlfriend. But Russ had barged right in, pounding his chest like some enraged gorilla claiming his mate.

Yet if she looked deep inside herself, she had to admit that she'd never meant enough to any man to inspire that kind of possessiveness. Men were something she played with, not inspired. She used them for what she desired, exactly as they did with her, and then she discarded them without any concern for their feelings. Not once had she let herself care.

Savannah sat in the brown leather chair at Brad's master console, turning the chair around to face the couch that Chelsea had plopped down on.

Not feeling at all like sitting still, Joslynn did exactly what she always did when anxious. She paced. "You might as well get it over with. Go ahead and scold me for whatever you think I did wrong."

"I don't think you did anything wrong," Savannah said, leaning back in her chair.

Jos whirled to face her. "Then why did you drag me down here?"

"I thought you and Russ could use a breather before things got ugly."

"That was a good call," Chelsea added. "He needed to cool down." Her gaze shifted to Jos. "So did you, although he was worse."

With a nod, Savannah said, "Lately, Russ *always* needs to cool down. At least he did before you two started going out."

Chelsea nodded as well. "Ethan told me Russ had changed some since you've been dating."

"But not today," Savannah said. "His temper was in full flight again. I don't think I've ever seen a man that jealous."

Jealousy. Another outdated practice Joslynn could really do without. If Russ was jealous, that meant he didn't trust her.

She trusted him. She did. If she'd seen him dancing with some cute girl, she wouldn't have flipped out. No, she would have simply walked up to them and…

Yanked the bitch's hair.

Which meant she was jealous, too. Which meant she thought Russ might betray her. Which meant she cared.

Oh, who am I trying to kid? I care. I care a lot.

"But I don't *belong* to anyone," she insisted.

After long, silent moments passed, Chelsea cocked her head. "Can I ask you something?"

Jos replied with a terse nod.

"Would it really be so bad to belong to Russ? I mean…you like the guy. He obviously likes you. You're dating. Doesn't that mean you belong to each other?"

The very question Joslynn was asking herself. Why was she protesting so vehemently when it might be exactly what she wanted—what she needed?

"It's just semantics, you know," Savannah said. "Nothing but semantics. You two are in a monogamous relationship. That's all that's happening. It's not like he owns you."

"Or you own him," Chelsea added. "You two just want to be together and not go out with other people. That's what a relationship is."

Could it be that simple?

"I suppose…" Joslynn let out a weighty sigh. "Russ just threw me for a loop up there."

"I imagine he did," Savannah said. "But you *were* dancing with Marc. From Russ's point of view, he probably saw flirting."

"I wasn't flirting with him!" Jos insisted.

Or was I?

She hadn't set Marc straight right away, even though she was aware of his interest. While she might've been thinking about Russ, she hadn't considered how he might feel should he see her with Marc.

"This relationship stuff is harder than I thought it would be," she finally admitted.

Both of her friends laughed in response, which finally brought a hesitant smile to Joslynn's lips.

"So what do I do now?"

Standing, Savannah placed a gentle hand on Jos's arm. "First, you let him apologize."

"Do you think he will?"

Chelsea chuckled and came to stand by them. "If they guys talk some sense into him, that's exactly what he'll do."

"What do I do after he apologizes?"

"You do the same," Savannah said. "And then you let him know that you only have eyes for him."

* * *

Russ shoved his hands in his pockets and tried to ignore the glares Brad and Ethan were shooting at him. He was aware that he'd stepped in a big pile of shit where Josie was concerned. He really didn't need a lecture, but it appeared they were both ready to give him one anyway.

"Exactly how many times did you get your bell rung when you played football?" Ethan asked him.

"What's that supposed to mean?"

Brad let out a snort. "He's saying you must have brain damage, 'cause we both warned you not five minutes ago not to act like a fucking caveman."

"I didn't act like a fucking caveman!" Russ insisted, not realizing how stupid he sounded parroting back the words until they were already out of his mouth. Not only that, but it simply wasn't the truth. He'd marched right up to Marc and staked a claim on

Josie as though she were a plot of land. What in the hell was wrong with him?

There might be women in the world who would appreciate an old-fashioned male, one who was full of raging jealousy at the mere sight of her anywhere near another man, but his girl-friend sure as hell wasn't one of them. He had to wonder what Chelsea and Savannah were saying to her at that moment and if they might calm her down enough that she would talk to him once he could get his head on straight.

If he could get his head on straight…

His life was a mess. Everyone had been warning him that he was out of control, but he'd ignored them. All it took was a cus-tomer saying the wrong thing and he blew his stack. Something went awry—a missed appointment, an inconsiderate driver—he went ballistic. It was amazing he hadn't found himself in a heap of trouble.

What had caused him to become so hostile?

Dad's diagnosis?

Or the fear he would follow in his father's footsteps?

Things had been better since he'd started hanging around Joslynn. She'd promised to help him with his stress level, and she was making progress. But he still had a long, long way to go. His reaction to seeing her with Marc proved it.

What if his little dog and pony show over her innocent dance with Marc made her pull back? Trust was a tough thing for her to give. Every time she'd offered someone her trust, that person had betrayed her. By acting like a jerk, he'd all but accused Josie of being unfaithful. Right now she had to view Russ's actions as another betrayal and probably thought he didn't trust her.

How was he supposed to convince her that he was sorry for his behavior? And how was he going to get her to believe he wanted to change?

Because he did want to change. He *had* to change. Not only to keep his relationship with her growing stronger, but he knew that his parents needed him. He wasn't about to let them go through this ordeal on their own.

But who would help him when it became his turn?

You can't think like that.

He gave his head a shake to banish his worry and focused on the problem at hand.

"I need help," Russ admitted, more to himself than to his friends. "I don't want to lose her."

A firm hand settled on his shoulder, and he glanced over to find Ethan grinning at him. "Good thing you've got friends like Brad and me."

"Yeah," Brad added as he closed the cover of the grill. "Friends who will help you stop looking like an asshole in front of the woman you love."

The word slammed into Russ, as though he'd run headfirst into a wall.

Love.

I love Josie.

Brad let out a chuckle. "I can see you've had an epiphany, my friend. I take it you didn't realize—"

"That I love her." All of a sudden it was so easy for Russ to say.

With a chuckle, Ethan slapped Russ on the back. "Now you just have to find the courage to tell Joslynn."

* * *

Joslynn watched Russ as he ate, wondering if she should say something to break the ice.

He hadn't said much to her since she'd come back from her visit to the basement with Savannah and Chelsea, which made her wonder if he was still angry.

Brad grabbed his beer and stood up. "I have an announcement."

"That sounds ominous," Russ said. He turned to smile at Jos. "Maybe he's firing me."

Glad his mood seemed to have eased, she smiled back at him.

He took her hand in his and gave it a squeeze.

"It would cost too much to fire you," Brad said. "And I'd have to train someone else. So, no. You're staying, Russ."

"Damn," Russ said with a faux grumble.

A lopsided grin filled Brad's face. "Savannah isn't going to be able to headline for us after August."

Ethan's brows gathered. "Did her recording company finally twist her arm to get her on a national tour?"

"Nope," Brad replied. "She's got…other plans. Let's just say that she'll be too busy to sing for a while."

From across the table, Savannah winked at Joslynn.

That playful gesture told Joslynn exactly what Brad was about to tell everyone. Her feet started a happy little dance under the table.

"We're gonna have a baby," he said, raising his longneck.

Chelsea got to her feet as quickly at Jos, and both hurried to hug Savannah.

"When are you due?" Joslynn asked.

"The beginning of October," Savannah replied before taking Jos's hand in hers. "And I expect you to be there with me the whole time. In fact, Brad and I were hoping you'd deliver the baby."

"Of course." Joslynn grasped her friend's hand tightly. "So long as the doctor agrees and there aren't any complications. One little thing goes wrong, though, and the OB takes over."

"Sounds like a plan." After giving Jos's hand a squeeze, Savannah let her hand fall away. "Does Caroline know?"

"We told her this morning," Savannah replied. "That's why she's with my mom. They're going shopping for things for the baby. I told her we should wait to see if it was a boy or a girl, but she's already convinced she's going to have a sister."

Chelsea chuckled. "You can always exchange girl things for boy things later if you have to."

Moving back around the table to sit at Russ's side, Joslynn leaned in to kiss his cheek. He turned his head so she caught his lips instead. When he eased away, she followed for another quick kiss to show him how happy she was.

"I guess we have a problem," he said as he looked to Brad. "Who's gonna take the headline spot while she's on maternity leave?" His glance shifted to Ethan. "Unless you guys happen to know another country music star who might be willing to fill in for a while." He tossed a win at Chelsea.

"Sorry," Chelsea replied. "I've got the Australian tour that starts in July."

Russ shifted his gaze to Ethan. "Well, then. Looks like you'll have to sing, partner."

"Fuck you," Ethan replied in a teasing lilt. "I'll be in Australia with my *wife*."

"Wife?" Joslynn was on her feet again. "You're getting married?"

"Yeah," Chelsea said. "I finally decided to keep the guy. We were going to tell everyone tonight, but…" She stared at Brad. "Someone decided to let their own cat out of the bag first."

"When?" Savannah asked, reaching over to lay a hand on Chelsea's arm.

Ethan rubbed the back of his neck. "About that…" Then he looked at Chelsea.

"We were married last Wednesday by a judge," she announced.

The table erupted in happy noise as the men slapped Ethan on the back and Joslynn and Savannah converged on Chelsea.

* * *

Russ shook Ethan's hand. "I can't say I'm surprised. I knew when you two tied the knot you'd keep it private."

"Yeah," Brad added, "but I figured we'd be there."

Ethan shrugged. "You know me. Once I made up my mind, I didn't want to wait. And Chel didn't want anyone to have a chance to find out and alert the press. Her assistant, Addie, set the whole thing up. She got the license, sent us to a judge, and…voilà. I'm a married man."

"Wait 'til the reporters get wind of this." Russ felt a little sorry for them. They'd had to celebrate one of what should be their happiest days in absolute secrecy to keep from having the wedding blasted all over the place. "I can't believe no one picked up on you getting a marriage license."

"Addie gave the clerk a nice financial incentive to keep the news to himself," Ethan replied. "Chelsea is going to have her publicist make a quick announcement early next week. That's why we wanted to tell y'all today. Sorry you guys couldn't stand up with me."

Brad cuffed Ethan's shoulder. "We're just glad you were able to have some peace and quiet instead of flashes going off in your face."

Cocking his head, Russ considered his partners. Their lives were changing for the better. A new wife. A baby on the way. Everything was lining up perfectly for both of them.

Then he glanced to Joslynn, and a warm contentment filled him. She was sitting with Savannah and Chelsea, and the three were laughing and hugging and swiping away happy tears.

Maybe my life is lining up perfectly too…

Unless I end up like my father.

* * *

Joslynn sighed, her heart full of happiness for her friends.

Savannah had always confided that she hoped to give Caroline a brother or sister, and the joy of the baby news was clear. And knowing how much Chelsea loved Ethan, Jos wasn't surprised they'd married. Add the fact that they'd done so without any disturbance by the paparazzi made the event doubly special.

Just seeing their lives play out so perfectly made Jos think of Russ. A quick glance saw him with a grin on his face as he spoke with Brad and Ethan. As though he knew she was watching him, he looked in her direction. The heart-stopping dimple was there, making her heart skip a beat.

She'd never thought much about her future aside from her medical career. Marriage and family seldom crossed her mind. Yet as she felt herself smile at Russ in return, those notions flooded her thoughts.

Something about being with him was so natural.

With other men, she'd often felt smothered, as though she couldn't be herself when she was with them. Sure, she enjoyed dating. She enjoyed sex. But she didn't enjoy simply being with them. Even when she and Russ weren't doing anything special, she was comfortable with him.

He fits.

With a shake of her head, Joslynn left the thought behind, not wanting to examine it for fear of finding herself in too deep.

Only time would tell.

* * *

Every time he stepped into Josie's home—the Cottage—Russ was struck by how damn clean the place was. The carpet bore the lines left in the vacuum's wake without a footprint to be found. The kitchen was spotless, the gleaming surface of the stainless-steel sink and appliances reflecting the light. There wasn't a single dish in the drain tray.

She had to hate his place. "Organized chaos," his mother always called it. Russ wasn't sure the "organized" was accurate, although he was always able to find what he needed with minimal searching. Josie probably arranged the clothes in her closet by color and style. Were the hangers evenly spaced?

Most of his clothes ended up on the floor or draped over some furniture.

"Want a drink?" she asked as she hung up the hoodie she hadn't worn in the coat closet.

Leaning his hip against the kitchen island, he shook his head. After the shitty way things had gone at the cookout, he wanted to clear the air. He wasn't about to cloud his thoughts with booze.

She walked past him into the kitchen and plucked a glass for herself from the cabinet. Setting it aside, she pulled a can from the refrigerator and poured herself some soda, which she sipped as she stared at him.

"Quite a night, huh?" he asked.

"Oh yeah. A new baby. A wedding. A shame we didn't have something to top it," she replied with a wink.

He reached out to run his hand down her arm. "Maybe one day."

Letting out a little snort, she took another sip of soda.

Unsure of what that derisive noise meant, Russ frowned. Since his revelation back at Brad's place, he'd felt a nagging need to find out if Josie had developed feelings for him. Not that he expected her to love him. Not yet.

But he wanted her to open up to him.

He *needed* her to.

"We should talk about…things," he said. "About us. About why I was so jealous." Standing in the kitchen seemed too impersonal, so he nodded at the sofa. "How about we sit down?"

She took a rather long drink before setting the glass on the countertop. Then she led the way to the couch.

He joined her, leaning forward to rest his forearms against his thighs and feeling awkward. What he wanted was to hear that she cared, even if only just a little bit. Deep down, he thought she did—*hoped* she did.

He wasn't leaving until she told him one way or the other.

God, he felt vulnerable, sitting there with his heart in his hand, hoping she'd take it from him and protect it instead of tossing it right back at him. Not that he was about to tell her that he loved her. After spending so much time with Josie, Russ knew exactly what would happen if he admitted the intensity of his feelings.

She'd freeze him out.

Although he was being impatient—another of his bad personality traits—he wanted to know if he even had a chance for the "something more" he wanted from her.

Simply having her sitting by his side was making it difficult to think. Everything about her called to him. The warmth of her thigh against his. The sweet scent of her perfume. It took all his concentration not to grab her and kiss her. At least when she was in his arms, he could feel that she wanted him.

"I feel like I should apologize again," she said.

"Funny, I was just about to say the same thing. I shouldn't have reacted the way I did to you dancing with Marc."

Joslynn turned to smile at him. "I've learned something important, which makes me understand why you were so upset."

Russ smiled back. "And what was that?"

"Relationships aren't easy."

A laugh spilled out as he leaned back, and he was pleased she laughed as well.

Then she reached over to take his hand in hers. "I didn't realize dancing with some other guy was that big of a…thing."

"And I didn't realize how jealous I could be. You know, I've never been jealous before."

Her brows knit. "Really? Not once?"

"Not once." He shrugged. "I'm not like Ethan and Brad. I haven't dated all that much. Never had a relationship that was very long-term."

"A guy that looks like you? An NFL player? I find that hard to believe."

"A lot of the players slept around. I'll admit it. I didn't." He shrugged again. "Maybe my parents taught me better. It just wasn't something I wanted to do."

She squeezed his hand. "At least we're starting out on equal footing since I've never really settled on one guy before. This is new for both of us."

Russ was fighting an internal battle to just say "fuck it" and drag Joslynn to the bedroom. Holding her hand shouldn't be at all erotic. But it was. The way she rubbed her thumb against his palm was enough to make him hard.

Then a picture of her in Marc's arms made him see red for a moment, and he huffed out a breath, angry at himself for his irrational jealousy.

"What's wrong?" she asked.

He replied with a question of his own. "Do you know why it was so hard to see you dancing with Marc?"

"I thought we covered that."

"I didn't mean Marc; I meant dancing."

"What's bad about dancing?"

"Because it can be so…intimate." The sound system drew his attention. He got to his feet and strode across the small room.

The flick of a switch followed by a quick adjustment of the station and he found exactly what he was looking for. Soft jazz filled the room. With a crook of his finger, he said, "Dance with *me*."

Rising, she gave him a coy smile. "I don't know...Maybe I'm all danced out for the night."

"Dance with me, sweetheart."

She drew closer. "If you insist."

Before she could react, he tugged her against him and wrapped his arms around her waist.

Instead of resisting as he'd expected, Josie looped her arms around his neck and melted against him. Her body fit his as though she were made for him.

Swaying gently with the music, Russ brushed his lips against her ear and whispered, "Did you notice how well we fit?"

"I did," she whispered back. Then she rubbed her cheek against his shoulder.

"Doesn't that show you we belong together?"

This time she didn't reply, and he could almost feel her pulling back emotionally.

Frustrated and impatient, he stiffened. "I'm falling for you, Josie." When she shrugged in response, he released her and fought the urge to walk out. "Why can't you just admit that you care about me?"

"Words don't matter, Russ. Actions do. I'm here with you. That speaks volumes."

"Josie..."

"What do you want from me?" The panic was plain in her tone.

"I need to know that I matter to you. I need to hear the words."

She reached for his hand and squeezed. "Why can't I just show you?"

His lips pulled into a grim line. "Tell me how you feel about me."

Her hand dropped. "Why?"

Her hesitation worried him, and for a moment he wondered if he'd read her all wrong.

No. No. She cares.

She has *to care.*

"Because I have to know." A deep breath didn't help control his rising temper much. "Tell me how you feel about me, Josie."

She shook her head, and he noticed that her hands were trembling when she folded her arms around her middle.

Russ felt as though a band had wrapped around his chest and started to squeeze, stealing his breath. "If we're gonna stay a couple, I can't do all the work. You have to tell me you're in this too," he demanded. "I have to know that I'm not the only one whose feelings are on the line."

Her head bowed. "I...can't."

Although the part of him that loved her wanted to let her off the hook when he heard the tremor in her voice, he couldn't stop pushing her. Desperate with fear, he let his voice rise to a near shout. "Tell me you care about me, or I'm leaving."

Her head snapped up and she let out a gasp. "You'd do that? Over a few stupid words, you'd walk out?"

"You promised to be honest, and that's all I'm asking. Be honest and tell me that I matter to you."

"You're being unreasonable," she insisted.

"Why can't you say it?" he demanded.

Joslynn stomped into the kitchen and tossed the glass in the sink. When she turned back to face him, she was breathing hard.

"Say it, Josie."

She threw her hands in the air. "Fine! I care for you! I admit it! Why was it so fucking important that you hear it?"

Russ reacted as fast as lightning. His hands gripped her shoulders as he walked her backward, pressing her back to the wall. Face hovering so close to hers that her choppy breath brushed his lips, he savored the anticipation of kissing her. Once he let his lips meet hers, he would never be able to stop touching her until they were both naked in her bed.

So he waited, looking deeply into her dark eyes, pleased to see passion simmering there. "Because it means we don't have to wait anymore. I'm going to make love to you now."

CHAPTER THIRTEEN

Joslynn never had a chance to catch her breath. Accustomed to being the aggressor and enjoying her power over her lovers, she wasn't given time to even try to take the reins. The way Russ was kissing her, touching her, flooded her senses.

She loved how he was taller than she was. Most of her lovers had been fairly close to her height, which gave her a bit of an advantage. She could always look them directly in the eye, and in her mind, being eye to eye gave her a level playing field.

Everything about the intimacies she shared with Russ was different. She had to rise on tiptoes to kiss him, which was easier if she draped her arms around his neck. Rubbing against him was so erotic.

His scent surrounded her, filled her, as did his taste. Their tongues mated, chasing from one mouth to the other as he slid his palms down her back to cup her ass. Then he pulled her hard against him.

She let out a low moan when she felt his erection rubbing against her. "I want you," she whispered.

Instead of replying, he buried his lips against her neck, nibbling and licking and driving her insane.

After tilting her head to give Russ more access to her sensitive neck, Joslynn raked her fingers through his hair, loving the way the buzz cut tickled her skin. By the time he worked his way up to her ear, she was panting with desire.

"I want you," she said, her voice a little louder and full of demand.

His deep voice rumbled against her temple. "Patience." When he ran his tongue around the ridges of her ear, she shivered.

Patience? Was he nuts?

One thing she'd learned about sex was that desire could be fleeting. If his blood was running as hot as hers at that moment, the two of them shouldn't be wasting time. With anyone else, she would already be leading him to her bedroom.

It was clear that Russ Green wasn't about to be led anywhere. He was piloting this encounter, and all Jos could do was hang on tight and enjoy the ride.

* * *

The huskiness in her voice was almost his undoing.

Russ wanted to take his time, to make their first time together special. He might not have the experience with women that Ethan and Brad did, but his feelings for Josie were inspiring all sorts of creative ideas on what he wanted to do to her. With her.

Her gorgeous face and stunning body had haunted his dreams

from the moment he'd seen her emerge from that Georgia pool. Now that he knew she was every bit as stunning inside as out, he only wanted her more.

Kissing her sent blood racing through his veins and set his heart to hammering. Her tongue was wild, each stroke sending his desire climbing. It took all his concentration to stop touching her long enough to unbutton her black blouse. His fingers felt thick and clumsy, but he worked his way down until he could part the front and reveal her bra.

It was a vivid purple. A surprise but something that suited her well. There was nothing conventional about his Josie.

Before he could go to work on removing more of her clothing, she pulled his shirt out of his jeans and lifted his polo over his head. "Oh my..." she said, staring at his bared chest. When she raked her fingers through the light patch of hair over his pecs and licked her lips, heat rushed to his cock.

Unable to find any words, he banished her blouse to the floor. Holding eye contact, finding her sensual gaze incredibly arousing, he unzipped her jeans and helped her wriggle out of them. They puddled around her ankles, and she kicked them aside. Only then did he allow himself to take in all of Joslynn.

Her body was incredible. Not that he didn't already know that. What she wore as she ran revealed her shape quite well, and the swimsuit she'd worn had shown off each curve. But seeing her bare skin, knowing that for that moment he could touch, could taste every inch of it was almost enough to make him lose control. He leaned in to kiss the butterfly tattoo over her heart. "Sweet Lord, you are the most beautiful woman I've ever seen."

"Flattery will get you just about anything you want, Mr. Green." She leaned forward to lick one of his nipples.

Russ hissed out a breath. "I don't say anything I don't mean."

"Neither do I," Josie replied before giving his other nipple the same attention. Her fingers nimbly unfastened his button-fly jeans, and he pushed them down and then stepped out of them.

"A briefs kind of guy," she said. "But I have to admit, I didn't expect them to be baby blue."

He shrugged, having better things to focus on than his choice of underwear. Cupping her face in his hands, he kissed her again as she wrapped her arms around his waist. When they finally broke the kiss long enough to catch his breath, he knew he couldn't wait much longer to make her his.

"Put your legs around me," he said, placing his hands against her hips.

"Shouldn't we—"

"Come on, Josie. Go." As he lifted, she did as he asked, wrapping her legs firmly around his hips.

Turning, he headed toward the bedroom.

* * *

None of her lovers had ever made Joslynn feel the way Russ did—as though her pleasure was more important than his own. The way he touched her, kissed her, conquered her made her feel cherished.

Almost loved.

He set her on her feet next to the bed, and then his hands seemed to be everywhere. Touching her hips. Caressing her shoulders. Covering her breasts. After he popped the clasp, he helped her shrug out of her bra. "You really are beautiful. Absolutely beautiful."

The heat of a blush took her by surprise. After all her years working in medicine, she wasn't easily embarrassed. She'd seen and heard just about everything.

Then Russ had told her she was beautiful and she'd found herself humbled by his praise.

He gave her compliment after compliment, and she felt her blush grow hotter. So she tossed him a compliment of his own. "You're built like a brick house."

A smile bloomed on his face.

"I mean it. You could probably still play football."

"Fuck football." He grabbed her hand and pulled her roughly against him. "I have better things to do." His mouth covered hers in a kiss that was almost brutal.

They were both way past playing. Joslynn returned the ferocity of his kiss as their hands fumbled to get what little that remained of their clothing out of the way. As she pushed his briefs past his hips, his erection sprang forward. She let the briefs fall and wrapped her fingers around his thick cock.

He closed his eyes as if savoring her touch, so she stroked the silky skin, loving the feel of the hardened flesh. She considered dropping to her knees to take him in her mouth, but he brushed her hand aside and drew her back into his embrace. Then his lips were on hers again before he swept her into his arms and laid her on her bed. He came down on top of her as she parted her thighs.

No man had ever picked her up like that before. She was too tall, too muscular. Yet Russ made her feel almost...delicate. As he kissed her, she reached over and fumbled in the nightstand drawer to retrieve a condom.

As though sensing her desperation, he moved to his side and allowed Joslynn to roll on the condom.

"*Now*, Russ," she said.

* * *

Those two words hit Russ as hard as an NFL tackle. Her want and need were plain, want and need that matched his own. Josie spread her legs wider, grabbed his cock, and guided him home.

She was so hot, so wet. Unable to temper his pace, he withdrew and then plunged in again. As she wrapped her legs around his hips, he lost all control.

And she was there with him, her hips rising each time he pushed into her, and she scored his shoulders with her nails, the sting only adding to his pleasure. Holding on to just enough discipline to wait for her, he caught the first tremors of her release, her flesh rippling around his cock until he lost the battle to hold back. Thrusting into her one last time, he let out a near shout at the strength of his orgasm.

In that moment of utter bliss, he realized one very important thing.

Joslynn Wright belonged with him.

And he was never going to let her go.

* * *

As light streamed through her bedroom skylight, Joslynn woke up in Russ's arms, which came as a huge surprise. Not once in her life had she slept the whole night with another person in her bed. Yet here he was, letting out slow, even breaths that were not quite snores as he lay there gloriously naked. Since they'd kicked the quilt and sheet down to the foot of the bed, she was able to lean up on an elbow and get a good eyeful of the man she'd finally made love to.

There wasn't an ounce of fat on him, and his muscular chest would've inspired a sculptor. Although he was relaxed in sleep, his stomach still bore the outline of six-pack muscles. His arms were thick and well defined. He looked like what he'd been once upon a time—a quarterback.

Memories of the night brought a smile to her lips. Russ was a fantastic lover. The men she'd previously slept with had a bad habit of being a bit selfish in bed, often thinking only of their own pleasure. Not Russ. He'd made it quite clear that her pleasure was as important as his. And he'd definitely pleased her. More than once.

As she stared at his cock, her eyes widened as it slowly began to grow. Her gaze shifted to capture his. Those blue eyes were now open and fixed on her.

"Good morning," she said, not at all ashamed of having been blatantly staring at his body.

Instead of returning her greeting, he cupped her neck and pulled her into a lingering kiss.

Although Joslynn might have been content to make love to him again, she was desperately in need of caffeine. Her important schedule had been derailed by being awake when she should've been sleeping, and she felt punchy. Sluggish. If they were going to burn up the sheets again, she wanted to be at her best. That required coffee.

"Breakfast first." She stroked his now firm cock. "Then dessert."

His heavy sigh brought a smile to her lips. "If you insist."

Rolling away from him, she got to her feet. "I do." Opening her closet, she grabbed two things—her favorite Japanese-print silk robe and an oversized terry-cloth robe that she used on especially cold nights. She handed the bigger garment to Russ. Then she donned the silk and tied the belt. "I'll make some coffee, and then I'll make us some food."

* * *

Russ picked up his empty plate and carried it to the sink, and Joslynn couldn't help but be surprised yet again. The man had a way of constantly challenging her preconceived notions about men. He'd helped prepare their egg-white omelets without being asked, something she found endearing. Normally she liked to be self-sufficient. Opening her own doors was better than appearing to be a weakling who needed to wait for some man to help her out. Since they were sharing the meal, she was quite pleased to allow him to share the preparation and cleanup as well.

While he loaded the dishwasher, she took care of putting away the leftovers. As she bent over to return the egg carton to the bottom refrigerator shelf, she let out a gasp when he grabbed her hips and rubbed up against her from behind.

Smiling, she pushed back, loving the feel of his erection

against her bottom. "I take it you're ready for dessert," she said as she straightened up.

Russ turned her to face him, wrapped his arms around her, and lifted her off her feet. As he walked backward, he shut the refrigerator door with a kick. The seductive smile on his face fired her blood. "Absolutely."

He set her down on the table, and she let her legs dangle over the side, suddenly noticing he'd cleared everything from it, including the small vase of flowers she always kept there. Then he produced a condom from the pocket of his robe.

"You're a Boy Scout," she teased.

He winked. "Always prepared." Flicking open the tie on his robe, he stepped between her thighs and leaned down to kiss her.

Joslynn couldn't remember the last time she'd become so hot so quickly. Seeing him naked and aroused—and knowing that she was the reason he was in that state—turned her on. She plucked the condom from his fingers.

As his hands worked on removing her robe, she opened the package and rolled the condom on his cock. Her arms around his neck, she kissed him, pushing her tongue past his lips and hoping she could excite him as completely as he'd excited her. She grasped his bottom lip between her teeth and tugged.

Russ growled, the sound racing straight to her core. This time wasn't going to be slow and teasing. No, this would be fast and rough and exactly what she needed.

Using his hips to ease her legs farther apart, he stared deeply into her eyes as he entered her. The intensity Joslynn saw there stole her breath away. Then he captured her mouth in a searing kiss and pressed home.

She moaned into his mouth before gripping his shoulders tightly to ground herself as he thrust into her again and again. Everything inside her tightened until the heat uncoiled through her limbs in a burst. He came only a moment behind her.

Although her breathing was still choppy, she smiled. "I think it gets better each time."

He returned her smile. "That's because we care about each other, Josie. I told you. It makes all the difference."

CHAPTER FOURTEEN

Russ matched Josie stride for stride the first five miles. He didn't have to call "uncle" until mile six. As she'd done every time they'd run together, Josie slowed to a walk so he could catch his breath.

The last two weeks had been close to perfect, as though the two of them were always meant to be a couple. When they weren't working, they were together. Mornings were spent running or relaxing. Afternoons she caught up on her sleep—or they made love. Russ worked most evenings at Words & Music, and three nights a week Josie worked at the ER.

It was a nice rhythm.

"We going to Shamballa?" he asked when he wasn't gasping for breath.

"Don't we always?" she responded with a grin. "You're really showing progress. Getting stronger every day. Before long, I'll get us in a half marathon."

"In your dreams," Russ said, following her back to his SUV. "You work tonight, right?"

She nodded.

"I'm heading into Words and Music. Since Brad went with Savannah to her Boston concert, I'm taking a few management shifts for him."

After digging the key out of his pocket, he unlocked the doors. Once inside, he looked at Josie as she buckled her seat belt. "I just wanted to tell you how much these workouts are helping me."

The smile she gave him was so relaxed, he wondered if their time together had been every bit as relaxing for her. "I'm glad. You know, there are other things we can do to help with your stress."

He started the engine. "I haven't felt stressed lately." Probably because his mind and body were both content, Words & Music was running smoothly, and things had quieted down at the Green home.

Russ had never enjoyed the type of peace he'd known in the time he'd spent with Joslynn.

"I'm glad, but…it's not quite that easy." She rubbed his thigh. "You have to admit, the last couple of weeks have been pretty low drama."

Blessedly so, but he wasn't going to admit it aloud and jinx himself.

"I really need to get you to one of my yoga classes. I'm sure you'd love it, and it's so relaxing."

"C'mon, Josie. I'd look ridiculous trying to bend myself into some of those positions."

"They're called poses," Josie corrected. "And you'd do great."

As he pulled into a parking spot at Shamballa, he said, "I'll think about it."

"I'll get you there. One day," she said.

* * *

Late that afternoon, Russ was driving to Words & Music when his phone rang. A glance to the SUV's view screen showed his mother was calling. A quick touch of the screen, and he said, "Hey, Mom. What's up?"

Her voice echoed through the SUV. "Um…do you think you can come over?"

The fearful tone of her voice sent adrenaline running through him. "What's wrong?"

"Oh, it's nothing. Really. I just could use a little help."

He'd learned over the years that the more Yvonne Green downplayed something, the worse it was in reality. Fighting his growing anxiety, he glanced in the review mirror and then eased to the right lane so he could turn at the next intersection and head toward his parents' house. "I'm on my way now. Tell me what happened."

"It was silly. Daddy didn't mean any harm."

"Mom…" Russ tried not to get angry that she was being evasive, but the less she told him, the more his imagination ran wild. All that stress, all those feelings of anxiety that he'd kept at bay came flooding back. "What did he do this time?"

"He locked me in the basement."

"He what?" Russ shouted.

"Calm down, Russell. I don't think he meant any harm. I went down to fold a load of laundry. When I was just about done, I heard the door shut. Then I heard that old lock we had on the top of the door. Remember? We had it there—"

He'd heard the story a million times. "To keep me from falling down the stairs when I was little. I know." He was finding it difficult to rein in his anger. This was a reminder that the man Russ had looked up to his whole life was ill.

And he wasn't ever going to get better.

"I'm almost there, Mom. Hang tight."

* * *

No one answered the front door when he pounded on it, so Russ used his key to let himself in. "Dad? Dad, where are you?"

Worried that his father wasn't responding, Russ hurried to the kitchen and opened the bolt at the top of the basement door. Pulling the door open, he found his mother waiting a few steps down. "Are you okay?"

"I'm fine." Yvonne pushed past him into the kitchen. "Where's your father?"

"I don't know."

She cupped her hands around her mouth and bellowed, "Baron! Baron!"

"I'm checking upstairs," Russ said. Jogging to the foyer, he stopped panicking when he saw his father on the top step.

Rubbing his eyes, Baron stared down at him and frowned. "I was napping. What's all the shouting about?"

Yvonne grabbed Russ's arm to move him out of her way. Then she hurried up the stairs. She alternated between scolding and hugging her husband while Russ let out a heavy sigh.

Funny, he didn't feel much relief. He never did after that damned disease made his father do something stupid. His heart was still slamming in his chest, and he couldn't seem to relax the fists he'd clenched his hands into.

"Why did you lock me in the basement?" Yvonne demanded as Baron followed her down the stairs.

Baron glared at her back. "I did no such thing." Then he glanced to Russ as though he'd just noticed he was there. "What are you doin' here?"

Moving aside so they could pass him and head to the kitchen, Russ replied, "I came to let Mom out of the basement, Dad."

Yvonne poured three cups of coffee and handed a mug to Baron and then one to Russ, who leaned back against the counter.

"I'm sure it was an accident," she said.

Temper still climbing, Russ dumped the coffee in the sink and all but tossed the mug in. "Why did you lock her in, Dad? And why didn't you let her out when you heard her yelling?"

"I didn't lock her in," Baron replied.

Russ closed his eyes and tried to hold tight to what little patience remained. "You *did*."

"I went to do the laundry, honey," Yvonne said in what seemed like a far-too-calm tone. "I heard you click the lock at the top of the door. I'm sure you didn't do it on purpose."

Baron thought it over for a minute. "I guess I did." He looked at the open door. "I thought…" His brows gathered. "The door was open, and I thought Russ might fall down the stairs."

"Makes sense," Yvonne said with a nod. "We put that lock on there to keep you from getting hurt when you were a kid, Russell."

Makes sense, my ass. "I'm not a kid now. There was no reason to lock the damn door. Hell, Dad, I don't even live here any-more." Russ took a few deep breaths so he'd stop shouting. Baron couldn't help what was happening to him. Yelling wasn't going to change anything.

"Innocent mistake," Yvonne insisted.

"I went upstairs to do a crossword puzzle and I must've fallen asleep," Baron added. "I didn't hear her knocking."

With a hesitant smile, Yvonne shifted her gaze to Russ. "No harm, no foul. Thanks for helping us out, Russell. Were you head-ing into work?"

Tossing his mother a curt nod, he frowned. "I need to go. Are you two okay now?"

"We're fine," his father insisted.

* * *

Russ was still upset when he left his parents' house, and he picked up a hefty speeding ticket on his way to Words & Music.

* * *

The crowd was rowdy all evening, as though they sensed Russ was in a tempestuous mood and were committed to making him mis-erable. By the time the partiers fully took over the bar, all he had remaining of his self-control was one thin thread.

A group of six men, all wearing ridiculous baseball caps that labeled them as a bachelor party, were especially obnoxious. The best man, or so his hat claimed, was the worst of the lot. Russ had already warned him several times to stop making sexual remarks to the waitresses. Not only were the party members harassing the staff, but they were so loud that the other patrons began to complain.

When the best man pinched one of the waitress's asses, that last thread snapped.

Russ went to the groom and leaned down, frowning. "I'm afraid I'm going to have to ask you gentlemen to leave." Although the words were made with a clenched jaw, he was rather proud of himself because he thought he'd masked the hostility flowing through him very well. "The last round is on the house, but it's time to call it a night."

The best man, clearly listening in, started laughing. "Hey, don't I know you?"

Russ shook his head, not wanting to engage the worst of the troublemakers. "I'll give you a few minutes to settle your tabs and then—"

"You used to play for the Colts, didn't you?" The best man let out another loud guffaw. "Anyone ever tell you that you sucked as a quarterback?"

Hands clenched into fists, Russ turned to walk away. Adding this situation to what had happened with his father and all of the calm Josie had helped him find became a distant memory.

He wanted to hit something. Hard.

A rough grip of his upper arm made him whirl back around. The best man had narrowed his eyes and was glaring at him. "I guess you knew you sucked, 'cause here you are, bein' a bouncer in some fuckin' bar for minimum wage."

Instead of smacking the guy's hand away, Russ leveled a hard stare at him. He reminded himself that the best man was drunk and not in control of his actions, but if Russ didn't get away soon, he wouldn't be in control of his own, either. "Let. Go. Of. Me."

With a snort, the guy let his hand fall away. "Pussy."

Turning on his heel, Russ planned to head to the office to try to cool down. He'd promised himself he wouldn't get into another fight, especially with a patron, no matter how obnoxious and insulting that patron was.

But his heart was pounding like a jackhammer in his chest and his ears were ringing. Every muscle was tense, and his vision began to tunnel.

He'd gotten only a few steps away when a mug went flying by his head, splashing beer on him before smashing against the wall.

That was all the provocation he was going to take. Russ rushed the best man, grabbed his shirt, and started walking him backward until he collided with the bar. "I should knock your lights out, you bastard."

"Fuck you, you has-been."

A strong hand took a hold of Russ's fist as he cocked it back so he could break the best man's nose. Shifting his anger to whoever was restraining him, Russ growled at Ethan standing there. "Let go."

Instead of saying anything to Russ, Ethan shot a hard look at the groom. "Get your friend out of here. Now."

"Not until I beat some manners into this asshole." Russ tried to pull his hand free.

"You're not hitting him." Ethan's voice was calm, considering the tension in the air. "Go to the office. I'll meet you there."

When the best man let out a snicker, Russ jerked against Ethan's tight hold. Before he could cock his fist back to take a good punch, the groom grabbed his best man's arm and pulled him away.

Russ would've followed if Ethan hadn't put himself between him and the retreating bachelor party attendees. "Get outta my way, Ethan."

"I'm not letting you beat that guy up."

"He was begging for it!" Russ insisted, pointing at the door where the men were fleeing.

Anger flowed through him in heavy waves, and he flushed hot. As his light-headedness returned, he suddenly heard a rushing noise in his ears, so loud that it drowned out all other sounds. He couldn't catch his breath. The harder he tried to draw in air, the less air he seemed to get, until he was panting like a hard-run dog.

Sparks of light began to dot his vision before it narrowed as though he were suddenly in a tunnel, drawing closer and closer.

And then the world faded to black.

CHAPTER FIFTEEN

The first thing Russ became aware of was the stale smell of beer. Then he realized that he was lying on the floor next to the bar, looking up at the worried faces of Ethan and three waitresses. "What the hell happened?"

"You passed out," Ethan said. "I was just about to call 911." He frowned. "Maybe I still should."

"Don't you dare," Russ said, rubbing his hand over his face and trying to orient himself. His mind felt as though he'd had too much to drink. Everything was a fog. "I passed out?"

"Fainted dead away," the blonde said, sounding concerned.

Fainted? "No way."

"'Fraid so, my friend." Ethan extended his hand. "Let's get you off that dirty floor."

"Slowly," the waitress cautioned. "You don't want him to faint again."

"I didn't faint!" An absurd thing to say considering he was letting his friend help him to his feet from where he had been lying on the floor. The stares and speculative chatter of the people surrounding him made his temper rise.

Thankfully, Ethan dismissed everyone with a few words and took Russ's elbow. "Let's go to the office."

Jerking his arm away, Russ snapped, "I'm fine."

"C'mon, Russ. We can talk in the office."

He decided to follow Ethan because at least he could have a little bit of privacy to figure things out.

When they reached the office, Ethan let Russ enter first, then closed the door. "What happened?"

Russ flopped on the couch. "It wasn't my fault. That fuckin' guy picked a fight."

"That's not what I'm talking about now, although we'll definitely speak about it later. Why did you faint?"

When Russ's anger at Ethan's choice of words began to brew, the same things that had happened before he'd passed out started all over again. His breath came in gasps as his heart slammed against his rib cage. Fighting the feeling, he replied, "I didn't *faint*. Women faint."

Ethan dismissed Russ's words with a flip of his hand. "Fine, you *passed out*. It's just semantics."

Russ tried to figure out what had happened as his body slowly calmed. He'd never felt as bad as he had back in the bar, and he worried for a moment that something was physically wrong with him.

Ethan leaned back against the desk and folded his arms over his chest. "I should take you to the ER."

"Hell with that." If he showed up at the hospital and told Josie what happened, he'd not only be embarrassed, but she'd worry.

As he continued to calm down, Russ began to wonder if perhaps Ethan was right. If there was something wrong…

Like he needed one more fucking thing to worry about.

"I can run you over," Ethan said. "Look, I don't think anything's wrong. But you did fai—um…pass out. Least you can do is make sure you didn't hit your head or something."

Russ's hand rose to the back of his head and rubbed a knot forming there. He'd had his bell rung enough times that he knew this wasn't a bad injury. "I'm fine."

"Go. For me."

"Ethan…"

Ethan gave him a frown. "Joslynn will have a fit if you don't."

Russ rolled his eyes, but Ethan was winning the argument. In all honesty, he was a little worried.

But all the rigmarole that went along with an ER visit was beyond his patience tonight.

Pulling his phone from his pocket, Ethan began tapping at the screen.

"What are you doing?"

"Texting Joslynn." The phone chimed a response. "She says they're dead tonight and to bring you over."

"I'm not up to all that paperwork," Russ grumbled.

Ethan pecked at his screen again and was rewarded a few seconds later with a text chime. "She says she'll look you over first. If everything's fine, you won't have to stay." Another chime. "No need for paperwork that way." Pushing away from the desk, Ethan put his phone back in his pocket. "C'mon, let's go. I'll drive."

When rolling his eyes made him dizzy, Russ agreed with a grunt.

* * *

Joslynn had just finished charting her last patient when Russ walked through the ER double doors. She'd been on edge since Ethan texted. As the woman who cared for him, she was worried. That woman internally warred with the nurse practitioner, who had her suspicions about what happened.

But she needed more information.

Putting aside her tablet, she grabbed a pulse oximeter and went to meet him. "Hi, guys." She gave Russ a good looking over, already beginning her assessment.

"Why don't we head back to one of the rooms?" she suggested, resisting the urge to take Russ's hand in hers.

"I thought you said no hospital nonsense," Russ said, grumbling like an angry bear.

"I did. But I want to check a few things myself, okay? If everything looks fine, there will be no reason to do anything else."

Instead of arguing, he complied and came to stand at her side.

She glanced to Ethan. "Are you staying?"

He nodded.

"Hopefully we'll be back soon."

As Ethan made himself comfortable in the empty waiting room, Joslynn held the ID card that always hung from her lab coat pocket up to the scanner. The doors to the treatment area opened. "Let's see what's up. Okay?"

"I'm fine, Josie." At least he followed her, which meant he wanted answers too.

"You look fine, but indulge me so I won't worry about you."

That remark actually made his mouth twitch into a hesitant smile. "You're worried about me?"

She wanted to reply with an emphatic, "Duh!" Instead, she said, "Of course I am."

Even though all but one of the treatment rooms were empty, she led him past the first two halls and turned at the third. She entered the last room and shut the door after he joined her inside. "Hop up on the table for me."

Russ took a seat on the gurney, looking like a child being forced to comply.

Clearing the oximeter, she said, "Please hold out your right hand." When he did, she clipped it onto his index finger. Then she grabbed the blood pressure cuff. With practiced ease, she took his blood pressure and then let out a relaxed sigh. While it was slightly elevated, there was no danger. After putting away the cuff, she took off the oximeter and was relieved to see his oxygen level and pulse were both fine.

She set the oximeter aside and then slung her stethoscope back around her neck. "So what happened, Russ?"

"Not sure exactly." He rubbed the back of his neck the way he always did when he was nervous. "There was this bachelor party…"

After waiting for him to expand, she finally realized he wasn't going to. "And?"

"The best man was an asshole. I guess I lost my temper when he kept insulting me."

"So you got in a fight."

"No, not exactly." His eyes found hers. "I didn't hit him, okay?"

"Good."

"I was…exchanging words with Ethan, and I couldn't seem to catch my breath."

She could easily paint a picture of what had happened. The best man had probably gotten mouthy. Russ had come close to roughing him up. Ethan had stopped him. Russ had unloaded that anger on Ethan in response.

A sigh slipped out. She'd been so proud of Russ and how he was finally getting a grip on his stress and anxiety.

What had changed tonight?

Instead of psychoanalyzing him, Joslynn focused on the fainting spell. "You said you couldn't catch your breath?"

He nodded.

"Did you have any other symptoms?"

He thought it over a moment. "Something wasn't right with my eyes. My vision got blurry. And…narrow."

"How long were you out?" she asked.

"Ethan said it wasn't long. He didn't even have a chance to call 911. Thank God." His hand rose to the back of his head. "I think I hit my head when I went down."

Joslynn went behind the gurney to check for any injury. There was a small swelling, but she didn't think he had a concussion. Just to be sure, she checked his pupils and had him do a few motor skills exercises.

"So what do you think happened, Josie?"

The healer in her responded to the thread of fear in his voice. "I think you're fine, Russ. I can't be positive, but I think you had a panic attack."

"A what?"

"An anxiety attack. I think the fight—"

"I didn't fight," he insisted.

"Okay, the *near* fight set it off." Normally, she'd try to talk to the patient about the stress in his life and perhaps suggest a trip to the family physician if the stress was chronic. She might even discuss anxiety illnesses or the possible need for some pharmaceutical intervention. But she knew Russ wouldn't listen to any of that.

So she took his hand. "You're fine. I think the stress just got the better of you tonight. I guess I'll have to try a few new weapons to help you cope."

"I'm okay, then?"

Joslynn squeezed his hand. "Yes, you are."

When he didn't immediately hop off the gurney, she wondered if she might be able to figure out exactly what had set off the attack. "Any problems tonight? Other than the obnoxious bachelor party?"

Russ shrugged and glanced away.

Which meant there *was* something else.

The knowledge came in a flash, and she was a bit angry at herself for not seeing the connection sooner. "Did your mom call?"

His head snapped up. "What?"

"It's just…when something happens with your father, you get…upset. What happened?"

He let out a long, drawn-out sigh. "He accidentally locked Mom in the basement. I had to go let her out."

Thankful that there hadn't been a major incident, Joslynn wrapped her arms around Russ, feeling the need to comfort him. She could only imagine how difficult it had to be for Russ to watch Baron slowly mentally deteriorate. She was happy to feel him slide off the gurney and put his arms around her waist.

Russ was changing her views of how relationships worked. Whenever she'd previously been faced with adversity, she'd handled it with independence and strength. Yet now she was nearly overwhelmed with the need to comfort Russ, and in turn, it seemed as though he needed whatever comfort she could offer.

The phone to the ER rang, and she eased back and pulled it from her pocket. "Give me a second." She answered the call and then slid the phone back in her pocket. "I need to go."

"So I'm okay?"

"You're fine."

"What do I need to do to keep it from happening again?" he asked.

"We need to get a little more serious about lowering your stress," she replied. "I have some ideas."

CHAPTER SIXTEEN

Just getting Russ to come to her beginner yoga class had been an ordeal. Joslynn finally had to promise him that if he didn't like it after ten minutes, he could leave. Now the pressure was on for her to make him want to stay.

Ever since his panic attack two night ago, she'd been turning ideas around in her mind on how to help him. After the weeks they'd spent together, she'd been encouraged. He'd acted—and felt—better. More in control.

But one episode with his father and he'd tumbled right back into stress hell.

She couldn't fix things for the father, but she could try to help the son.

Russ looked uncomfortable, arms folded over his chest as his gaze skipped from student to student. At least there were two other guys this evening. She hoped their presence would make him feel less awkward.

She handed him one of the extra rolled mats and pointed to a spot just to her right. Then she worked on getting herself ready to teach.

Heaven knew she needed a good stretch from the stiffness that had settled on her. Russ was to blame. He'd been right about having them wait to know each other before they'd made love. It had been better because of their strong feelings for each other. But he'd been correct about one other thing as well—now that they were intimate, they were intimate often. Almost every time they'd gotten together. And she found herself a bit stiff and sore from their amorous activities. The man could be quite…creative.

He was the best lover she'd ever known.

More and more, Joslynn found the notion of making a long-term commitment to him less alarming. In moments of inner honesty, she admitted that the notion of losing him was untenable, and she knew should they break up, her life wouldn't be the same. She needed his comfort, his humor, his body. Yet she couldn't stop herself from thinking that Russ was going to become a permanent part of her life.

Exasperated with the avenue her thoughts traveled, she glanced up as a student appeared in the doorway. Her lips drew into a concerned frown when she saw it was Marc. With all the thoughts of Russ coursing through her, she wasn't sure she was equipped to deal with a guy who was really nice but would probably upset Russ. Why was he even here?

"Joslynn!" Marc waved as he walked through the double doors to enter the yoga studio. He came to stand in front of her. "Fancy seeing you here."

She'd never seen anyone as big as Russ move so quickly. Eating up the floor in long strides, he came to stand at her side. As he directed a rather scorching scowl at Marc, Russ folded his arms over his chest again. His legs were braced in what could only be called a "fighting stance."

Marc's body language was no less belligerent, and he was clearly taking offense to Russ standing close to her. Although neither said a word, each directed a focused, hard stare at the other.

"I'm surprised to see you here, Marc," Jos said, hoping to break the stilted silence.

"When Savannah told me how relaxing yoga was, I had to come find out for myself," he replied. "Especially when she said you taught the beginner classes."

Something that sounded a bit like a closemouthed laugh came from Russ, which only made Marc narrow his eyes. "Admit it," Russ said. "You came to see if Josie and I broke up."

"Fine," Marc said. "I admit it. Since it appears you're together, I know when to say when." He smiled at Joslynn. "Now I just want a nice relaxing yoga session."

Joslynn sighed at their macho behavior. She hadn't led Marc on, and it wasn't her fault if he showed up to satisfy his curiosity. "Class is getting ready to start. Why don't you get your mat ready, Marc? Russ, you should take off your shoes."

They acted as though they hadn't even heard her and just stood there glaring at each other.

When it dawned on her they were both suffering from jealousy, she shook her head and turned her back on them. She'd made it clear she was committed to Russ, so Marc had no reason to feel as if he had some claim on her. And Russ should be confident in her feelings. She was learning to express them more freely and had never given him a reason to doubt her.

She wasn't some prize for the two men to fight over, and she refused to let them ruin this class for her. "Go on." She waved them both away. "Go to your mats." When they were out of earshot, she muttered, "And grow up."

At the front of the room, Joslynn went about her job. "First pose, Sukhasana." As she sat cross-legged and set her hands against her knees, she led her students in some deep-breathing exercises. She did her best to try to clear her own troubled thoughts so she could enjoy the session.

But her mind wouldn't settle, and anger began to blossom, blocking all the soothing effects of the deep breathing.

How dare they treat me like some kind of trophy to battle over!

Despite her tumbling emotions, she was cognizant that her students were watching her and waiting for direction. She called out the second pose and demonstrated the downward facing dog.

Her body seemed to be her enemy as each new pose became a fight. Her muscles refused to stretch, and when she tried to demonstrate Vrksasana, she came close to falling on her face. To try to cover her bobble, she moved between her students, helping them perfect the balance pose and hoping they didn't realize exactly how much she was failing at the relaxation she was trying to teach them.

Why am I so jittery? And so tired lately?

She spent the most time with Russ, who seemed to enjoy himself, judging from the smile on his face as he tried to get his large body to bend and flex into the different poses. As she tried to help him hold the Vrksasana, he let out a loud laugh when he had to put both feet on the floor. Although he knew talking was verboten, he whispered, "Don't think I can do this one, Josie."

With a shake of her head, she put a finger to his lips.

He retaliated by kissing it before she pulled her hand back.

A self-conscious glance to Marc revealed a scowl hot enough to set Russ's mat on fire. She couldn't tell if he was angrier at her or Russ since he kept shifting his focus between them.

Dismissing Marc from her thoughts, she returned to the front of the studio and tried to focus on making this class pleasant for her students. By the time she demonstrated the last pose, the Shavasana, she felt a lot better than she had when class had begun.

Her students rewarded her with a smattering of applause before they rolled their mats and left to seek out their next adventures.

Heading to Russ, she waited as he rolled up his mat. "That was…interesting."

"Sure was," Marc said, butting into the conversation. "You seemed a bit distracted, Joslynn."

"She was awesome," Russ countered as he took her hand in his. "I normally hate stuff like this, but Josie made it fun."

"Yeah, it was fun," Marc said.

Russ's hand settled on her shoulder. "Shouldn't we be going?"

"I guess I should head out," Marc said. "This was great. Maybe I'll come to your next class."

"There are other yoga instructors," Russ said, anger clear in his tone.

"Yeah, well…" Marc smiled at her. "Thanks again, Joslynn. Maybe I'll see you around."

Glad the tension in the air eased with his parting, Joslynn let out a sigh.

So much for relaxing with yoga tonight.

She wanted to scold Russ, but considering his anxiety attack, she abstained. But she couldn't seem to stop frowning at him.

The hand on her shoulder squeezed.

Joslynn glanced up to see Russ looking down at her, the concern plain in his eyes. "I'm sorry," he said.

She simply quirked a brow.

"I promised I'd stop acting jealous."

A point in his favor that he'd realized his error. Another point since he'd apologized without prompting.

So she offered an apology of her own. "I'm sorry Marc came to class. I talked about yoga at the barbecue, but I never expected he'd ask Savannah about my classes. How about we get some juice? Shamballa sound good?" Russ took her hand in his again and gave her a gentle squeeze. "I've got a better idea."

* * *

Well aware he'd angered Josie at the yoga class, Russ wanted to make things up to her. Instead of going to the café, he'd taken her back to the Cottage and was making juice for her from scratch.

Since she'd started him on his "destress" program, he'd been eating better as well as exercising. He'd consumed more fruits and vegetables in the last few weeks than he probably had in the last six months. Tonight he was creating blueberry-banana Greek yogurt smoothies, which he hoped she'd like.

But then he'd had that panic attack and wondered if all the good he thought he'd done was entirely wasted.

There'd been no reason to be jealous of Marc. Not really. It was clear the man was attracted to Josie, but she hadn't given him any more notice than she had the other students.

She sat on one of the kitchen island bar stools, watching him as he worked. There hadn't been much conversation on their drive from yoga class, and because of the noise of the blender, there wasn't much being said now. But there needed to be.

Although he'd apologized for his reaction to Marc, he probably needed to discuss it with her. His feelings for her would always have a touch of jealousy. It was simply a fact.

Pouring the purple mixture into two glasses, he stuck a straw in one and then handed it to Josie.

"Thanks," she said before taking a drink. Then a smile filled her face. "You're really getting a knack for these."

"Thanks." He took a long drink of his own.

She chuckled and pointed to her upper lip. "You've got a little…"

Although he could feel the smoothie mustache, he loved teasing her. "A little what?"

Instead of telling him, she set her glass down, hopped off her bar stool, and came to him. Stepping close enough they almost touched, she rose on tiptoes to lick his upper lip clean.

When she tried to step back, he wrapped his arms around her waist and pulled her against him. He captured her lips and proceeded to kiss her until she put her arms around his neck and sagged against him.

As he nibbled at her ear, he whispered, "Do you know how sexy you are doing yoga?"

"I am?"

As he kissed his way to her neck, he said, "Hell yeah. How about we try a couple of those poses now?"

Her breath caught, which meant her thoughts were traveling the same road as his. "Now?"

"Now. Naked." He eased back so he could work her shirt over her head. He tossed it toward the sofa as she kicked off her shoes. He followed suit and then whipped his T-shirt off, not caring where it ended up.

Josie took his hand and led him to the bedroom. Most of the women he'd known were hit-or-miss where sex was concerned. Not Josie. Her sex drive seemed to be every bit as high as his own, and his need for her grew with every minute he spent with her. He'd never wanted a woman like he wanted her, and he was fine with that. More than fine.

After they both finished undressing, he rolled on a condom and then inclined his head at the bed. "What was that one pose? The one where you had us on hands and knees, sucking in our stomachs and then arching our backs?"

Her responding smile was seductive. "The cat-cow."

"Looked more doggie style to me."

"Let me see if this is what you want…" She crawled up on the mattress, positioned herself on all fours facing away from him as she wiggled her shapely ass.

Russ found himself unable to speak as he knelt behind her. Tracing her spine with his fingertips, he was pleased to see she arched her back into his touch. He pressed his erection against her, rubbing her core as he mimicked the act he craved.

Josie pushed back against him, glancing over her shoulder, still smiling. "Don't make me wait."

"I don't want to hurt you."

Another rock of her hips against his cock. "You won't."

Entering her slowly, he held tightly to her hips.

She was clearly having none of his gentleness, forcing herself back until he was impaled to the hilt. A gasp fell from her lips as she let her head fall forward.

"Are you okay?"

"Shut up and fuck me."

Hearing those forceful words inflamed him. His girlfriend always knew exactly what she wanted. Her demand filled him with need, and he thrust into her again and again as his thighs slapped against hers.

* * *

Joslynn clenched her hands in the quilt, anchoring herself for the storm racing through her.

Her muscles tightened as the familiar knot blossomed inside her until she came, feeling as though electricity were racing from her core to her limbs. She let out a shout, one echoed by Russ after only a few more thrusts.

He collapsed against her back, wrapping his arms around her waist as though needing to hold her through his own storm.

Easing from her, he headed to the bathroom for a few moments.

Her skin covered in a light sheen of sweat, Joslynn shivered as she scrambled under the covers. Although spring was well established, she couldn't shake the winter cold from her bones. The older she got, the more the low temperatures bothered her—a lingering side effect of her chemotherapy, and one that would never leave her.

Russ had a contented grin on his face as he flicked off the bathroom light and then slid under the quilt. As she rolled closer to him, he put his arm around her shoulders and held her close. "That was pretty amazing."

"It just seems to get better."

"You sound surprised."

She laid her check against his chest and draped her leg across his thighs. "I guess I am."

"I love you, Josie."

Everything inside of her reacted as though she were in danger. She scrambled off the bed and grabbed a robe, donning it and tying the belt tightly. "Don't you dare say that."

Russ sat up and frowned. "What's wrong?"

Everything. Every. Fucking. Thing.

Fight or flight had full hold of Joslynn's mind. Although this was her home, she needed to run. Fast and far.

Didn't he realize that those words would destroy everything they'd shared?

There was no such thing as love. There was desire. Passion. Respect. Even some kinds of affection.

But love?

Love ruined everything. It always had in the past, so she couldn't help but believe the future would hold nothing but more of the same.

She didn't want his love.

Jerking some clothes from her bureau, she dressed, not exactly sure where she'd escape to, but she had to leave. She had to put some distance between herself and disaster.

Russ was behind her as she put on her panties and some sweatpants, but he didn't try to stop her. A good instinct on his part, because she wasn't sure how she'd react if he touched her. Would she strike out?

No. She could never hurt him. She cared too much for him.

So why did she feel the need to get the hell away from him?

"Josie..."

His voice was a whisper, and she couldn't help but respond to the comforting gentleness she heard as he drew out her name. Clutching her shirt to her bare chest, she trembled.

"It's going to be okay, sweetheart," he said before settling a hand over hers.

Emotions in chaos, she tried to take a few deep breaths, which turned into gulps. She was hyperventilating, and her vision began to narrow into a tight tunnel. If she didn't get a grip, she was going to end up passing out the same way Russ had.

Russ's arms were around her, and she rested her forehead against his chest. Then she did something she hadn't done in longer than she could remember.

Joslynn burst into tears.

CHAPTER SEVENTEEN

Nothing made Russ more uncomfortable than a woman weeping. Yet as Joslynn dropped the shirt she'd held and leaned against him, he put his arms around her and smiled. Thankfully, she couldn't see his expression with her head bowed. She'd never understand that he wasn't mocking her. Instead, he smiled because her vulnerability gave him hope.

She'd finally revealed a chink in the armor that surrounded her heart. She didn't love him. Not yet. But for the first time, he believed she could. Even more, he believed she *would*.

Rubbing his chin against the top of her head, he let her cry until she was reduced to sniffles with a few small hiccups. "Feeling better?"

Joslynn bumped his jaw as she raised her gaze to his. "I can't believe I was crying. I never cry."

Russ wasn't sure what to say to that. Didn't all women cry? He'd seen both Savannah and Chelsea cry quite a bit. His mother was a champion crier. And there were many reasons why they wept. When they were happy. When they were sad. When they were pissed.

Why should Josie be any different?

That had to be the dumbest question he'd ever asked himself. She wasn't anything like other women. None of the rules seemed to apply to her. Of course she didn't cry often. She was so damn strong that she probably saw any show of emotion—especially tears—as a weakness.

Her job in the ER had to make her feel like an emotional yo-yo, and she'd probably learned to keep a tight rein on what she was feeling. It wasn't that he doubted Josie was a woman with deep and powerful sentiments. She just wasn't going to show those emotions to other people.

Then it dawned on him exactly why he understood her so well. "You're Ethan," he blurted out before he could stop himself.

Her reddened eyes searched his. "I beg your pardon?"

"You're a female version of Ethan."

She bent over to grab the shirt she'd dropped and jerked it over her head. "I'm not sure if that's a huge compliment or a horrible insult."

Letting out a chuckle at her teasing tone, Russ put on his pants. A glance around for his shirt yielded no results, which meant he'd probably left it in the other room. "Neither, really. It just dawned on me that you and Ethan approach life—at least the emotional part of life—the same way."

"This discussion obviously requires wine." She headed out of the bedroom, and he followed right behind.

A loud yawn slipped out as he located his shirt and donned it. Pulling a green bottle out of the refrigerator, she frowned.

"I'm sorry. I've destroyed your sleep schedule since we started dating."

Although she was right, he wasn't going to complain. Staying up nights hadn't bothered him all that much. He might yawn through his shifts at Words & Music, but he still did his job. He always tried to catch up on his sleep when she worked.

But tonight he was suddenly exhausted. A glance to the clock showed it was approaching eleven. Since Josie would be up until the wee hours of the morning, he had a long night ahead of him.

After she poured herself a glass of wine, she sat on the couch. "Now that I'm properly braced, explain to me why I'm like Ethan."

Russ joined her. "He doesn't like to show how he feels either. Keeps everything bottled up just like you do."

"You do that, too," she said. "That's why you have a tendency to blow up."

"But I eventually let it out, even though I tend to do that with my fists." He chuckled, but she glared at him. Since he didn't want this discussion to switch to his temper problems, he got back on the original topic. "Ethan *never* does. People think he's cold—that he doesn't have feelings."

"I don't keep things bottled up," she insisted.

"With your job? I think you'd have to just to survive. After a while it probably gets to be like you don't feel anything at all."

* * *

Joslynn gathered her brows, thinking hard about everything Russ had said.

"I have to keep things to myself," she insisted. "There's so much...misery coming through the doors at work that I have to control every word, every facial expression." She couldn't burst into tears every time she had to treat an abused child or the victim of a drunk driver. In unpleasant tasks, things like telling people they have diabetes or cancer or stitching someone back together after a horrible accident, an NP couldn't freely express her emotions. If she didn't keep a cover on things, she'd spend each shift a blubbering mess.

What good would she be to her patients then? They didn't need someone to break down and sob over what had happened to them. They needed a kick-ass, take-charge person to help them through a rough time. They needed someone who could hold herself in check.

"I get that," he said. "But you don't have to guard yourself with *me*."

While that was comforting, she couldn't help but wonder why was it so difficult for her to connect with another person.

She needed him to understand. "You know, until I met Savannah, I never had a close friend, not even during school."

"That's sad."

"Not really," Joslynn said with a shrug. "It was how I wanted it." She'd focused on beating leukemia and then learning everything she could to turn herself into a good nurse. Friendships had been pretty low on her priority list.

Her connections with men were even more detached. Joslynn held men at an emotional distance. "Do you know how hard it was to admit that I...that I care for you?" she asked.

"Yeah, sweetheart," he said, lying down and putting his head on her lap. She raked her fingers through his short hair. "I know. And I'm proud of you."

The problem with expressing her feelings was that she'd seen too much in her life. Not only had she gone through cancer treatment, but in the time she'd spent in the infusion center, she'd watched a lot of people—even innocent children—battle that bastard disease and die from it.

And then there was work. Mangled children. Abused women. Gunshot victims. That was why she didn't show her feelings. That was why she was so... What was the word Russ used to describe Ethan?

Oh, yeah. Cold.

Is that what people thought of her? That she was cold? That she was some automaton that had no feelings at all?

Russ scattered her thoughts when he let out that soft almost-snore of his. He'd fallen asleep with his head resting on her lap.

With a sigh, she finished her wine and set the empty glass on the end table. No matter how hard she fought the feeling, Joslynn cared for Russ. As she stroked his hair and watched him sleep, a smile started in her heart and spread to her lips. The battle was over. She was going to let him in.

All the way in.

* * *

Russ opened his eyes, wondering why his neck was so sore. Then he saw Josie's face above him. If his neck was stiff, she was going to be in a world of hurt judging from her position. He'd still been snoozing on her lap, and she'd fallen asleep sitting up with her chin resting against her chest.

He had no idea what time it was—a problem he'd had a lot since he'd met her. His "day" had always been a few degrees from normal since he owned a place that was open until the wee hours on the weekends, but now that he was in a relationship with a woman who worked night shifts, he'd gone even farther afield.

Maybe one day they'd sync their lives.

He really needed to get up and stretch out his stiffness. "Josie," he said softly.

The woman woke up faster than anyone he'd ever known. Her head jerked up, a motion followed closely by a drawn-out groan as her hand went to the back of her neck.

"Stiff?" Russ sat up and started to rub the tightness where her neck met her shoulder. "I'm sorry I didn't wake up sooner so you didn't get a crick."

She let out another groan as he dug his fingers into the knots that had formed in her muscles. "I was stupid for not lying down."

As he gave her a neck massage, he leaned in to brush a kiss on her lips. "Good morning, by the way."

Her eyes darted to the large clock by the front door. "It's already six. We should be at the park, warming up for our run."

"How about we skip the run today and I take you out for a nice breakfast?"

Rolling her shoulders, she smiled. "Like I'm letting you off the hook that easy."

Russ yawned, resigned to a morning run.

"Didn't you get enough sleep?"

"I'm fine."

Josie's smile faded, and she brushed his hands away. "There's something I want to talk to you about…"

The ominous tone raised his radar a notch. He quirked an eyebrow.

"I'm thinking about switching my shifts in the ER to days," she said.

His eyes widened in surprise.

"You can close your mouth now," she teased.

Shutting his jaw, which had slackened at her announcement, he had to resist the urge to get to his feet and cheer.

Then he realized exactly what she was doing. Josie was suggesting that she change her entire lifestyle to suit his needs.

He shouldn't have been surprised. He'd been doing the same thing by staying up through the nights on days she didn't have ER shifts, although it hadn't been a huge hardship since his schedule was already crazy.

Russ wasn't about to let her do something so extreme. Simply knowing that she was committed enough to the success of their relationship to take that major a step was all the reward he needed. "You don't have to do that, sweetheart. Things are working fine the way they are. I don't want you to do something that drastic just because I yawn from time to time."

"I've actually been thinking about it for a few weeks." She wrinkled her brow. "I suppose that's something couples should talk about, isn't it?"

He nodded, a bit perplexed that she could be her age and have never learned the rules. Not that he was an expert, but he knew the game. "How old are you?" he blurted out.

At least her smile returned. "Didn't anyone ever tell you it's not polite to ask a lady her age?" She tossed him a wink. "I'm thirty-one, Russ. And exactly how old are *you*?"

Loving how she turned the question back on him, he grinned. "Thirty-four."

"What made you ask my age?"

He gave her a shrug.

"Seriously, why was my age suddenly so important?"

Since she was sounding irritated, he told her the truth. "I was thinking that by the time a woman was your age, she should know how couples decide important things."

This time she was the one who shrugged. "I've always made important decisions on my own."

"*Every* decision? What about when you were a kid? You know, when you were sick?"

"My mom always said it was my disease, so she let me make the call on what treatment I wanted. The oncologist would give me my options, and I'd choose what I wanted to do."

What was he supposed to say to that? A preteen facing her own mortality and the parent who hadn't run away dumped all the important decisions that had to be made directly in Joslynn's lap.

If he ever met her mother, he hoped he could keep his anger under control. "How do you two get along now?"

She snorted. "We don't. We're not close. She lives in California, and I haven't even talked to her in five years. She's got her own life out there. I've got mine here."

"No wonder. Shit, Josie…She should've been more involved. She really let you choose treatment?"

"It was what I wanted," she insisted. "Even then, I was bossy. Besides, there weren't many options. The doctor said it was pretty straightforward on what worked best." The smile she gave him seemed so phony that he reached out to put his arms around her.

Pushing him away, she got to her feet. "I'm heading to bed." She picked up the empty wineglass from the night before and carried it to the sink. "I need some more sleep before I go to the hospital tonight. I spent most of last night watching TV while you snored." She winked.

Russ followed her to the bedroom, refusing to end such an important discussion so abruptly.

She stood next to the bed, folded her arms under her breasts, and stared at him. "What?"

Obviously, discussion about her illness was going to get him nowhere, so he focused on the choice she had to make. "We still haven't talked about you switching to days. I don't want you to do that for me."

"Like I said, I've been thinking about it for a while. The administration proposed it several weeks back, and at first I just blew it off. But now that we're together... Well, it might make things simpler. Working the night shift is tough. I make it work, but the switch might be good."

He sat on the edge of the mattress and patted the spot next to him. "Why would it be good?"

Josie dropped down beside him. "I could be on sync with the rest of the world. You. Savannah. It just seems like I miss a lot of things because of sleeping during the day."

"I have to admit, it would be nice to spend time with you when one of us isn't snoring."

"I don't snore!"

"Yeah, you do. But it's cute," he said, and kissed her nose.

"So how does a couple make a decision?" she asked.

Russ took her hand in his. "First, they talk about the pros and cons."

"All right." Josie pursed her lips as she thought for a few moments. "Pro, I would be on the same schedule as most of the civilized world."

"True."

"Pro, I could teach more yoga classes since I won't be starting work in the evening."

He nodded, glad she was catching on. It wasn't as though he'd made a lot of joint decisions before, either. But he wasn't about to let her start making choices based on what he wanted. She'd grow to resent him if that choice turned out wrong.

"Pro, you and I could spend more time—at least more quality time—together."

"I'm glad you think that's a pro."

A frown filled her face. "Why wouldn't I see it as a pro? I care about you. Of course I want to spend time with you."

He grinned. "Told you it would get easier to say."

The frown swiftly changed to a smile. "Yeah, it is."

Giving her hand a squeeze, he said, "Any cons?"

"You know what? I really can only think of two."

"First?"

"I'll lose my late-shift pay, but I don't really need the extra money."

"Second?" he asked.

"I'll need a few days to adjust my days and nights." She cocked her head. "You know, I really think it would be a good change for me…and for us."

That statement earned a kiss.

"What do you think, Russ?"

"I think it makes sense to work days. I just didn't want you to do it only because of me."

"I wouldn't do that," Josie insisted.

He let out a chuckle. "I don't think you would, either."

This time she was the one to offer the kiss.

"So I'm doing this. I'll talk to my boss when I get to the hospital tonight. It'll probably be a few weeks before I switch over."

Flopping back on the bed, Russ waited as Joslynn lay down and snuggled up against him. Then he kissed the top of her head. "And that, sweetheart, is how a couple makes a decision."

CHAPTER EIGHTEEN

Y ou made it!" Russ said, waving his arm at Joslynn. Her last night shift at the hospital had ended this morning, and he'd expected that she'd go home and sleep. Adjusting to working days would probably take a while.

She waved back as she jogged over to meet him at the team bench. "I did. Are you surprised?"

"A little. I know you're probably exhausted after working last night."

Shrugging, she set her bag on the grass. "Tired but stressed. Last shift was rough. Figured watching a little softball might shake the bad thoughts right out of my head."

Russ took her hand and gently pulled her closer. Then he kissed her, letting his lips linger against hers even though people were staring. "I'll take you home after this. How about a nice massage? Then you can sleep."

Her smile always hit him on a visceral level. "That sounds like heaven."

"Geesh, Russell. Are you bringing in another ringer?" The grating voice of Robert Campbell, owner of the Black Stallion, almost stole away Russ's good humor. While he could normally stomach Robbie's over-inflated ego, Russ didn't like the way he was eyeing Josie.

Introductions were probably in order, despite the fact he wanted to keep her to himself. She was sure to recognize the name, because Russ had told her several stories about the competition between Words & Music and the Black Stallion. While both venues were extremely popular, Russ and his partners liked to best Black Stallion whenever they could, probably because Robbie Campbell could be such a horse's ass. Not only did they compete to book talent, but the two bars played in touch football and softball leagues with several other clubs. Ethan especially liked to brag about beating their biggest rival. His favorite thing was to tease that by marrying Chelsea, he'd taken away Robbie's most profitable act. All Russ cared about was being able to rub Robbie's nose in any loss.

"Josie Wright," Russ said, "this is Robbie Campbell."

"I own the Black Stallion," Rob added.

"Ah, so you're here to get your butt kicked," Josie said with a cheeky grin. "I suppose you're used to it. I mean, Words and Music always has a better crowd than the Black Stallion."

Russ didn't even bother smothering his laugh at the deep blush that spread up Rob's neck to reach his face. While the rivalry between the two clubs was well known in Nashville, Russ and his partners had the upper hand since both Chelsea Harris and Savannah Wolf were frequent headliners.

"She doesn't have a uniform," Rob grumbled. "Can't play without a uniform."

Josie glanced to Russ. "Got another T-shirt lying around?"

He hadn't expected her to even consider playing. Whenever the Words & Music staff faced off against the Black Stallion employees, things had the potential to turn ugly. "I do. But you don't have to—"

"I'd love to play. It'll help take my mind off that crappy shift. Are you playing fast or slow pitch, Robert?"

"Fast pitch," Rob replied. "We're serious about this game." His gaze traveled from her head to her toes, lingering too long on her breasts.

Russ wanted to punch him in the nose, but Josie must've followed his train of thought because she narrowed her eyes at Rob. "Serious is the only way I play."

Rob dismissed her with a flip of his wrist. "Fine. Whatever. Play, then. Girlfriends and siblings are eligible, and it's clear you're dating this idiot. Hope you enjoy losing."

Recognizing her coy smile, Russ decided to wait to ask her what she knew that he didn't. "We'd be happy to have you, Josie."

"Whatever," Rob said again. "Just get your roster to the umpire before you're disqualified." He stomped away, leaving little clouds of dust in his wake.

As soon as he left, Russ shook his head. "You don't have to play just 'cause Robbie's being an asshole."

"I know."

"So what are you hiding?" he asked.

She glanced down and dragged her toe across the dirt. "Who said I'm hiding anything?"

"Oh, please. I know that smile, that smug smile."

Her grin grew. "Did I ever tell you my college intramural team won every single game we played whenever I was on the mound? I'm a pretty good pitcher."

"That's impressive."

"So…let's go kick that windbag's ass."

* * *

Her energy restored, Joslynn donned the T-shirt in the restroom while Savannah chuckled.

"What?" Joslynn asked as she used the mirror to adjust the shirt.

Savannah's reflection smiled. "I haven't seen you look so happy before. Russ is good for you."

"Yeah, he is."

"And you're good for him."

"I am?"

With a nod, Savannah said, "What's it been? A month?"

"Six weeks." *Great.* Now she'd become one of those women who tracked the time of how long she'd been with her boyfriend.

What's wrong with that? her heart asked.

More and more she'd been listening to that heart, which in and of itself was a huge change. Her whole life had been about logic—about leading with her wit and not her emotions.

"He brings out the best in you," Savannah added. "And vice versa."

Turning to lean back against the counter, Joslynn adjusted her ponytail. "You're right. We're good for each other." Before this turned into some overly mushy discussion, she switched the topic. "Where's Caroline? Figured she'd be here as a cheerleader."

"She spent the night with my parents. They're bringing her here in a little bit. Love me some softball, so pregnant or not, I had to play."

"Just don't do any headfirst slides," Joslynn teased. "Where's Chelsea? Figured she'd be here too."

"She's in Miami. At least I think that's where she is." A laugh rose from Savannah. "That woman tours so much, it's impossible to keep track of what city she's in."

"Is Ethan playing?"

Savannah shook her head. "He's on the road with her this time."

Joslynn's eyes widened.

"I know, right? Who would've expected him to ever go on tour?"

"Not me. You told me how much he hates publicity."

"He does, but as much as you've been good for Russ, Chels has been good for Ethan. He doesn't mind dealing with her fans anymore. Not that he'll ever be like his parents. They embraced their celebrity. Ethan tolerates Chelsea's."

Joslynn checked her watch. "We should get out there."

As she walked with Savannah to the dugout, she took inventory of the people warming up on the Words & Music team. She recognized some of the waiters and waitresses, although she didn't know all their names. Leslie Guinan was playing catch with her sous chef. The surprise was seeing Leslie's brother jogging from the parking lot toward the field. After Marc showing up at the yoga class, Joslynn worried about Russ. But he'd promised not to be jealous, and she was willing to give him the benefit of the doubt.

Following Savannah to a large plastic tub full of equipment, Joslynn tried a couple different gloves before she found one that would work. She also grabbed a softball. Just as she turned to ask her friend if she was ready to catch a few pitches, Marc came up behind her and swiped the ball from her mitt.

"Wanna warm up?" he asked, tossing the ball lightly in the air and catching it a few times.

Before she could answer, Russ was there, his voice a rumbling growl. "*I'll* warm her up. I'm catching today, and I need to get a feel for her pitches."

"You're pitching?" Savannah asked.

"I'm going to try," Joslynn replied. "It's been a few years since I played. I should take a few swings with the bat too. Hope it all comes back to me."

"I'm sure it will." Marc nodded at her and then Russ before trotting over to his sister.

"You two have fun," Savannah said. "I'm gonna go warm up with Brad."

Russ grabbed a catcher's mask from the tub. "I forgot he was going to be here."

"I imagine he's a pretty good athlete," she said, picking up another softball since Marc hadn't returned the one he'd taken from her.

"I sure hope so. It would be great to watch Robbie go down."

Joslynn gave him a quick kiss on the cheek. "Let's see if I can help with that."

* * *

Russ grinned as he tossed the ball back to Josie. She wasn't a good pitcher; she was a *great* pitcher. She'd just struck Robbie out swinging, and the way he grumbled profanities under his breath as he walked away from the batter's box was music to Russ's ears.

Although he hadn't intended to bring in a ringer, that was exactly what she'd turned into, and he was loving every minute of watching the Black Stallion staff go down in flames.

"One more out," he said as he punched his mitt. Then he held up a finger to his team. "Only one more out." He eyed the runners on first and second, threatening with a glare should either decide to make a move.

Since Words & Music led three to nothing, all his team needed to do was get out of the top of this inning. They wouldn't even have to bat if Josie could strike out the next batter. Unfortunately, the next man up to the plate was the head bouncer. Built like a brick house, the guy took a couple of swings before spitting in the dust and stepping into the box. He'd gone two for two with a single and a ground-rule double, so he was capable of doing some damage. And Josie was tiring. She might've struck out Robbie, but this bouncer was another story.

Squatting, Russ readied for the pitch.

Josie looked determined as she focused hard on the batter. Then she wound up and took a long stride as she launched her pitch.

The clang of metal echoed as the bouncer got a solid piece of the ball—a line drive toward the shortstop—Marc. He had no time to react as the ball caught him right in the face, and he went down hard.

Russ tried to keep track of the runners, but Josie sprinting toward Marc distracted him. When it dawned on him that Marc wasn't getting up, Russ forgot all about the game and hurried out to see what could be done to help.

She fallen to her knees and cast aside her mitt. "Marc? Can you hear me?"

Thankfully, Marc groaned in response. As he attempted to sit up, she held his head still.

"Don't move," she cautioned. "Let me see how badly you're hurt."

Russ grimaced as he noticed that Marc's eyes were already starting to swell. Blood trickled from both nostrils, which meant the poor guy probably had a broken nose. "What do you need, Josie?"

"Call 911. We need to get him to the hospital."

* * *

Joslynn was finally able to take a moment and talk to the people who'd followed Marc to the emergency room. Leslie remained at her brother's side, but both siblings wanted Joslynn to head out to the lobby and ease all the worried minds.

Everyone from the Words & Music team was there, as were several from the Black Stallion team. She did notice, however, that neither Robert nor the brute who had hit the line drive had bothered to show up.

As the teams gathered around, Joslynn offered them a smile. She was quite accustomed to explaining things to patients and their families, but she'd never faced such a large group. "Marc is going to be fine. He told me to let y'all know that he has a broken nose and a concussion. We're going to keep him here tonight just to be on the safe side." She directed her gaze to Russ and Brad, both of whom looked extremely relieved by the news, as did Savannah. "He's probably earned himself a few days off to recover."

"Absolutely," Russ said, coming over to take Joslynn's hand. "Whatever he needs."

Her first instinct was to jerk her hand back. She still wasn't used to public displays of affection, but to so brazenly declare they were a couple in front of the ER staff?

To hell with it!

Not only did she hold his hand, but she gave him a quick kiss on the cheek. Turning back the large gathering, she said, "I know some of you would like to see him, but it's probably best if you allow him to get some rest. Leslie said she'll post on social media when he's ready to have visitors."

As the softball players turned to leave the lobby, Joslynn turned to Russ. "Leslie was hoping you and Brad could take Marc's car back to his place."

"Sure," Brad replied. "Russ and I will take care of it."

"Think you can bring my Kia here while you're at it?" she asked.

"Why don't you come with us now?" Russ asked. "After Brad and I get Marc's car home, I'll follow you to your place."

"I should stay with Marc."

His brows knit. "Why? You're not on the clock now."

"I'm the one who brought him in. I should stay until I hand him over to the plastic surgeon."

"Plastic surgeon?"

She nodded. "He's going to have to get that nose put back together unless he wants it to be crooked from now on."

"My nose has been broken twice—that I know of. Could be more. I never needed a plastic surgeon."

Brad cuffed him on the shoulder. "A broken nose gives a face character."

"A broken nose," Joslynn countered, "can cause all sorts of problems if it's not corrected."

With a scoff, Russ said, "Last time I broke my nose, coach had the trainer snap it back into place on the bench and then sent me in the next play."

"Then your coach was an idiot of the highest order." When she saw Francie waving to her, Joslynn knew the plastic surgeon was on his way for the consult. "I should go. The surgeon's coming, and I should explain a few things to Marc and Leslie before he gets here."

Russ nodded. "Want me to come back and get you later? You could text me."

Josie shook her head. "If you and Brad could please bring my car here, I can go home after I make sure Marc's settled."

"Can do," he replied. "After that I'm heading to see Mom and Dad. Want me to head to your place after?"

"Up to you, but I'm due about twelve hours of sleep. Expect to see nothing but my closed eyes." She brushed a kiss over his lips. "I'll go get my keys."

CHAPTER NINETEEN

Russ and Brad had driven back to the softball field to get Josie's car and took it back to the hospital. Then Russ made sure Brad got home. Russ was every bit as tired as Josie had claimed to be. After a quick visit with his mother and father, he planned to head home, take a hot shower, drink a cold beer, and get a good night's sleep.

He hadn't heard from his mother today, which hopefully meant Baron had enjoyed a good day. At least there were still plenty of them, thank God.

But the bad days were sometimes *really* bad.

What kind of future was Russ offering Josie?

He thought again about getting the genetic test his father's doctor had offered. The stronger his feelings for Josie grew, the more he wondered if getting the blood draw was the right thing to do, to find out if he potentially faced disaster.

How would she react if he had the gene?

How would I *react?*

For the first time since they'd discussed it, he wondered if her inability to have children might be a good thing. While he loved her and would enjoy raising a family with her, Russ knew that if he could pass along the early-onset Alzheimer's gene, it would be reckless and cruel to have kids.

But what if he didn't have the gene? And what if Josie discovered that her leukemia hadn't left her sterile?

It was stupid to keep questioning the future when he didn't have any answers.

He pulled into his parents' driveway still debating with himself. A glance to their porch found his father and mother sitting on the swing, Baron's arm around Yvonne's shoulders.

The picture of contentment.

Out of his SUV, Russ joined them on the porch, taking a seat on one of the Adirondack chairs. "How are you two?"

"Five by five," his father replied. "Did you win the game?"

At least Baron's memory was trusty today since he remembered the softball game. Russ shook his head.

Baron shot him a glare. "Why not?"

"A guy got injured before it ended," Russ replied. "Had to hang it up to get him to the hospital."

With a concerned frown, Yvonne said, "What happened?"

"Line drive to the face," Russ said.

His mother's frown intensified.

"It was Leslie's—our chef's—brother," he explained. "Josie rode with him to her hospital and was taking care of him when I left."

"I hope you know that girl's the best thing that ever happened to you, Russell," Baron said.

"I know, Dad."

"So when are you going to propose?" Yvonne asked.

Since Russ asked himself the same question at least ten times a day, he smiled at his parents' enthusiasm. "It's kinda early in the game."

Baron shook his head. "Nonsense. The moment I met your mom, I knew."

"She's been mighty good to us," his mother added. "Comes around or calls pretty much every day to see how we're doin'."

That frequency was news to Russ, although he wasn't truly surprised. Once Josie made a commitment, she gave it her all.

"Well?" There was a sharp demand in Baron's voice.

"Well, what, Dad?"

"When are you gonna stop fightin' what you feel for her?"

"*I* don't fight it," Russ replied. "*She* does."

"Then it's up to you to make her realize how great the two of you are together."

* * *

Joslynn sat behind the wheel of her car and started the engine. She was so damn tired. Seemed she felt a little less energy every day, and she hoped once she got her days and nights straightened out, her fatigue would improve.

Despite being tired, she found herself hoping Russ was there when she got home. There was just something right about sleeping at his side, something she would be able to do more often with her new schedule.

As she opened the door, she could hear the strains of a

guitar—not a recording, but Russ playing an actual guitar he must've brought from his house. Putting her keys on the hook, she kicked off her shoes as she listened to him play. She hadn't realized how talented he was.

He glanced up and smiled at her, one of those heart-stopping smiles. "Hi, sweetheart."

Sitting down next to him on the sofa, Joslynn gave him a quick kiss. "I'm happy you're playing for me."

"I am, you know. Playing for you, I mean."

"No, I don't know what you mean," she admitted.

"Just listen for a minute, okay?"

She nodded.

He began a song. It was unfamiliar to her, but Joslynn was quickly captured by the haunting melody—so clean, so clear, yet stuffed full of emotion. But it ended rather abruptly.

"Is that one of Brad's new songs?" she asked. "Savannah told me he's working on a new album for her. I'd like to hear the rest."

His lopsided smile raced through her like an electrical charge. "I can't play the rest."

"Why not?"

"I haven't written it yet."

Surely she'd heard him wrong. "Wait…*you* wrote that song?"

He nodded and set the guitar aside. "I started writing one for shits and giggles. It didn't really go anywhere. Then I started this song. There are lyrics." He shrugged. "They're not ready to share yet."

"You wrote a song."

"I wrote a song for you."

Joslynn was having a hard time wrapping her mind around

what he'd told her. How could she possibly inspire a man to compose such a beautiful piece of music?

Because he loves you.

For the first time, she believed it—she believed that Russ loved her.

And you're falling in love with him.

In the past, her realization would've been a reason to put as much distance between the two of them as she could. Not this time. This time she wanted to put her arms around him and never, ever let go.

Standing, she took his hand and pulled him to his feet. Although he gave her a puzzled tilt of his head, he didn't say a word as she led him to her bed.

What was there to say? She understood now—understood his jealousy. If another woman approached Russ, Joslynn would be inclined to attack. Russ was hers.

He belongs to me!

Oh yes, *now* she understood.

And she needed to feel him deep inside her body.

As though he'd caught her desire, he kissed her while their hands scrambled to remove clothing. Finally naked, he stared down at her, pulling the tie from her hair to let it spill around her shoulders.

She tried to take charge, but he wouldn't allow it. Instead, he backed her up to the mattress so that she sat on the edge. He pushed her to lie down with her knees hanging over the side.

Russ knelt as he draped her legs over his shoulders. She let out a surprised gasp as he pressed a kiss to her core. He licked between her folds, and she surrendered to the passion. When he gently sucked on her sensitive bud, she almost came off the bed.

"Easy there, Josie," he said.

She hadn't realized that she'd been squeezing her legs together so tightly. Relaxing her muscles, she stroked his head as he went right back to bringing her closer and closer to climax. When her release raced through her, she called to him to join her. Instead, he sent her flying a second time.

Joslynn tried to catch her breath as he grabbed a condom from the nightstand and tossed it by the pillows.

Russ crawled up on the mattress as she backpedaled to get to the middle.

Rising to her knees, she clutched his shoulders and turned him until he was flat on his back. "My turn." After brushing her lips against his neck, she worked her way down to his chest. She swirled her tongue around each nipple. A couple of kisses to those ripped abs, and then she grabbed his cock and licked him from root to tip. His hissing breath made her smile.

He laced his fingers through her hair as she stroked him with her tongue. "Josie…"

The way he said her name made a thrill race through her, and she took as much of him as she could into her mouth.

* * *

Russ wanted the feelings Josie sent pounding through him to last forever. The heat of her mouth on his cock. The silkiness of her long hair brushing against his skin. The sweet taste of her still on his lips.

Before he could tell her he was insane to get inside her, she rose over him. After rolling on the condom, she straddled his hips and guided him home.

He couldn't hold back, thrusting into her tightness again and again, showing her with his body everything he felt in his heart. The moment he felt her clench around him, he surrendered to his orgasm, letting the fire rush through him as he poured himself into her. Through choppy breaths, he told her how much he loved her.

With what little strength remained, he rolled away and managed a quick cleanup. Josie ran into the bathroom when he was done and came back out in one of the oversized shirts she liked to sleep in.

"Are you staying the night?"

Russ loved how her voice was full of hope. "I'd like to if you don't mind."

"I'd love for you to stay." As he held up the sheet, she slid back into bed beside him before snuggling up to his side and draping her leg over his thighs. "That was amazing."

He kissed her nose. "It was more than amazing. I'm not sure there's even a word that can describe how good that was."

A lusty yawn made her whole body shake. "I'm done."

"I imagine you are. Get some sleep."

Holding her close, Russ tried not to be disappointed when she fell asleep almost as soon as she closed her eyes. After what they'd just shared, he'd hoped she might admit that she loved him too.

Josie *did* love him.

She *had* to love him.

Because he would be utterly lost without her.

CHAPTER TWENTY

Three days later, Russ came back from the grocery store to find Josie's car parked in his driveway. He eased his SUV beside the blue car, watching as the garage door opened to reveal an organized space.

The mess was gone, replaced by large plastic containers that had been labeled with a thick black marker. The floor had been swept, and hanging from one of the beams in the middle of the ceiling was a brown punching bag.

"What the hell?" he said more to himself than to her. She must have spent hours making sense of the crap he'd accumulated and, having nowhere else to store it, shoved into that garage.

Josie, dressed in a red tank top, black spandex shorts, and sporting fingerless workout gloves, took a couple of punches at the bag before glancing up to smile at him. Her hair was pulled into a tight ponytail, and she had the same intense expression on her face she always had before she ran his ass into the ground at the park. "Hi, baby."

Baby?

He raised his eyebrows at the endearment.

"Would you prefer 'honey'?"

"Nah. Baby's fine with me." Russ watched her take a few more swings at the punching bag. "What's up with the new equipment?"

She stopped hopping around like a boxer and shook her hands out as though they stung. "I figured out something important."

After accepting a welcoming kiss from her before she danced away and hit at the bag again, he took a seat on a wooden stool he didn't realize he owned. Heaven only knew what other treasures she'd found when she'd organized his garage. "What did you figure out?"

"That yoga just isn't going to work for you."

He threw his hands in the air and let out a cheer. "Thank you, God!"

Joslynn laughed. "Yeah, I was a little slow on the uptake with that one. Sorry. I was hoping you'd learn to love it."

"Since we have some of our best sex after you drag me to yoga, I shouldn't complain." He waggled his eyebrows at her.

When she got close enough, he tugged her into his arms and gave her a proper kiss, loving how she sagged against him and let out a telling sigh when he ended the kiss.

"So why the punching bag?" he asked.

Heading back to land a solid hit on the bag, she smiled. "Since you can't run or stretch away your stress—"

"I love running with you," Russ protested.

"I'm glad." Josie grabbed the bag to stop it from swaying. "I hoped that if you work your frustration out on this, maybe the jerks you need to toss out of the bar won't make you so…hostile."

"It was one guy, Josie. One drunken asshole who grabbed a waitress's ass."

"And it was enough to give you an anxiety attack."

* * *

Aware that his temper was rising, Joslynn didn't press the point. Ethan had painted a little more descriptive picture of what had happened at Words & Music, but she focused on why she'd gone to so much trouble to clean up his disaster of a garage and hang the punching bag.

"This," she said, shoving the bag to set it swinging, "will help you channel your anger." She retrieved a pair of gloves she'd bought for him and handed them over. "Go change your clothes, put these on, and we'll give it a go."

He didn't take long donning his gray running shorts and a black T-shirt with the sleeves torn off. As he pulled on the gloves, she went over to him and brushed a kiss on his cheek. Then she went behind the bag and took hold of it with both hands. "Let's party, baby."

She underestimated his strength, and his punch almost knocked her over. Taking a tighter hold of the bag, she braced her legs farther apart. "Again."

Damn if he didn't grin and hit the thing harder.

Joslynn held her ground and grinned. "Again."

* * *

Joslynn put her hands against the tiled wall of the shower and let the hot water spray on her shoulders. Taking deep breaths, she focused on relaxing after a tough workout.

The punching bag had gone over better than she'd expected. Russ had hit the thing until his arms trembled with fatigue and her shoulders ached. Then she'd led him on a three-mile jog that had ended up with them back at his house making love on the sofa.

Something about their incredible chemistry always ignited when they worked out together. Didn't matter what activity they chose. Running. Lifting weights. Yoga. Whenever they finished, they reached for each other.

At least they had enough self-control to get somewhere private before the clothes came off.

Russ had popped into the shower first, and she'd joined him a few minutes later, knowing that if she got there too soon, they'd probably end up back in bed. After he dried himself with a towel, he rushed out of the bathroom, telling her that his phone was ringing.

Joslynn turned off the water and opened the glass door just wide enough to fetch a clean towel. As she dried off, he came back into the bathroom, towel draped around his slim hips. He was staring at his phone, and the startled look on his face frightened her.

"What's up?" Something was clearly wrong, so she hurried the drying process and stared at him through the glass.

"I'm not sure."

"What's that supposed to mean?" She stepped out of the shower stall.

"It was Mom. She sounded kinda…weird."

"What did she want?"

A frown filled his features. "You know, I'm not really sure. She just said that she'd called by accident and that they were fine. But her tone…"

"We should go over there."

His frown deepened. "She didn't act like she wanted me there."

"Tell you what…If we stop by the Cottage first, we can grab the cookies I made for them. Gives us an excuse to swing by."

Although his brow was still furrowed with worry, he nodded.

"I'll hurry," she promised. "If traffic is light, we can be there in thirty minutes."

* * *

Panic sizzled inside Russ, growing in intensity with each mile that passed as he headed to his parents' house. Although he normally drove a bit too fast, today he was pushing close to an unreasonable speed.

Josie didn't criticize him. Instead, she chatted amiably about how Savannah's daughter had an upcoming dance recital and how she was going to attend. Josie was astute and had figured out long ago the best way to calm him was to distract him, a tactic at which she was very skilled.

After they pulled into the driveway, she hurried to catch up with him as he practically catapulted himself from the SUV. She took his hand in one of hers, holding on to the container full of snickerdoodles with the other.

The door opened as they mounted the porch stairs, and he

heard her gasp when his mother stepped outside. Russ had a flashback to Marc Guinan after he'd been nailed by the line drive. He put his hands on her shoulders. "Shit, Mom. What happened?"

Yvonne burst into tears before rushing into his arms. All he could do was hold her until she settled down.

Josie went to the door, casting a concerned glance back at him before going inside.

Russ gave her a nod, knowing she was going to check on his father. A few moments later, Baron's angry shouts spilled from the house.

Torn between comforting his mother and protecting the woman he loved, Russ decided to stay with Yvonne. Josie was experienced in dealing with people, and she could handle herself.

This wasn't the first time his father had flown into a rage. Before the Alzheimer's diagnosis, Baron would go off the deep end from time to time—often for no apparent reason. It was one of the reasons they'd talked to a doctor. When he'd started his medications, he'd seemed to improve.

But today? Today Baron was shouting obscenities at the top of his lungs and had hurt his wife.

Although she was still softly weeping, Yvonne pushed away from Russ. "I need to go to your father."

"Let Josie handle him for a minute. Tell me what happened."

"I don't know what happened. One minute, he was fine. Then…then…"

"He hit you?" Russ clenched his hands into fists.

She gave him a nod. "I don't know why. Last time—"

"He's hit you before?" His anger soared and his teeth clenched. "When?"

Russ realized that his rage had no true direction. Baron wasn't in his right mind, and it wasn't as though there was anyone Russ could punch in retaliation.

"Only once or twice." Yvonne scrubbed away the remaining tears with the back of her hand.

The shouting had abated, which he hoped meant it was safe to go inside. "Let's have Josie take a look at your face." Thankfully, it didn't appear as damaged as he'd first feared. Her lips were swollen, and there was some dried blood around her right nostril. The dark shadow under her right eye would be even more colorful in a day or two.

He led his mother inside, finding Josie sitting on the sofa next to a now compliant Baron. She was holding his hands and murmuring to him in a low and soothing tone.

How many troubled patients had she calmed with the same sweet voice and gentle manner?

"See?" Josie said, putting a hand on Baron's shoulder. "Yvonne didn't leave, and Russ is here for a visit." Her gaze caught Russ's. "Baron had the wrong idea that his wife had left and a stranger was running around his house in her place." She patted his father. "Like I told you, she's right here."

Baron let out a snort. "That bitch thought she'd be tricky with me, pretending she lived here."

"She should've known better," Josie said. Then she glanced to Yvonne. "Why don't you come sit down?"

Despite having been abused, his mother didn't even hesitate as she hurried to her husband's side.

Josie rose to surrender her spot next to Baron. "Why don't Russ and I go get you two some milk and a plate full of the cookies I made for you? I imagine the cake I brought over Monday is long gone since chocolate is your favorite. Right, Baron?"

"Chocolate is my favorite," he said flatly.

Russ had grown accustomed to his father doing what Josie called "mirroring." Baron tended to repeat whatever he was asked, because he knew he was expected to say something. Since he couldn't think of an answer, he'd just parrot the words back to the person.

After Yvonne sat, Josie crouched next to her and held her head, looking over her battered face. Then Josie used her thumbs to wipe the remaining tears from Yvonne's cheeks. "I'll get you some ice for that lip, okay?"

Josie rose to her full height and took Russ's hand. "You two stay right there, and we'll get your snack." She led him into the kitchen.

* * *

Had Yvonne shown up at the hospital in that condition, the first thing Joslynn would've done was call social services. "Didn't any of those home health service names I gave her work out?" she asked when they were out of earshot.

Russ leaned back against the kitchen counter, folding his arms over his chest the way he always did when he was closing her off.

"She didn't call, did she?"

He shook his head. "I called a couple myself, but Mom wouldn't meet with any of them."

"Russ, your mother needs help, and she needs it yesterday. I thought she'd agreed."

"She probably said that because it was what you wanted to hear and it got you off her case. She told me she didn't want anyone coming in to help my dad. It took me forever to get her just to let me hire someone to clean the house."

"You're going to have to insist."

"I can't tell my parents what they have to do, Josie."

So many times, patients' families needed to be persuaded to do the right thing, even if it was staring them right in the eyes. Baron's condition had advanced beyond the point of Yvonne handling his care solo, and Russ needed a little tough love to realize that time had changed his role as child to the role of parent. It happened to everyone eventually. "You saw her face, right?"

He winced.

"Your father is more than she can handle alone now. Both of us know it. We need to convince her."

Holding his hands out in front of him, palms up, he gave her a frown. "What do you want me to do? Lock him in a nursing home?"

"No." *Not yet, at least.* There would be some more hard choices that would need to be made in the near future, and Russ would have to make them. Joslynn had no doubt Yvonne would do everything in her power to keep Baron home, but that was in no one's best interest if his symptoms kept escalating.

A tear slipped from the corner of her eye, and she quickly swiped it away. In the months she'd been with Russ, Joslynn had developed a deep affection for his parents. They were wonderful people, the kind of people who didn't deserve something this horrible to be happening to them. The NP in her knew what should be done, but she felt more like a daughter with the Greens, which made the advice she was giving so damned difficult.

"Then what, Josie?"

She took no exception to his exasperated tone. She was every bit as frustrated and angry over the situation. "Let's start with getting an aide." There was no reason to make Russ think about the evitable. For now she'd do everything she could to help Yvonne in her desire to keep Baron home. And that would require a lot of help. "You're going to have to insist. Just like you did with the maid service."

"Mom's gonna pitch a fit."

"Then let her go right ahead and pitch a fit."

At least Russ smiled. Not a genuine smile—more one of relief that someone was stepping in and forcing him to put his foot down with his parents.

I should've done this earlier. That was what he needed to make the situation better—someone to give him a nudge. "We can go through the hospital social worker or you can call and interview some of the people yourself."

"I'd rather you pick someone." He pushed away from the counter. "I'll go tell my mom."

"It might not be a bad idea to have her go for an x-ray. I don't think her nose is broken, but better safe than sorry. I'll make her an ice pack while you talk to them."

"I'll see if she'll go." Grabbing Joslynn's hand, he squeezed gently. "Thank you, sweetheart."

Fighting the urge to cry, she gave him a nod.

"I'm getting the DNA test." Russ said the words in such a bland tone that it took her a moment to realize their importance.

"So you want to know?"

"I *have* to know."

She brushed the back of her knuckles against his beard-roughened cheek. "Want me to go with you?"

"I'd like that."

"Since you're being so brave, maybe I'll follow your lead and get those fertility tests," Joslynn said.

"You don't have to," Russ said.

"Quid pro quo. Besides, we both need to have all the information. It's the only way we can make smart choices."

"Since you're going with me, then I'll go with you. I love you, Josie."

I think I love you too…

CHAPTER TWENTY-ONE

Hi, baby," Joslynn said as she answered the phone.

"I'm gonna stay late," Russ said. "Ethan is out of town with Chelsea, and Brad wanted to be with Savannah and Caroline. I'm gonna close."

"Okay. I'm still working on that quality-of-care report anyway. How are things there?"

"Fine." The word was clipped and terse.

"Are you okay?" she asked.

"Fine."

A few stilted seconds ticked by, raising her radar a notch when he didn't elaborate. It had been three weeks since the incident at his parents' house, and she'd thought things were going better. Russ had helped Yvonne hire some help, and knowing his parents were in good hands had seemed to relax him. He'd even told her he didn't feel as if he had to constantly worry about them any longer.

Why did he suddenly sound so stressed?

"I gotta go," he said.

"Want me to stay up 'til you get here?" Joslynn asked.

"I'm going home tonight."

It was a rare thing for him not to come to the Cottage and sleep at her side. "Are we still running in the morning?"

"Fine."

"Is that the only word you know?" she said, hearing the frustration in her voice. She tried to soften it. "Russ, what's wrong?"

"Nothing. Look, I need to go. Bye, Josie."

He hung up before she could say another word.

* * *

He's not coming.

After a night of worry, she'd hoped to find out what was up with Russ when he came to their morning run. But he was nowhere to be seen.

With a frustrated sigh, Joslynn stopped stretching. She shielded her eyes against the sun and fruitlessly scanned the parking lot again.

He's really not coming.

Trying to control her irritation, she began her run. There had to be a good reason he hadn't bothered to text her to let her know he wasn't going to meet her for their morning workout. Russ was always considerate, so what bothered her most was how out of character this was.

The first mile was agony. No matter how hard she concentrated, she couldn't find a rhythm. Her thoughts were too consumed with Russ. Irritation had yielded to worry. What if something had happened to him? What if something had happened to his parents?

Head spinning, she toughed her way through the second and third mile and then threw in the towel. Her body might crave the exercise, but her brain wasn't cooperating. After she was able to figure out what was happening with Russ, maybe she'd try again.

Back at her car, she frowned when she checked her phone. No new calls or texts. She hit redial to try again.

"You've reached Russ Green, but you've also missed him. You know what to do."

Not bothering to leave yet another message, she reached out to Yvonne, who answered after the first ring.

"Good morning, Joslynn."

The friendly, relaxed qualities in Yvonne's voice didn't ease Jos's mind, but she was well trained at hiding her emotions. "Good morning. Russ wouldn't happen to be there, would he?"

"You just missed him. He came by to talk to Karlee about her schedule."

"I'm really glad you hired her. She's a great nurse. She'll do a good job."

"She's very sweet. Reminds me of you," Yvonne said. "She's got that same way with Baron that you do. Want me to see if I can catch Russell?"

As if Joslynn would let his mother know how much trouble she was having getting in touch with him. "No, thank you. I'll try his cell."

Sliding into the driver's seat, she debated with herself over what to do next. The relationship she and Russ shared had been sailing along so smoothly, she hadn't anticipated the choppy waters she suddenly found herself in.

Oh, stop being so melodramatic.

Russ being busy didn't constitute choppy waters. He'd probably had a shitty night at Words & Music and just needed some peace and quiet.

She became irritated with herself over how much she was fretting his absence last night and this morning. Since when had independent Joslynn Wright become a woman who wrung her hands when her boyfriend didn't answer his phone? She hated women like that—weak, spineless women who were only happy when they were with a guy.

No man will define me.

Slamming her phone onto the center console, she started the car and began to back out of the parking spot.

The phone rang. Russ's ringtone—"Didn't See You Coming."

She should ignore him the way he'd been ignoring her.

She didn't. Instead of a polite greeting, she said, "You've reached Joslynn Wright, but you've also missed her. You know what to do."

"I suppose I should apologize."

"Ding. Ding. We have a winner." The wounded sound of her own voice made her wince. "No big deal, Russ. You missed our run. So what?"

"Yeah, I have to say I was surprised you answered. Figured you'd be five miles in by now."

"Then why did you call? Did you *want* to get my voicemail?"

Since he didn't reply, she took that as confirmation. Instead of talking to her and apologizing for standing her up, he'd planned to be a coward and leave some pathetic excuse of a message.

Why was he playing games with her? It was so out of character, and he was well aware how much she despised that kind of dishonesty. "If you didn't want to run, you should've just said so."

Great. Now she sounded even *more* hurt.

"It's not that." Silent seconds dragged on. "Look, I gotta go. I want to meet Dad's nurse and talk to her about the schedule."

"You never did lie well, you know."

"I've gotta go. We can talk later. Bye, Josie."

"Bye, Josie"?

Not "I Love You."

Just "Bye, Josie."

Like last night, she realized.

"Bye, Russ."

Joslynn threw herself out of the car and launched into another run. It took ten miles for her anger to abate. Only then did she reach out for help.

"Savannah? Can I buy you and Chelsea lunch?"

* * *

Joslynn spotted Savannah and Chelsea the moment she walked into the restaurant. Although only Savannah waved, both women had friendly expressions.

No wonder. Their men hadn't suddenly turned into walking, talking jackasses.

As she took a seat, Savannah's gaze searched hers. "What's wrong?"

Two emotions fought for control of Joslynn's brain: the urge to burst into tears and the desire to slam her fists against the table. Either outburst would be accompanied by her tattling about Russ to her friends.

"I shouldn't have done this." The whispered admonition was for herself, not Savannah and Chelsea, but they cast her worried glances.

"What happened?" Chelsea asked.

Joslynn sighed as the inevitable happened—she morphed into one of those women who bitched about her man to other women. "Evidently, I'm dating Dr. Jekyll."

A frown formed on Savannah's face. "I take it Russ just turned into Mr. Hyde."

"They all do eventually," Chelsea added. "Thank God it's usually temporary and over something stupid."

"What did he do?" Savannah asked. "Leave wet towels on the floor? Forget to put the toilet seat down?" Her teasing tone and smile faded quickly in wake of Joslynn's stern frown.

"He lied to me." The worst indictment Joslynn could ever make. Russ had promised her honesty, the same honesty she'd promised him, and she'd never wavered. And she'd given him something she'd given to only a handful of people.

Her trust.

And he'd rewarded her by lying to her. "When I called him on it, he didn't say a fucking thing."

She hadn't realized that she'd clenched her hands into fists until Chelsea laid her hand over one of them. "Calm down. We'll figure this out. Together."

"Figure it out? He *lied* to me!"

Chelsea eased her hand back but seemed to take no offense to Joslynn's outburst. "About what?"

"About where he was."

"Why don't you start at the beginning?" Savannah suggested.

After taking a deep breath, trying to regain some calm, Joslynn told her tale. "He didn't stay at the Cottage last night, which is no big deal. He had a late shift at the bar, and"—she shrugged—"sometimes we both need our space. We were supposed to meet for our run this morning and he didn't show."

"That's not like Russ," Chelsea said. "The man's always five minutes early."

"I know, right? And he didn't call at all last night. He always calls when he gets home from work. Doesn't matter how late it is." When he called after work, he always apologized, telling her he hoped he hadn't woken her up. Then he'd always say that he just wanted to hear her voice before he went to sleep. "I checked this morning to see if he'd texted or if I missed his call. Nada."

Savannah frowned. "I'll bet you had trouble sleeping, didn't you?"

Joslynn gave her a curt nod. "So I figured he'd meet me at the park. He never misses a run."

"And he didn't show up at all." Chelsea shook her head. "Why don't they realize how much we worry about them?"

Throwing her hands up in exasperation, Joslynn admitted, "But I don't *want* to worry about him! I don't want to be some clinging girlfriend who's always checking on where he is and who he's with!"

"What did he lie about?" Chelsea asked. "Specifically?"

"The jerk called when he thought I'd be running. Seemed upset to get me and not my voicemail."

"Coward's way out," Savannah said. "Brad does that, too. Stupid guys acting like naughty kids who're trying not to get punished."

"Ethan's got the same problem," Chelsea added. "You're not in this alone, honey. Not by a long shot."

"Russ said he couldn't run because he was on his way to his parents' place to meet with the home health nurse. But he obviously didn't know I'd just spoken with his mom and she said he'd just left. So where was he really going?"

And who was he going with?

Suspicion. A trait that Joslynn wanted no part of.

"See?" she practically shouted at her friends. "See why I didn't want a relationship? They always end badly. I was better off just screwing around when I was in the mood!"

Thankfully, there weren't many people in the restaurant to turn and stare at her outburst. Ashamed and embarrassed, she braced her elbows on the table and put her head in her hands. "Why did I do this to myself?"

"You love him."

Joslynn's head shot up at Savannah's matter-of-fact statement.

"She's right," Chelsea said. "You wouldn't be this upset unless you loved him."

"I *hate* him." Joslynn recognized the words for a lie the moment they fell from her mouth. Judging from their smiles, her friends did too.

"As they say, it's a thin line," Savannah said.

"What am I going to do?" Joslynn was in uncharted waters, and she needed their experience to guide her through this.

"First," Chelsea said, "you're gonna calm down. Then we're gonna talk this out."

Savannah nodded. "Exactly. Things aren't all that bleak." When Joslynn started to sputter, Savannah held up a hand. "He lied, yes. But we all know Russ isn't a liar, which means there was a good reason—something he thought justified the lie."

Chelsea was nodding as well. "Now we just need to figure out what that reason is."

* * *

Russ had never been so miserable. Even worse, his mother's intense stare told him she knew exactly how he felt.

But did she know *why* he felt that way?

He hadn't shared his news with anyone, because part of him was having trouble accepting the test results. Denial seemed an easier place to dwell.

He knew he should tell Josie. She knew something had changed.

But he couldn't tell her. The news wouldn't change the way she felt. He had no doubt she'd be his greatest advocate and that she'd do anything and everything to help him.

Russ would never put her through what his mother was going through with his father.

Never.

"Russell…" She tapped the spoon against the rim of the pot before setting it aside. After putting a lid on whatever she was cooking, she grabbed her cup of coffee and took a seat across from him at the kitchen table. "Talk to me."

He shifted his coffee cup between his hands. "Mom...stop."

"Not until you listen to me."

Unfortunately, he knew that stubborn set of her jaw quite well. He'd seen it far too often when he was growing up. It was almost as intimidating as Baron's counting to three when Russ was young.

"You don't have to stay here again tonight," she insisted. "Now that we've got Karlee coming in so often, your father and I are doing well. Go home. Go be with Joslynn."

Be with Joslynn.

Exactly what he wanted most in the world.

The one thing he couldn't do.

Seemed as though he had to fight the urge to pick up his phone and call her every single minute, to tell her what he'd discovered and beg that she help him face a bleak future.

Fight it he did, though. Knowing what he now knew, how could he hold on to her?

She deserved so much better.

"Russell, honey? Are you even listening to me?"

"I'm listening, Mom."

"We're fine now," she insisted. "I've got Fiona and Michelle here on Mondays to clean. Karlee is coming in almost every day to help with Dad. There's no reason for you to stay with us at night."

Russ's first instinct was to remind her that her black eye might've faded, but he could still see exactly where Baron had hit her. Just seeing her that day had made something inside Russ click into place, as though he discovered the solution to a question he hadn't even realized he needed answered. He'd realized that he was looking at his own future in everything Baron did, and he also realized that he couldn't put Josie through the same ordeal Yvonne was enduring.

As everyone kept pointing out to him, Russ was already out of control. He could barely leash his temper now. How bad would things get when that fucking disease got its claws in him, as genetic testing had told him was entirely possible? Would he abuse Josie the way Baron had abused Yvonne?

The mere thought sent a shudder racing through Russ. "I know I don't need to stay. I just…I just want to be here in case…"

"I've known you since you drew your first breath on this earth, Russell Grant Green. You think I don't know what you're thinking?" Yvonne let out a snort. "You're blaming yourself because you didn't protect me."

Instead of answering, he just shifted his nearly empty coffee cup to his other hand.

"Who exactly do you think you'd be protecting me from?"

Dad. When he's not Dad.

Russ shrugged.

His mother reached over, picked up his cup, and set it out of his reach. "Your father would never hurt me, Russell."

Your black eye says otherwise. "He might not mean to."

"So by staying here every minute you're not at work, you think you'll keep him from ever hitting me again?"

He gave her a curt nod.

Waving a dismissive hand, she said, "That's foolishness."

"Mom, he hit you. More than once."

"And each time, he wasn't in his right mind."

"So that makes it okay?"

Yvonne reached out a hand to him, and Russ reluctantly grasped it. "Oh, honey. Nothing about this is *okay*. Not a dog-gone thing. Yes, he laid hands on me when he was in a bad way. But I learned each time. I'm a smart cookie, Russell. I never make the same mistake twice."

"You can't know what sets him off," he insisted.

"Not exactly, but I'm learning to read him, to keep track of his moods. I know my husband as well as I know my own mind. I can see the changes coming now, and that's when I do all the things that Joslynn taught me. I have the meds to calm him down. Now that I've got Karlee, I've got someone to call before he gets too out of hand. I'm not fighting this alone anymore."

While that made perfect sense, all Russ could think about was how to keep the women he loved safe. If he was at his mother's side whenever he could be, he could protect her.

But there was only one way he could protect Josie, only one way he could be sure she wasn't the one worrying about his moods and whether she had the right tranquilizers around when he flew into an Alzheimer's-induced rage.

And that was to set her free.

Knowing that she would fight him and try to convince him that he wasn't doomed to follow in his father's footsteps, Russ was going to have to do whatever was necessary to push her away. His future now seemed set in stone.

One day he would suffer from Alzheimer's—and the mere mental picture of him striking Josie made his blood run cold.

God, how he loved her. Everything about her, from her fierceness to her intelligence, made him happy. Yet now it was that love that was going to force him to stay away from her. She deserved better. She deserved a man who was whole now and would be whole the rest of his life.

Russ couldn't promise her that. Not anymore.

"Go home, Russell," his mother said. "Go see that sweet Joslynn."

"And leave you to fend for yourself?"

Her narrowed eyes were followed by her wagging her index finger at him. "You're one stubborn son of a gun, you know that? Before you were a twinkle in your daddy's eye, I made him some promises. For better or worse. In sickness and in health. Well, by God, I have seen a little worse and a little sickness. But I won't pass that responsibility off to you, no matter how much you want me to." Standing, she came over to him and cradled his face in her hands. Then she kissed his forehead. "You're a good boy, Russell. With the cleaning service and now Karlee, you've helped me more than you know. But Baron is my husband. Let me be his wife."

* * *

"Everything looks good, Joslynn." Christina Adams, Joslynn's gynecologist, lifted the ultrasound transducer and then handed Joslynn a towel.

As she wiped the blue gel from her lower abdomen, Joslynn stared at the monitor. She had some training in reading ultrasounds, but she wanted to be sure she was seeing things correctly. "So that's a mature follicle?"

"Yep. Nice, ripe egg," Christina replied. "And the uterus and right tube are normal. The left ovary might be atrophied from the chemo, but the right works. I can't guarantee you'd achieve a pregnancy, but I see no structural reason you can't conceive. We can draw blood and check hormone levels, too, but I don't think we need to."

Pulling her gown closed, Joslynn sat up. Although she had a smile on her face, she wasn't surprised to feel a tear slip from the corner of her eye. She quickly swiped it away. "No thanks. This told me plenty. Although…I do have my annual blood work tomorrow."

Christina returned the smile. "Just let my nurse know which lab, and she'll send in orders to piggyback the hormone testing. I'm glad this all seems to be good news." Standing, she grabbed her tablet. "Any questions for me?"

Joslynn shook her head. "Thanks so much."

"You're quite welcome. You can go as soon as you're dressed. No need to stop by the desk on your way out." The phone in her pocket rang for the third time since the exam began. "Please excuse me. I need to run."

"Of course. Thanks again."

Alone in the room, Joslynn allowed a few happy tears to fall. She'd convinced herself at an early age that she didn't want to have kids of her own, that there were plenty of other important things in life. While she wasn't sure she wanted to be a mother, she was pleased that she now had that option.

After she dressed and left the office, she sat in her car, staring at her phone. Her first instinct was to call Russ and share the results with him. But she couldn't follow through.

Something was up with him, something that was stressing him out. After she figured out what that was, she'd help him with it and then she could share her news. The way he'd sounded last time they talked, he was liable to totally misconstrue what she was saying and feel pressured to have kids with her.

A quick and very scary thought raced through her mind. Did he have news of his own? Had he gone for his genetic tests?

No. He'd promised her she could go with him when he talked to the genetic counselor. She'd told him how important it was for her to be at his side. The only reason he wasn't with her today the way they'd planned was because he hadn't returned any of her calls so that she could arrange for him to go with her.

Angry at being so completely ignored, Joslynn jammed her phone back in her pocket. She'd sent plenty of texts and left several voicemails.

Now it was time for Russ to pull his head out of his ass and reach out to her.

CHAPTER TWENTY-TWO

The Cottage was cleaner than it had ever been, which meant Joslynn had a serious problem. Every time she felt something in her life was out of control, she tried to seize that control back in one of the few ways she could—by fussing with her house.

Fussing? In the week since Russ had become harder to reach than a reclusive celebrity, she'd repainted the master bedroom, added new light fixtures to both bathrooms, and put up a new backsplash in the kitchen. If the man didn't straighten up soon, she would probably remodel the entire house.

When she wasn't tackling some project, she was at work or running. Yoga was a no-go, which made her frustration worse. She needed the process to relax, but she couldn't turn her brain off long enough to let any endorphins flow. Instead of enjoying the stretching and the breathing, she found herself launching from one pose to the next just to get the damn sessions over.

Why was this happening? When she'd finally accepted that

she'd fallen in love with Russ, he'd begun treating her like she had a contagious disease.

What in the hell happened?

This was all her fault. Instead of following her usual, safe pattern with men, she'd caved. She'd agreed to open herself up, to open up a heart she'd believed was cold. And she'd fallen in love with Russ Green. She'd committed to a relationship with him. She'd even found the courage to explore the scary question of her fertility.

What had that relationship brought her? Where there had been trust, companionship, and caring, there was suddenly loneliness, silence, and anger.

Well, that was all ending. *Now.* One way or another, she was going to pin him down and find out exactly what was going on and why he'd done the unexpected one-eighty.

How odd to pick up her phone and have it immediately begin to ring. Had Russ realized how desperately she needed to talk to him?

Instead of her boyfriend, the call was from her family doc's office. "Joslynn Wright."

"Joslynn, it's John Blunt."

Her heart leaped into her throat. Usually when she had her routine blood work drawn, she received a call from his nurse, saying her numbers were fine. Why would the busy doctor take the time to talk to her during the workday?

Maybe he'd accidentally received her hormone workup and wanted to tell her about it himself. "Dr. Blunt. Hi. What's going on?"

"I don't need to put on the kid gloves with you, Joslynn. The numbers aren't what I'd like to see."

Terror flooded her mind, making her vision tunnel and her breathing speed. "Which numbers?"

"Mostly white differentials."

"Chemo?" she whispered.

"Now, let's not get too far ahead of ourselves," he replied. "Let's run some new blood work and get you in here for a physical. If those aren't what I'd hope, then we'll do a PET."

"When?"

"For the physical, let me check my schedule…Can you make it in on Friday at one?"

A glance to the calendar hanging on the refrigerator showed her open on Friday. "I can be there."

"Good. We can draw blood then, or you can swing by the hospital lab when you're at work so we have the results by Friday. I'll leave orders in the system."

"Thank you, Dr. Blunt." Such an odd name for a doctor, yet a trait she admired in any caregiver she worked with.

"Hopefully, this is nothing," he cautioned. "I know you're an NP, so don't start thinking about things too hard. Okay?"

"Okay," she lied, knowing damn well she'd do nothing but think about the ramifications of her screwed-up blood tests until she drove herself into a panic attack.

"This could be nothing. You know that as well as I do." He sounded so hopeful.

"Right." Already searching for reasons for the abnormal tests, her first thought was that her summer allergies were kicking in. That was why her whites were "off." Allergies. Nothing but allergies.

But that didn't account for her increasing fatigue, or for her losing several pounds with no change in her diet. Her intuition had been whispering that something wasn't quite right, which had prompted her to get her annual blood screenings done a few weeks earlier than necessary.

"Are you okay, Joslynn?" Dr. Blunt asked.

"I'm fine." *Just fine. Always "fine."*

"Then I'll see you Friday."

"See you then." After ending the call, she stared at the phone, marveling at how one phone call—a few simple words—could spin the entire world off its axis.

No matter how much she tried to heed the doctor's advice to wait, to not overreact, her thoughts shouted at her.

I have cancer. Again.

It had always been the thing she feared most, and yet she'd always understood that it was a possibility. While the odds were that her acute myelogenous leukemia hadn't returned, survivors of childhood leukemia had a much higher risk of developing other forms of cancer. A PET scan was likely to reveal hot spots somewhere on her body. A section of colon. A swollen gland. Her pancreas or her liver. Something would scream at the radiologist that cells were dividing and multiplying there at an alarming rate that could equal only one thing.

Cancer.

Bad news followed right on the tail of good.

Russ. She'd have to tell Russ. She *wanted* to tell Russ, to have him take her into his arms, kiss her hair, and tell her everything would be all right.

Joslynn almost called him right then and there before remembering that even if she tried to call, there was no guarantee he'd answer.

Emotions brewed inside her, twisting and turning, rising higher and higher until she hurled the phone at the wall. It made a dent in the sheetrock before falling to the tile, still in one piece.

* * *

Russ had to resist the urge to groan when he walked into the office at Words & Music and found his two partners waiting there with frowns fixed on their faces.

"Let me guess…" He shut the door. "I forgot our monthly partners' meeting again."

Ethan turned to Brad. "You know, I'm not sure what's worse. Dealing with him or dealing with Savannah and Chelsea when they're on a mission."

"The women," Brad replied. "Definitely the women." He leveled a glare at Russ. "Which is why we're here to deal with *you.*"

Moving past where the two of them sat on the couch, Russ took the chair behind the desk. Considering the hostility in Brad's voice, it felt good to have a barrier protecting him. This little ambush was most likely about what was happening between him and Joslynn, but that was none of their business.

Russ let the charade play out. "What are you talking about?"

"Do you know what a ripple effect is?" Ethan asked.

"No, Ethan. I don't. Just like I don't have a single clue what in the fuck you two are talking about or why you're here."

His anger seemed to have no effect on Ethan. "When you toss a small stone in the pond, it makes ripples that expand as they spread out."

Russ rolled his eyes. "Thank you for that wonderful science lesson."

"You threw the stone," Brad said. "And you rocked *our* boats."

"It's been a decade since we smoked weed together, but damn. You two sound stoned."

"What did you do to Joslynn?" Ethan asked.

"I beg your pardon?"

"He asked what you did to Joslynn," Brad replied.

Leaning back in the chair, Russ folded his arms over his chest. There was no way either of them would ever understand why he was making the difficult choice of easing away from her, and he didn't feel any need to explain it to them.

He was setting her free, and there wasn't a thing they could say that would change his mind. "First off, what happens between Josie and me is none of your damn business. Second, I didn't do anything to her." *Except ignore her.*

Two loud snorts echoed through the room.

"What did Savannah and Chelsea tell you?"

"Nothing specific," Brad admitted. "Just that Joslynn was really upset and it was your fault."

"That's it?" Russ shouted. "They said she was really upset and you two planned this inquisition?"

"Inquisition?" A scoffing laugh slipped from Ethan. "Overdramatic much, buddy?"

Russ shook his head. "Josie never gets upset. It's not in her DNA."

DNA. The fucking source of the problem. But he wasn't going to burden his partners with what he'd learned. They'd know. Eventually.

Not yet, though.

"Look," Brad said, "it's like this, Russ. When my wife says to fix something, I fix it. And she wants me to fix whatever you did to Joslynn. So I'm here to do exactly that. What did you do to her, anyway?"

"I don't have time for this." When Russ started to stand up, his partners jumped to their feet as though they'd use physical force to keep him there.

"Sit down, Russ," Ethan cautioned.

The anger inside Russ made him clench his hands into tight fists, and it took all his self-control not to turn his rising fury on his best friends. What happened between him and Josie was no one's business but their own, despite what Savannah and Chelsea—or their husbands—seemed to think.

At that moment, he had enough demons to battle as he waged a war neither of them knew a damn thing about. Everything inside him wanted to go to Joslynn, to drop to his knees and beg her forgiveness for the cold shoulder he'd given her. He wanted to hear that she loved him enough that she'd face his bleak future at his side.

But then images of his mother's battered face would fill his mind, and he'd know that there was no way he'd ever put Joslynn through an ordeal like that. What he was doing by distancing himself was letting her down easy and sparing her a future of misery.

He scowled at his partners. "Look, you two might let your women carry your balls in their purses, but I'm not about to. Stop bitching at me and let me get back to work."

Russ stormed out of the office before he broke down and told them what was wrong.

And how there wasn't a fucking thing he could do to change it.

CHAPTER TWENTY-THREE

Russ sat in his SUV, staring at the Cottage and wondering how he was going to be able to find the courage to do what needed to be done, no matter how painful it would be.

Joslynn was in there, waiting for him. When he'd finally made the call to tell her that he needed to talk to her, she'd let out a rather shaky laugh and told him she needed to talk to him too. She'd all but demanded that he come by, and there had been something in her voice that had made him feel an urgency where before there had been only dread.

With a resigned sigh, he forced himself out of the SUV and headed to the blue front door with the pretty flowers she'd painted there.

She opened the door before he could press the doorbell. "Come in," she ordered before softening it with a whispered, "please."

Following her inside, he declined her offer for coffee or iced tea. Reminding himself over and over that he was doing this for her, that he was doing the right thing, he took a seat on the over-stuffed chair instead of sitting by her on the sofa.

It's like ripping off a bandage, Russ. Just do it.

Dressed in faded jeans and a purple short-sleeved shirt, she leaned back against the cushions, making an X of her arms and cupping her elbows as though she was cold. Her eyes were fixed on him, and there was a sadness in those dark pools that he knew he'd put there.

Did she know what he was there to do?

After several stilted, silent moments passed, Russ worked up his courage. "First, I want to thank you for all you've done for my parents."

Her brows gathered, and the sadness was replaced with a budding anger. "That's what you came to tell me?"

"Well, no…I just needed to say it. Things are going so much better for them because of everything you helped them do."

"And your way to thank me was to treat me like a leper for two weeks and only deign to talk to me at your convenience?"

He winced.

"Let me ask you something…What exactly did I do, Russ? What did I do wrong to make you avoid me?"

The acerbic edge to her voice was deserved. Josie had a right to her anger. He *had* avoided her, but not for anything she'd done—because he'd been too much of a coward to just set her free.

"You said 'first.'"

Her comment brought him back from his thoughts. "Pardon?"

"You said 'first,' that you wanted to thank me for helping

Baron and Yvonne 'first.' What's second?" Her icy tone sent goose bumps across his arms.

"Before that, tell me about what you said was so important," he insisted, knowing that as soon as he sank the knife into her, she'd never want to speak to him again.

She shook her head. "What's 'second,' Russ?"

Standing, he slid his hands in the front pockets of his jeans, feeling awkward. "I've been doing a lot of thinking the last couple of weeks." Which was true. If he told her about the genetic testing, she would insist on staying with him. That's why he went alone to get the results, to protect her if it was bad news. Had she heard the results, he could never set her free. Even now she wouldn't let him go unless he hurt her.

No matter how much it killed him to do so.

"Clearly," she said, "all that thinking has taken up all of your time and made it impossible to answer your phone calls or texts." Each word dripped with disdain.

"I'm sorry about that, Josie." He rubbed the back of his neck before shoving his hand back in his pocket. "I was… busy."

"And I'm president of the United States."

Taking the clipped sarcasm as his due, Russ bit back any retort. "Look, we've had a lot of fun together. Right? I mean I've really enjoyed being with you." *I love you.* "But…" He just couldn't seem to make himself look her in the eyes.

"But you're breaking up with me. Is that what you came to tell me?"

The rage in her voice wasn't what finally made Russ focus on her face.

It was the hurt.

The moment he saw the twisting emotions playing across her features, he almost changed his mind. Were he not doing this for her own good, to spare her the agony of being tied to a man whose future was likely to be full of pain and sorrow, he would've gathered her into his arms and promised to never, ever hurt her again.

Then he saw his mother's battered face in his mind's eye. "Yeah. I guess I'm breaking up with you."

* * *

Joslynn wasn't surprised. Russ's behavior the last two weeks had all but screamed his intentions. Despite knowing what had been coming, she thought she was doing a good job of hiding her tumultuous feelings.

Until he actually said the words.

There would be no tears. Especially not now, and most definitely not in front of Russ Green.

Tears for him?

Fuck him. Fuck him and the fucking horse he rode in on.

How had she allowed this to happen again? She thought she'd learned her lessons well, that she would protect her heart from this kind of pain. Her father. Tim. There was no way she should've found herself in this situation, getting her feelings shredded by a guy.

I love him.

And he said he loved me.

Fuck. Fuckety fucking fuck.

She wanted him out of her house, and she wanted him out

right now. But she'd stay civil. It was the one way she could be sure he didn't know exactly how much he'd hurt her.

"Well, then…" A deep breath kept her emotions under tenuous control. "What else is there to say?"

"You okay, Josie?"

"Fine." Her teeth tugged on her bottom lip as she stood up.

Russ came to stand in front of her and held out a hand. "We can still be friends, right?"

Everything inside her wanted to slap his hand away as hard as she could. Instead of touching him, she crossed her arms under her breasts and headed to the front door. "It's not like we'll see each other much, but being friends?" A quick shake of her head as she opened the door. "There's no reason for that. We're breaking up, then we're done. Period. And I'd appreciate it if you'd leave now."

He walked to the door as though someone had weighted his feet down with lead. Stopping when he stood in front of her, he put a hand on her arm. It was clear that he wanted to say more, but she didn't want to hear anything else.

She shrugged his hand away. "Good-bye, Russ."

"Josie…"

"Good-bye."

Why he was so reluctant to go was beyond her. The man should be leaving skid marks since she'd let him off the hook so easily. She hadn't pulled the stereotypical whining, weeping girlfriend who was begging him to stay. She'd given him the freedom he'd wanted and was ready to let him waltz right out of her life. No strings attached.

"I still want to know what you wanted to tell me." His voice was breathy and soft as though his throat was clogged.

"I don't care what you want."

Those blue eyes took on a hangdog expression, and no matter how much she didn't want to react to it, she did. "Is there anything I can do?" he asked.

Her teeth were digging in her lower lip hard enough to draw blood. No words would come, not even angry ones. Joslynn only shook her head.

"I guess I'll be seeing you, then."

She shut the door as soon as he'd cleared the threshold, clicking the dead bolt and hoping he heard it slide into place—and that he knew it was more than just shutting him out of her home. Never again would she let him back into her life.

Fool me once…

A tear spilled over her lashes, and she furiously swiped it away. Stripping as she hurried to her bedroom, she got into her running attire as quickly as she could manage and was out the door and on the move less the five minutes after Russ Green walked out of her life.

* * *

Three days later, Joslynn almost smiled at the Care Bears adorning the scrubs of the nurse taking her blood pressure. She loved the scrubs that nurses donned at her hospital.

But there was nothing in her life to smile about, and once Dr. Blunt did this physical, she might well find herself in another fight for her life.

The room was chilly, and wearing nothing but the stupid gown made Joslynn feel exposed. She always went out of her way to try to make her ER patients feel more comfortable when they were in similar attire. But despite helping a person cover with a sheet or a blanket, she knew those gowns equaled vulnerability.

The nurse closed her laptop and tucked it under her arm. "The doctor will be in shortly."

"Thank you."

Waiting for him wouldn't be easy. Not only because she was type A and needed to constantly be doing *something*, but because this visit had so much at stake. Before coming here, she'd stood in front of her mirror and visually inspected everything from head to toe. There wasn't a single thing that looked "wrong" to her. She'd checked her breasts, her groin, searching for lumps and finding nothing suspicious.

But cancer wasn't always visible on the outside.

The door opened, making her jump since she hadn't expected Dr. Blunt so quickly.

"How are you feeling, Joslynn?" he asked as he set his laptop down on the counter.

"Still really tired. Although I'll confess to running an awful lot lately." More than was probably healthy, but it seemed as though the only way to hold her emotions at bay was to run until she was too exhausted to think.

"I see you're down seven pounds," he commented as he scrolled through the data the nurse had entered. "Try not to drop any more weight."

She nodded, well aware that if she had a battle against disease in her near future, she needed to build herself up so she could face it. At least he talked to her like one professional to another instead of doing the handholding that she despised. Sure, she might treat patients with kid gloves, but she hated someone treating her as though she were made of glass.

"You didn't get more blood drawn yet?" he asked.

She shook her head. She just hadn't been able to force herself back to the lab.

"Then we'll do that now." He turned to her and smiled. "Maybe it will give us some answers."

She shrugged.

"Let's get this physical done, then, shall we?"

* * *

"You *what*?"

The volume of his mother's voice made Russ flinch. "You heard me," he said in a near whisper. The last thing he wanted to do was tell his parents a second time that he'd broken up with Josie.

Baron tossed him a scowl, stood up, and walked behind the sofa where Russ sat. Then he gave him a good smack to the back of the head. "What is wrong with you, Russ?"

Russ frowned over his shoulder at his dad.

"Why would you do that, Russell?" Yvonne asked.

Although he'd known his parents would have objections, it wasn't as though Russ could give them the true reason. His father was having a good day. Russ wasn't about to tell Baron that he'd let the love of his life go to spare her the ordeal of caring for an Alzheimer's victim.

His heart ached. Walking away from Josie had been the equivalent of driving a sword into his own gut. The pain had been devastating, but he wasn't about to sentence her to the kind of life his parents were living.

"Let me ask you a question," Baron said.

Russ gave him a nod.

"When did you break that girl's heart?"

The sharp question only increased Russ's pain. "Three days ago."

"And yet she was here this morning."

It took a moment for his father's statement to register. "What?"

"It's true," Yvonne said with a nod. "She came by after breakfast to bring us some information on a new physical therapist she says we should work with."

Russ ran his hand over his face, trying to figure out what would possess Josie to go to his parents' house after he'd broken up with her. "Are you kidding me?"

His mother shook her head. "She didn't say a word about you or what happened. Said we should call her if we needed anything."

Absolutely flabbergasted, Russ couldn't think of a single reason why Josie was still checking on his parents. "Why would she do that?"

"You don't know?" Yvonne asked. "You really don't know?"

Baron let out a snort. "Ain't got the sense God gave a goat." Damn if he didn't give Russ another smack to the head.

"Stop it, Dad." He rubbed the sore spot. "No, Mom. I really don't know."

"Because she promised me she'd always be there if we needed her."

The promise didn't surprise him. Josie was a thoughtful person, and she always followed through with anything she said she'd do. But now that they were no longer a couple, that promise should've been nullified. What kind of person kept caring for an ex's parents after the end of a relationship?

A kind, dedicated person like Joslynn. An NP who genuinely liked the people she cared for. He'd seen the way the tie between her, Yvonne, and Baron had grown. He shouldn't have been so shocked that she still came by to check on them.

"She takes care of us because she loves you." Yvonne came to sit next to him on the couch. Then she patted his knee. "I have to confess, Russell, that when you said you had something to tell us, I'd hoped you were going to say that you'd proposed to Joslynn."

Like he'd do that to her.

I sentence you, Joslynn Wright, to life with a man who will one day forget who you are and hit you when he's angry.

She glanced back at her husband. "We were both hoping you two would marry."

"I wouldn't do that to her," Russ blurted out.

Yvonne gripped his leg. "What did you just say?"

"Nothing."

"Answer your mother," Baron insisted.

This wasn't a discussion he wanted to have, so Russ jumped to his feet. "I need to go."

"Don't you *dare* walk away," Yvonne said. "What did you mean that you wouldn't do that to her?"

Hands on his hips, Russ kept his back to his parents. "I don't want to talk about this."

Baron put himself in front of Russ. "I think I understand." He reached out to put his hands on his son's shoulders. "Come sit down. Please."

With a heaved sigh, he gave his father a nod and went to sit next to his mother again.

"This ain't about you and Joslynn not getting along." Baron's eyes caught Russ's, and there was naked pain in his father's blue eyes—eyes that looked so like his own. "This is about me."

"Dad…"

Yvonne kept shifting her gaze between Baron and Russ. Then her mouth became a surprised O.

"I need to go," Russ said. His parents had enough problems. They didn't need to have this discussion, one that would just make them feel worse about Baron's illness.

"Russell!" Yvonne said. "Tell me you didn't break up with that angel because of us!"

"I didn't break up with her because of you." Which, thanks to the way she'd asked, was the truth.

"Now you're lying," Baron said. He frowned and glanced to his wife. "He feels sorry for you, Vonny."

"Dad, stop. Please."

"He doesn't want Joslynn to find herself in your shoes." A tear slipped from Baron's eye.

Russ swallowed hard. His father had never been one to show his emotions, yet another thing that Alzheimer's had changed. But today was a good day, and Baron had control of his mind. Which meant he could see the effects of his illness on his family, exactly what Russ hadn't wanted to remind him about. And he wasn't about to make them feel some sort of misplaced guilt that he'd inherited the Alzheimer's gene.

"Oh, Russell." Yvonne shook her head. "You're worried that one day you'll be like your daddy."

Baron was nodding and frowning, having swiped away the tear.

All Russ could do was nod. He was too choked up to say a word.

Looking to his wife, Baron said, "Let me ask you somethin', Vonny. On the day I asked you to marry me, if someone would've told you that we'd be where we are now, would you have changed your mind?"

"No, sir. Not for nothing." His mother looked back at Russ. "What do you think love is? A guarantee of happiness?"

"No," Russ snapped. "I don't think that."

"Yet because of your daddy's problem, you think you're guaranteed *unhappiness.*"

He sure hadn't thought of it that way. "It's more than that."

"Then tell us," his father said, his tone as terse as Russ's had been.

Head bowed, Russ shook his head.

"You had the test, didn't you?" Yvonne asked. "That's why you pushed Joslynn away."

"Mom…"

"You have the gene, right?"

Russ's shoulders sagged as he nodded.

"Oh, Russell. I'm so sorry."

"It's no one's fault, Mom."

Baron's chin trembled. "I'm sorry, Russell. I'm so sorry."

"Dad…" Russ hurried to Baron and embraced him. "There's no blame. None at all."

After a long hug, Russ finally let go only to find himself gathered into his mother's arms. He held her as she softly wept.

When he let her go, she took his hand. "This doesn't mean you have to leave Joslynn."

"Yes, it damn well does."

"What if you could switch places with her?" Yvonne asked. "What if she was the one who had the chance of getting something like your daddy has?"

The blunt talk in front of Baron bothered Russ, and he worried his father felt as though they were being cruel to speak so openly about his diagnosis. Then it dawned on him that they'd never really discussed how Alzheimer's had changed all their lives. Maybe this talk was past due.

His mother pressed the point. "Would you want her to walk away from you for something that *might* happen to her years in the future?"

When he didn't answer, she stood and went over to take Baron's hand. "Go on home, Russell, and think on that for a while," she said. "If the potential for a hardship is enough to send you running, well, then…Go on and run. She deserves a man with more guts."

CHAPTER TWENTY-FOUR

He *what*?" Savannah shouted loud enough for a few of the customers in Shamballa to turn and stare at her.

Joslynn hunched a little lower in her chair. "Russ broke up with me." It was humiliating to have this discussion. She'd never wanted to be the kind of woman who whined about some man.

Ah, but Russ wasn't "some man." He'd wounded her heart, maybe beyond repair. Not only was she angry at him, but she was also furious at herself for allowing him that kind of power.

"That makes absolutely no sense," Savannah said. "The guy adores you."

"Obviously not," Jos drawled. Sarcasm wasn't her usual response, but then again, this situation wasn't something she'd gone through before. Even the time she'd spent with Tim in college paled in comparison to the commitment she'd made to Russ.

Is there a proper way to handle losing the man you love?

"How are you doin'?" Savannah asked.

"I'm fine."

"Yeah, right… The guys are going to have a fit."

"Can you just keep it low-key? I don't want his partners angry with him." Joslynn shrugged. "Besides, it's personal. It shouldn't affect anyone else."

Reaching across the small table, Savannah covered Joslynn's clenched fist with her hand. "Yes, it's personal. But you're my best friend, Jos. You're Chelsea's friend, too. And Russ, Brad, and Ethan are like brothers. You and Russ are family. Of course this will affect us."

All Jos could do was sigh and nod.

"Why?" Savannah asked.

"Why?" Joslynn let out a huff. "Beats the shit outta me."

"What did he say?"

"Something stupid."

"Don't they all?" Savannah gave her a lopsided smile.

Jos wasn't about to be cajoled out of her dark mood. "Something like 'we had fun, but it's over.'"

"What are you going to do about it?"

Incredulous, Jos pulled her hand back. "*Do* about it? Are you kidding me? I'm not doing a fucking thing about it. He wants his freedom? Voilà! He's free."

Savannah let out a weary sigh. "It's not going to be that easy, Jos."

"Sure it is. In fact, it's already done. Just let it be, okay?" For a moment Joslynn thought about telling Savannah about her doctor visit and her blood tests. Then she decided against it. The only person she really wanted to talk to was Russ, but that wasn't going to happen. No, Jos wasn't going to dump her health worries on Savannah until she was sure there was even anything to worry about.

Reverting to habit, she would handle things on her own.

Talking about Russ was only making her feel worse, so it was time to bring the conversation to an end. "Look, I need to go. I just wanted to tell you what was going on."

"What can I do to help?" Savannah asked.

Joslynn shook her head as she stood up and slung her purse over her shoulder.

"Please call me if you need anything, even if you just wanna talk. Promise?"

"Thanks. I'll see you soon." Her protective walls cracking at the sympathetic look on Savannah's face, Joslynn left in a hurry.

* * *

As soon as she got home from Shamballa, Joslynn hurried to change her clothes and don her running shoes.

She didn't mind running in the rain. Although it had been overcast at the beginning of her workout, the drizzle had started after mile one. That light misting turned into a downpour less than five minutes later. Still, she ran because it kept her from thinking about the mess that was now her life.

Dr. Blunt had found only one thing that concerned him, something she'd missed in her own head-to-toe inspection. Her thyroid was inflamed. The moment he palpated her neck, he told her she had a goiter. She'd glanced in the mirror and gasped when she saw the obvious bump against her larynx.

Thyroid problems are common for women, the NP in her kept preaching. Yet the panic in her kept screaming, *Cancer!*

A debate raged within her mind between the health-care pro-

CAN'T FIGHT THE FEELING

fessional and the frightened patient. If this was a thyroid problem, it would explain a lot of her symptoms. The fatigue. The weight loss. The insomnia. Plus, thyroid imbalances could be easily treated with medications. Her guess was that her gland had become too active and was forcing her body into a state of hyperactivity. In that case, she could take a prescription to slow down the hormone production and another medication to ease her symptoms.

But what if it is truly cancer?

There was no way to rule that out with simple blood tests. Dr. Blunt had ordered a biopsy to see exactly what was going on inside the gland. She would have that biopsy in a few days, and if it came back to show cancer, Joslynn faced chemo and possible metastasis to other parts of her body.

Her most basic instinct was to call Russ, to tell him what Dr. Blunt had found and to spill out her fears. In his typical way, he'd enfold her in his arms, press a kiss to the top of her head, and tell her that no matter what this problem turned out to be, he'd be there to help her through.

That had been the way he'd worn down her resistance in the beginning of their relationship—to hold up his parents' and grandparents' lives as examples of couples supporting each other through thick and thin. He'd promised the same in his relationship with her.

Liar!

She'd been foolish enough to believe him, to stop fighting her feelings and then let them guide her actions. She'd jumped into the deep end, allowing her heart to overrule her head. And she'd fallen deeply in love with him.

Fool!

Anger filled her, giving her strength and energy to keep running. The world went by in a blur as Joslynn kept striding, breathing in with each few steps and out with a few more. Her mind reeled, considering her connection with Russ and thinking through her numerous health options. Back and forth. Back and forth. One, then the other.

She ran a little faster.

She didn't dread the procedure. The process itself was simple and not horribly uncomfortable. The results would be more painful than the needle aspiration of some thyroid fluid and tissue.

Who will drive me there since Russ is gone?

You can drive yourself.

She could always ask Savannah. Or Chelsea.

You don't need *him!*

An image of Baron and Yvonne popped into her head, and she knew without a doubt that they would give their lives for their partner. She'd thought that was the kind of love she shared with Russ—it was the kind of love he'd promised, damn it!

She was weary, dog-tired of hiding her emotions. Her whole life seemed like a masquerade where she put on a disguise instead of showing people how she truly felt. Through the chemo and her fear that leukemia might steal her life, she'd used her "brave face." The nurses had been so encouraging and supportive, and she hadn't wanted to disappoint them with tears or whining. She'd pasted on a smile and endured the treatments, never once letting anyone know how terrified she was and how much she needed someone to hug her and tell her she would be all right.

At work she wore another mask—the poised NP, the woman

who understood exactly what her patients were enduring and would stop at nothing to help them through. She didn't dare show any fear, because that fear would be witnessed by people who needed her absolute confidence. So no matter how scary a situation was, Joslynn played her part and kept her facade firmly in place.

I'm fucking sick and tired of hiding who I really am and what I really feel!

Mile after mile, she lost herself in the loop of her thoughts. Worry over her situation would yield to her need to be with Russ. The love she had for him refused to allow her to separate the two.

Understanding dawned, and Joslynn almost skidded to a stop.

For the first time in my life, I don't want to handle something alone.

The world began to coalesce, bringing her back from where she disappeared to whenever she ran. As she became aware of where she was, she wasn't surprised to see she'd been following the route she normally drove to Russ's place. She'd let him leave without saying a single thing, without telling him exactly what she thought about him and the way he'd dumped her.

Well, she was damn well going to speak her mind now.

Slowing to walk, she caught her breath and gave a lot of consideration to exactly what she could say. Would she tell him she still loved him? Would she tell him she wished he'd tell her what had changed his feelings? Would she let him know how much she needed him, especially now?

The rain still fell, washing over her face, soaking her clothes and her hair. Didn't matter. The time for confrontation had arrived.

Choking back threatening tears, Joslynn pounded her fist against the door.

* * *

Russ scribbled down a few more lyrics before putting the pencil back between his teeth and playing a bit more of his song. The heavy rain and occasional thunder added to his melancholy mood, but he focused on telling Joslynn what was in his heart through this song.

His parents had given him so much to think about that he felt as though he were drowning in emotions. By the time he'd driven back to his home, he'd stepped inside, shut the door, and just stood there, thinking. Through his troubling thoughts and tumultuous emotions, only one thing rang clear.

I made the biggest mistake of my life.

Josie was the love of his life, and by walking away from her—no matter how important the reason—he'd ruined his future. And hers. He had no doubt now that she loved him.

The way she'd reacted to his announcement that he was breaking up with her told him how she felt. Oh, other people might see that stoic face she showed the public, but Russ knew better. He saw the vulnerability and how hard she was struggling to not tell him that he was breaking her heart.

That thought made him choke up, and he feared he'd spoiled things to the point she could never forgive him.

No, that was untenable. Josie had to take him back. She just *had* to.

While Russ wanted to jump back in his car and race over to her house, he forced himself to wait. If he charged into the Cottage, telling her he was wrong, she'd probably kick his ass right to the curb. No, he was going to have to find a way, a very special way, to let her know that he'd never stopped loving her and that he hadn't made his choice to leave because of anything she'd done.

Then he'd seen his guitar leaning against the side of his couch and he'd suddenly known exactly what to do.

He was going to finish her song, and then he was going to sing it for her at Words & Music.

Goal firmly in mind, he'd gathered together all his notes and tentative lyrics, and he'd gone to work. Things had been coming together nicely, and he had high hopes that he'd be able to show everything to Brad within a few days. After Brad helped him polish the melody and the lyrics, Russ would be able to give Josie a concert, and he'd beg her to forgive him.

A loud clap of thunder was followed closely by someone pounding on his front door. He wasn't in the mood to talk to anyone, and he sure didn't want to be interrupted. Had the pounding not continued beyond civility, he would've let the person believe he wasn't home. But whoever it was still kept beating against the door as though something was desperately wrong.

Russ set the guitar aside and got to his feet. Without even checking who was there, he jerked the door open, ready to confront the rude knocker.

Instead, he found Joslynn.

"Josie?" Sweet Lord, she looked like a drowned rat. Her ponytail was plastered against her neck and back, and rain dripped from her nose, chin, and hands. "Did you run all the way here?"

"You're a liar!" Face contorted as though she were in pain, hands clenched into tight fists, she took a few hitching breaths. "You're a liar! And I *hate* you!"

CHAPTER TWENTY-FIVE

Joslynn was not only furious with Russ; she was furious at her own behavior.

How had she ended up here, at his place, crying and shouting and embarrassing herself?

If this was love, she was better off without it. Yet she needed him—needed Russ now more than she ever had—to be with her should she have to battle cancer again. She also realized that should he face the same future as Baron, she wanted to be the one to hold his hand, help him through his fear, and if the worst happened, love him through the whole damn thing.

But he left me—he stopped loving me.

She felt like a rag doll that was so overstuffed she was ripping at the seams.

With a shake of her head, she turned on her heel, ready to run the hell away from this unnecessary confrontation. She had enough to deal with physically. Emotions were just too…hard.

Moving quickly, Russ snaked his hand around her upper arm. "Oh no, you don't. You get in here."

She shook her head again, unwilling to glance back at him so that he could see the tears that were filling her eyes.

He was having none of it. "Come inside, Josie. Please."

Joslynn finally forced herself to look at him. Through the hazy veil of her tears and the rain washing down her face, she saw something she hadn't expected.

Concern.

If he'd stopped loving her, why did he look so worried?

Everything seemed so muddled, and she was suddenly exhausted. How far had she run? She became aware that she was shivering, and before she could decide exactly what to do about it, Russ swept her into his arms and carried her inside. He didn't set her on her feet until he reached the master bathroom.

Without a word, he grabbed a couple of towels, put them on the counter, and then picked up the top one. Her clothes were so wet that she was leaving a puddle in the middle of his tile floor. The shivering wouldn't ease, and she tried peeling her shirt off with unsteady hands. The clingy material was plastered to her skin, and she couldn't seem to get the damn thing to move.

Russ brushed her hands away. First he gently pulled the band holding her ponytail and let her hair down before rubbing it with a towel. Once her hair wasn't dripping any longer, he helped to peel off her sodden clothes. She didn't resist, although she thought about it. But common sense won out. If she didn't get out of those wet clothes, she was never going to get warm. Since her energy had evaporated, she surrendered to his care, wondering why he was being so kind and gentle.

Once he had her shirt and pants off, instead of taking off her wet sports bra and panties, he marched into the bedroom, returning with a T-shirt and drawstring sweatpants.

"Take a warm shower and then put these on." He laid the clothes down next to the towels. "I'll go make some hot tea for you."

"Th-thank you." Shit if her teeth weren't chattering.

All he did was give her a nod before he left her alone.

* * *

Although he was worried about Josie, Russ stepped out of the bathroom to give her privacy. Her trembling had eased once he'd helped her get out of her soaked running gear.

He wanted to get into that hot water with her, to hold her as he soaped her body and helped warm her chilly skin. Taking a silent vow, he promised to do whatever he needed to make things up to her, to mend the hurt he'd caused.

Would she let him back in?

There was no way of knowing, but he worried he'd inflicted a fatal blow. Joslynn had finally let her walls down and had given Russ her trust. He'd spit on that trust, even if he had done what he thought was best for her.

Yet here she was at his place, showing him some pretty strong emotions.

A spark blossomed in his heart.

The shower started, and he let out a relieved sigh. She'd been so docile that helping her undress had been like stripping a mannequin. While she showered, he went about filling the water in his Keurig and trying to find the tea he'd bought weeks ago when he'd learned how much she loved it. The box hadn't even been opened, because they usually ended up back at the Cottage instead of coming here. Since she always started picking up his things and straightening up the place, Russ had figured she'd be more comfortable at her home instead of here.

As the Keurig heated the water, he found a clean cup and the sugar bowl. Once he had everything ready for her hot tea, he went to the couch to pick up the clothes he'd tossed there right out of the dryer instead of folding them. No doubt she'd start in on that chore when what she needed to be doing was sipping tea and relaxing.

How far had she run? His place was at least ten miles from the Cottage. To run that far in the pouring rain, especially when the temperatures had taken a nosedive? No wonder she'd been shivering.

The shower stopped, so he went ahead and made her tea. A few minutes later, she stepped out of the bathroom, wearing his clothes. She'd combed her damp hair and pulled it into a ponytail again.

That familiar feeling of comfort he'd always felt whenever he saw her was quickly replaced by pain when he remembered she wasn't his now.

Well, then…He'd just have to do something to change that.

"I made you tea," he said. "Go have a seat on the couch, and I'll bring it to you." Until the words had fallen out of his mouth, he hadn't realized how much they'd sounded like an order.

Surprisingly, she obeyed without a word.

Russ got her drink ready, handed it to her, and then crouched next to her.

She cradled the tea in her hands and blew over the surface before taking a cautious sip. Her eyes considered him over the top of the mug.

There was so much he wanted to say, but the words kept crowding together in his mind. After she'd taken only a few sips, he took the mug from her and set it aside so he could take her hands in his.

With a dark eyebrow quirked, she pulled her hands back and folded them together.

"Josie, I…" Why couldn't he spit out what he was thinking, what he was feeling?

Because it has to be perfect.

Russ tried again. "I've realized something—something very important. And I want to share it with you."

Still, she said nothing, although her gaze held his tightly.

"My mom doesn't resent my dad for getting sick."

She cocked her head. "What?"

"If you love someone"—he picked up her hands and cradled them in his—"you want to take care of them through the good and the bad."

A look of panic came into her eyes and her breathing sped.

He wasn't sure what that reaction meant, but he was glad there *was* a reaction. She still cared, which meant he had a chance to mend things. "I understand now that it won't matter if one of us has something horrible happen. Sharing the good times will give us the strength to get through the bad times."

She jerked her hands back. "What are you saying, Russ?"

"That I'm sorry. That I want to be with you through better and worse and all the in betweens. The whole nine yards, Josie. Sickness as well as health."

Her eyes narrowed, and fury swept over her features. "Who told you?"

"What?"

"Who *told* you?" she demanded, jumping to her feet.

Russ stood up as well, entirely confused. "Told me what? What are you talking about?"

"You feel sorry for me now, don't you?" She shook her head. "That's why you're being so sweet. You feel sorry for me!"

He reached for her; she turned away. "Josie, I have no idea what you're talking about."

* * *

What right did Russ have to look confused? He was the one to bring up her illness.

How had he found out? Joslynn hadn't told anyone yet—not even Savannah or Chelsea. There was no way he should know that she might have cancer again.

Yet here he was, talking about wanting to take care of her if she got sick. The man had dumped her like a bad habit. What other reason would he be telling her that he'd learned something important and then follow that announcement with his statements about better or worse and sickness or health?

"I don't want you to feel sorry for me," she insisted. "I don't want your pity."

His hands settled on her shoulders, and he turned her to face him. "I was trying to explain why I broke up with you."

This whole conversation was a train wreck. "But you couldn't have known about my biopsy back then…"

Eyes wide, he grabbed her by the upper arms, squeezing her almost too tightly. "Biopsy? What are you talking about?"

She'd been wrong. He *didn't* know. Joslynn wasn't about to explain until she figured out what he'd been trying to tell her. "Never mind."

"Oh, hell no. You don't get to 'never mind' me. What biopsy?"

She shook her head. "Tell me what you meant—about explaining why you broke up with me."

Judging from the harshness of Russ's features, he wasn't about to budge. But he surprised her. "I wanted you to know why I did what I did."

"You mean why you left me?"

He nodded. "When I saw my mother's face…That day, remember? When Dad hit her?"

Of course she remembered. It seemed as though Russ had turned to a block of ice that day. She nodded.

"All I could think about was protecting you."

"I can handle Baron."

"I wasn't talking about my dad; I meant *me*."

For all the words being said, Joslynn still couldn't make any sense out of what he was trying to tell her. "You'd hit me?"

"I'd cut my hands off before I'd hurt you."

"Then what…"

"When I get Alzheimer's. I meant when I get sick like Dad. I had the genetic test, and I carry the gene."

Everything suddenly clicked into place. Russ had left her to spare her caring for him if he became a victim of Alzheimer's.

"Russ, you don't know that you'll get sick. Yes, you've got the gene. But that doesn't mean you're definitely going to have Alzheimer's."

"I couldn't live with the thought that I would do to you what Dad did to Mom. I couldn't wish that kind of life on you."

The NP in her wanted to spit out all sorts of information about the disease to try to give him hope that he hadn't been given a death sentence. Then the lovesick woman in her hijacked her train of thought as she realized he hadn't left her because he'd stopped caring. Instead, he'd left because he cared too much. "You still love me."

"Yes, Josie. I still love you. But it might not be enough."

"Bullshit."

His eyes widened. "I don't want you to go through what my mother is going through with Dad."

"You still love me." She wanted to shout for joy, because her future—no matter how short that future might be—was once again full of love and light. He might think he was being noble by walking away to spare her a scary future, but she wasn't about to do the same thing. Her love for him was every bit as important as the air she breathed, and if she was going to stare cancer in the eye again, she needed him by her side.

That was, after all, what love was all about.

* * *

Russ could see her turning things over in her mind. Hopefully, she understood why he'd made the choice to go.

Instead of doing the honorable thing and making her leave, he wanted to pull her into his arms and soothe away the hurt he'd clearly caused her.

But one thing kept intruding, crowding to the front of his brain. "Josie, what did you mean about a biopsy?"

When she didn't answer right away, Russ's concern grew. She finally let out a sigh. "I've had some…bad test results."

His heart started pounding like a jackhammer, and his stomach plummeted to his feet. He'd been so concerned about his own potential future, he'd selfishly ignored hers. She was a leukemia survivor, but that was no guarantee that the disease wouldn't come back. "Oh my God. Is it…? Do you have…?"

"I don't know," she replied as though following his thoughts. "I'm waiting on some more blood tests." She picked up his hand and led it to her throat. "Right now, all I do know is that my thyroid is swollen."

Thyroid? As he stroked her slender neck, his fingers found a small bump. Surely something that tiny couldn't be a threat to his beautiful Josie.

Ah, but cancer started as one cell, didn't it?

Her chocolate eyes searched his. "You still love me."

In a voice choked with emotion, Russ reaffirmed what had always been in his heart. "I will *always* love you."

Joslynn took both his hands in hers. "Then what you should've known was that neither of us should ever go through something bad alone."

CHAPTER TWENTY-SIX

Even though there was more they needed to talk about, Joslynn didn't want to wait another moment for Russ to touch her. She smoothed her palms up his chest and leaned closer. Circling her arms around his neck, she rose on tiptoes to kiss him.

He enveloped her in his embrace, pulling her hard against him as though he wanted to absorb her. As his tongue slipped between her lips, she moaned, welcoming the invasion and returning the ferocity of his kiss. Each low growl rising from his chest fueled her, making her body respond with waves of heat and longing.

Russ lifted her so that she could wrap her legs around his waist. Somehow, he was able to keep kissing her and stumble his way to the bedroom. He set her back on her feet and went about undressing her as she helped remove his clothes. Garments were cast aside as hands explored, reclaiming what had once been so familiar and so arousing.

He pressed her back to the cool sheets and came down on

top of her, stretching the length of his body against hers. Then he cradled her face in his warm hands and stared down into her eyes.

Had he never confessed that he still loved her, Joslynn would've known simply by the love she saw reflected in those blue orbs.

Could Russ see the same kind of love in her eyes?

"I love you, Josie."

"I love you too, Russ."

"Oh, sweetheart." He kissed her. "I've been waiting to hear that for so long." He kissed her again and nudged her thighs apart before settling between them. The hard length of his cock nestled against her core as he shifted his lips to her neck, where he nibbled and then soothed each love bite with a lick.

Nearly mad with want, she reached between them to take hold of his erection and guide him to her entrance.

As Russ drove into her, Joslynn wrapped her legs around his hips, welcoming the feel of his heat deep inside her. Tears filled her eyes as tension built. He would push into her and then withdraw, each thrust harder than the last.

She came in a rush, a burst of bright lights dotting her vision as shivers raced across her skin.

He was right there with her, chanting her name over and over when he poured himself into her.

* * *

Russ had never known the kind of peace making love to Josie had just brought him. Things between them physically had always been great. Satisfying. But this time, there was something more.

Since he wasn't one to question his good luck, he simply savored the satisfaction thrumming through his body and thanked God that she loved him. He withdrew from her and rolled to his side, grateful that she followed to snuggle up against him. All he wanted to do was hold her like this for the rest of their lives.

Unfortunately, reality would intrude. Until it did, he could keep his arms around her and protect her.

Protect her from what?

Biopsy.

The word was tattooed on his brain. It meant only one thing. Her doctor feared cancer. Russ knew nothing about what a thyroid did or whether it was something she could have removed and live without. When he had a chance, he'd sit down at the computer and see what he could learn so that he could help Josie through this as much as possible.

She couldn't die. That just wasn't possible. He refused to even allow that thought to take root. If he had to spend every last dime he had, he would find a treatment for her. She'd beaten cancer before. She could surely do it again.

"What are you thinking?" she asked as she brushed her foot against his shin.

"That I was so very wrong," he replied.

"About?"

"About thinking I was doing the right thing by sparing you a scary future."

She kissed his cheek. "If you love someone, you want to be with them through the good and the bad."

"Exactly. I'm not about to let you do this thyroid stuff by yourself."

Rubbing her cheek against his shoulder, Josie let out a sigh.

"Do you want to talk about it?" Russ asked. With his parents' situation, everything was out in the open because his father's symptoms were so obvious. He'd had no idea whatsoever that Josie was even having health problems. Not once had she complained about pain or feeling poorly.

"I guess," she replied. "There's really not much to tell. At least not yet."

"How did you know you were sick?"

"I'm not even sure I am," she replied.

He squeezed her against him. "I want to know everything, sweetheart. I want to do anything I can to help you."

Another small sigh. "I have blood tests a couple times a year. Just to check my numbers. It's not like I was feeling terrible or anything. I might have had a bit of fatigue. Nothing that seemed too horrible."

"And the tests came back...bad?"

"Yeah. Not terrible. Just...off. The doctor is running them again and adding a few other tests. And he did an exam. That's when he found out my thyroid had some swelling—a goiter that could be anything from a tumor to just inflammation."

"All this is new to me, Josie," Russ said, feeling ignorant. "You'll have to explain what a thyroid is and what it does."

"I will," she promised. "Bottom line is that I'm supposed to have a biopsy of the lump."

"Well, then. We have the biopsy, and then, when we have the results, we figure out where to go from there."

She kissed his cheek before laying her head back against his shoulder. "Since you told me about having the Alzheimer's gene, I should tell you about my fertility testing."

"You got the ultrasound?"

"I did. One ovary is toast, but the right side is working. It might not be easy to conceive, but I can get pregnant."

"That's great, sweetheart."

"After you found out you had the gene, did you change your mind about having kids?" Josie asked.

"I don't really know how I feel about it," Russ admitted. "But when your biopsy turns out fine, we'll have our whole lives to figure things out."

* * *

Russ paced the waiting room, feeling like a caged animal. This procedure was the most important thing that had ever happened in his life, and there wasn't a thing he could do except wait to find out if Josie was sick—if she faced another battle for her life.

This time she wasn't fighting that war alone. The stories she'd told him of her childhood leukemia made his heart break for the young girl without someone to lean on through the scary ordeal. No one should have to face their own mortality. But to do so when a person had barely reached a double-digit age?

Life could be so fucking cruel.

Would it be cruel now? Would it threaten to take Josie away from him when he'd just discovered that he needed her as much as he needed air and water?

Stop it. Stop borrowing trouble.

A glance at his watch showed only three minutes had elapsed since his last check. The world seemed to have slowed to some odd new dimension where time passed more and more slowly as his anxiety rose.

She'd taken the time to explain exactly what was happening back in the treatment room. Her thyroid—a gland, she'd told him, that controlled metabolism—would have a thick needle introduced into it after the area had been numbed. The doctor would suction out some tissue and any fluid that might be causing the lump. He'd check things under a microscope to be sure he got what he needed, and then all Russ and Joslynn could do was wait until a pathologist figured out whether she had cancer.

If time was going slow now, he figured the week they had to wait for the report would be agony.

* * *

Joslynn had never been as relieved as when the endocrinologist said, "I think we might be done."

The procedure hadn't been terrible. Lying on the exam table and tilting her head back to expose her throat was uncomfortable, because the blood kept rushing to her head. She could feel her pulse pounding in her temples. The shot of Novocain hadn't been too painful, just a pinch of burning before her neck went numb. Then it was only a matter of the doctor getting a proper sample. She hadn't felt much of anything while he'd been working.

Without turning her head too much, she watched him squeezing some samples onto slides and then looking at them under the microscope. She wanted to ask him what he was seeing, but she knew better. He couldn't answer her anyway. Procedure was to have a pathologist do the actual diagnosing. Should this doctor say he saw nothing and the pathologist later find a malignancy, he'd open himself up for a lawsuit. Not that she'd even consider one, but some people...

"Good news. I've got all I need." He stepped away from the microscope and removed the drape from her throat. Then he offered a hand to help her sit up. "There was a lot of fluid, which is often a positive factor. But..."

Joslynn held up a hand. "I know, I know. I need to wait for the pathology report."

"Exactly." She started to slide off the table, but he put a restraining hand on her shoulder. "Give your head a second to clear. I had you back far enough you need to let the blood circulate for a few minutes so you don't get light-headed."

She gave him a nod and felt a rush of dizziness that made her realize he was right. "You did a good job," she said, feeling awkward. Is that how patients felt around her?

No. Probably not. Joslynn was really good at filling those too-silent moments with chatter that seemed to make her patients feel more comfortable. This doctor had been extremely quiet throughout the prep and the procedure. It wasn't a surprise that he had little to say now.

Finally feeling as if her circulation had stabilized, she eased off the table, testing to see if her wooziness had passed. She was anxious to see Russ, and although her hopes had risen with the doctor's words, she needed Russ to hold her.

Joslynn found him in the waiting room. The place was next to empty since it was near the end of the day. She marched over to him, and he smiled and opened his arms. She slipped her arms around his waist and laid her cheek against his shoulder.

"You okay?" he asked.

"Fine."

"Are you in pain?"

"My neck's still numb, but I doubt I'll have too much trouble when the numbness wears off. Nothing aspirin can't handle."

He squeezed her tight. "And now we wait."

Raising her head so she could catch his eyes, she nodded. "Now we wait."

CHAPTER TWENTY-SEVEN

Although Joslynn still wasn't sure why, Russ had asked her to meet him at Words & Music instead of going there with her. They'd planned to have dinner with Brad, Savannah, Ethan, and Chelsea and then take in the show on "open mic" night. Watching the diversity of new singers and novice bands could be very entertaining.

She had wanted a chance to talk to Russ before they met their friends. The doctor had called with her test results, and she was still a bit numb. Once the news settled in, she would need to explain everything to Russ.

Trying to push aside everything Dr. Blunt had told her, she worked her way through the crowd to get to the table where only Savannah and Chelsea sat. Having no idea where the men were, she wondered if perhaps they had some business to discuss about the bar before they joined the women.

Whenever they were out in public, Chelsea and Savannah always turned heads. At least their fans seemed to be allowing them some privacy tonight. Sure, there were a few phones being pointed at their table, which meant their pictures would be on social media. But no one was hounding either singer for an autograph or a selfie. The regular customers at Words & Music were probably accustomed to seeing the women since both were there often enough.

As Joslynn pulled out a chair, Chelsea held up her mug of beer in salute. "Glad you could join us!"

"Me too." Joslynn sat down.

"I'm really glad Russ came to his senses," Savannah said.

"Me too," Jos replied as she glanced to the empty stage. "I thought this was open mic night."

A conspiring look passed between Savannah and Chelsea.

"Yeah, well…The guys had a change of plans," Savannah said.

"At least for the start of the show," Chelsea added.

Joslynn knit her brows. "What do you two know that I don't?"

Her question was waved away by Savannah. "Want a beer?" She signaled to a tall, skinny waiter.

"Absolutely," Joslynn replied. She wasn't much of a drinker, only having wine from time to time. When the waiter got there, she said, "Budweiser and a large order of fried pickles. Extra dressing on the side."

He smiled. "Anything the lady wants." He shifted his gaze to Chelsea and then Savannah. "Would you two pretty ladies like refills?"

Both women nodded.

"I'm starving," Joslynn said. She picked up one of the peanuts from the bowl and cracked the shell. After setting the broken shells in one of the small galvanized buckets that sat on every table, she popped the peanuts in her mouth. Judging from the number of discarded shells, the other women were hungry as well. "I hope the guys get here soon. Peanuts and fried pickles aren't going to cut it. I want a steak."

Before she could say anything else, the lights dimmed. When she glanced to the stage, she was shocked to see that the stage manager, Randy, wasn't stepping up to the microphone to introduce the first act. Instead, Brad took center stage.

Confused, Joslynn turned to Savannah. "Brad's the emcee tonight?"

Savannah squirmed as though her seat had suddenly sprouted tacks. "Sort of…"

"Welcome to Words and Music," Brad said, waiting as the noise from the crowd quickly lowered. "Before we begin our usual open mic performances, we have a special…um…*treat* for you." His eyes wandered the room before settling on the table where Joslynn sat with Savannah and Chelsea.

Joslynn immediately suspected something special was in the works. Was Brad going to announce that Savannah was expecting? Or had Chelsea and Ethan finally decided to tell the world about their marriage?

She was about to ask if her friends knew what was going on, which she assumed they did, but choked on the words when Russ dragged a stool up to the mic. Sitting down, he grabbed the guitar slung over his shoulder and shifted it so he could strum the strings. Clearing his throat, he adjusted the mic that Brad had put in the stand before heading offstage.

"What's going on?" Joslynn asked. She looked back to their table to see wide smiles on both women's faces.

"Just wait," Savannah said.

"And watch," Chelsea added.

Heart hammering, Joslynn focused on Russ.

* * *

"Hi, everyone," Russ said, trying to control the way his voice wanted to crack with nervous energy. "My name is Russ Green, and I'm part owner of this place. I hope you'll all indulge me a little tonight. I want to do something special." He strummed the guitar before looking up and shielding his eyes against the stage lights. It took him only a moment to find Josie.

Her face was full of confusion, which was exactly what he wanted. She'd been so worried about hearing from the doctor, he'd been unable to distract her for very long. They'd planned the evening out to catch open mic night, and he'd suddenly had what had seemed like a brilliant idea. Now that he was sitting in the middle of the stage, he was no longer sure it was so brilliant.

How could he sing in front of all these people, let alone sing a song he'd written?

Yet here he sat, and he knew it was the right thing to do. Russ needed Josie to know that he was in this relationship for the long haul. To convince her that he meant it, he would have to tell her how he felt *before* any of her tests came back. He wanted her to know that, regardless of what might happen to either one of them in the future, he loved her.

After clearing his throat, he spoke into the microphone again. "I wrote a song for the woman I love, and I'd like to sing it tonight." He smiled at Josie. "This one is for you, sweet-heart."

Trying to focus on the song and not the number of eyes staring at him, Russ began to play.

* * *

Joslynn had never heard Russ sing before, but she remembered that he'd said he wasn't very good. Now she knew why.

The man was tone-deaf. Not just a bad singer, but entirely in-capable of carrying a tune. Had there been dogs in the place, no doubt they'd be howling.

Yet he still sang.

To her.

> *Days, months, or years. Doesn't matter at all.*
> *I'll be by your side through the worst and the best.*
> *As long as we're together, we can avoid a fall.*
> *I promise you that my love for you will pass the test.*

Her heart was soaring, so full of love for Russ and his off-key voice that she was amazed she wasn't floating like a cloud. Tears blurred her vision, and she found herself seeing only him as she stood and then walked toward him.

> *We may have fifty years or just a single day.*
> *We'll live all we can in the time God chooses to give.*
> *You'll hear my love in each and every word I say.*
> *Give me your heart and we'll learn how to live.*

The melody didn't matter. But Josie paid attention to the words, feeling each one land on her heart and brand it with the sentiments she now realized she'd needed to hear. She knew Russ loved her, but in the wake of the fear she'd had over being sick again, she'd found herself doubting that he'd want to stay if she faced cancer again.

The words to the song he'd written—the one he'd told her that she inspired—said exactly what she'd hoped. That from now until the end—whenever that end arrived—they were in this life together.

Just as she reached the stage, Russ finished his song. He quickly set his guitar aside and hurried to the edge of the stage. Then he jumped down and took her into his arms.

* * *

Nothing felt as good as holding Josie against him, knowing that she was his.

Now and forever.

After a few moments, Russ eased back to look at her. Her smile enchanted him.

"That was beautiful," she said in a breathless whisper.

Although he grinned in return, he knew better. He might not be able to get his voice to stay in tune, but he knew bad singing when he heard it. And his singing wasn't just bad; it was horrible.

"It was," she insisted.

He had to kiss her for that sweet and entirely full-of-shit pronouncement.

So lost in her—the feel of her soft lips, the scent of her sweet perfume—Russ didn't realize the crowd had begun cheering until the sound all but deafened him. Confused, he glanced at the stage as Josie did the same.

There stood Brad, Savannah, Ethan, and Chelsea. Brad picked up the guitar Russ had set aside, while Ethan held his own. Both of the women stood in front of the microphone.

Chelsea was the first to speak as she smiled down at Russ. "That was a really…um…*charming* performance, Russ. But maybe we can give you a helping hand."

Ethan and Brad began to play Russ's song. After the opening bars, Savannah and Chelsea blended their incredible voices to sing the lyrics. They had to have gotten the music and lyrics from Brad, and Russ was grateful to them for bailing him out.

As the first verse rang in his ears, Russ started to dance with Josie, swaying to the song that had come straight from his heart. While he wanted to beg her to marry him right then and there, he knew she wasn't one to put a lot of value on marriage. One day, maybe, he'd convince her to take the plunge. But even without the license, they were giving each other vows. Right here. Right now.

She looked up at him with those dark, sexy eyes and smiled. "Thank you, Russ. Thank you so much."

He returned the smile. "I'm glad you liked the song."

"You really meant what you wrote."

Since she'd made a statement instead of asking a question, he saw no need to answer. Instead, he kissed her, letting her know she was right—he *had* meant every word of the song.

When she ended the kiss, her smile remained. "I don't have cancer."

His eyes searched hers, finding the truth in her words. "Oh, sweetheart. That's"—he lifted her to spin her in a circle—"fantastic!"

Joslynn was laughing when he put her back on her feet. "I'll have to take some medicine to slow the thyroid gland down, but definitely no cancer."

Russ kissed her again as the song ended to thunderous applause.

* * *

Russ looked at each face sitting around the fire pit in Brad's backyard before settling on Joslynn.

She gave him a grin. "Thank you again for the song."

Ethan and Brad let out loud laughs, which didn't come as a surprise. They both knew how terrible a singer Russ was, and they'd still allowed him to go out on the stage. Only good friends would allow a guy to make an ass out of himself that way.

"Just promise us one thing, Russ," Brad said.

Although he was pretty sure he knew what assurance his partners wanted him to make, Russ asked anyway. "And what exactly is that?"

"That you will never—"

"And we do mean *never*," Ethan said.

"—sing at Words and Music again."

While the women laughed, Russ held up his right hand. "I solemnly swear that I will never sing at our restaurant again."

Brad and Ethan exchanged an enthusiastic high five.

"I do need to thank you both," Russ added. "And Savannah

and Chelsea. You made the song sound good, something I'd *never* be able to do."

"It was a good song," Chelsea said. "I'm really proud of you for writing it."

"It's a one-time venture," he assured everyone. "I'll leave the songwriting to Brad from now on." He smiled at Josie. "I did it to win my gal, and since she's here with me, I'll call it a success."

* * *

Joslynn had never felt so content, as though every piece of her life had fallen into the perfect place. She found fulfillment in her job, her health would improve as her thyroid imbalance was corrected, and she had Russ—a man who loved her enough to embarrass himself in front of a crowd just to show her how much she meant to him.

God, how she loved him.

And the love between them would only continue to grow.

How wrong she'd been to believe that she was meant to be alone, that she wasn't the kind of person to fall in love.

She'd never been so grateful to be shown the error of her ways.

"A toast!" Russ held up his longneck beer.

Ethan raised his beer as well and wrapped his arm around Chelsea's shoulder as she held up her own drink.

Leaning against Brad's shoulder, Savannah smiled and hoisted her glass of apple cider.

Russ launched into his toast. "There are three men here tonight whose lives have been forever changed for the better by three very special ladies."

"Here, here," Brad said before kissing his wife's forehead.

"Damn right." With a big grin, Ethan pulled Chelsea closer against him.

"Guys, I don't know about you," Russ said, "but if it weren't for my Josie, I'm not sure I'd want to face the future."

"I hear you, brother," Ethan said.

"Got that right," Brad added.

"So…this toast is to Joslynn, Chelsea, and Savannah," Russ said, lifting his bottle higher. "You took three lost men and helped them find their way home."

Did you miss Brad and Savannah's story?

Keep reading for an excerpt from
Can't Walk Away, available now!

CHAPTER ONE

My joint is jumpin'.

Brad Maxwell smiled to himself, wondering if other people's thoughts often reduced experiences to familiar song lyrics. Trying to ignore the old song that was now stuck in his head, he wiped a bar towel across the already clean wooden surface just as a blonde and a brunette made themselves comfortable right in front of him at the only two seats left open at the bar.

Dressed in jeans and a tight red top, the blonde locked her gaze on him and smiled in invitation—a smile he knew very well. How many times had he accepted one of those promising grins?

Too many.

Instead of returning the smile, Brad focused on business. There were plenty of other customers needing service, and he was ready to move on and not waste his time with meaningless flirting. "What can I get for you ladies?"

The blonde cocked her head. "How about some conversation?"

"I can do that," he replied. "What's the topic?"

"Whatever keeps you right here. I'd like to get to know you better."

No surprise that the veiled offer failed to get a rise out of him. The game had grown stale. Hell, he'd lived like a monk the last six months. With a shake of his head, he slid the bowl of pretzels a little closer to the women. "Sorry. Too many customers to stay rooted to one spot. How about a beer? Something to eat maybe?" A glance to the stage found the first act finishing their setup. "The entertainment should start soon."

The moment he took a step away to check the drink queue on his computer screen, she stopped him. "You're plenty entertaining." She gave him a flirty wink.

He felt not a single tickle of interest. After grabbing a menu, he laid it in front of her. "How about I get you something to eat? We've got great appetizers. Try the fried pickles."

With a pouting bottom lip, she scooped up some pretzels. "Just a vodka stinger." No doubt his abrupt rejection had made her omit any politeness in her request.

Brad arched an eyebrow at the brunette.

"I'll have whatever's on tap." Her attention was directed at the stage, although she spoke to him.

No wonder. The first act of the monthly Indie Night was stepping up to the microphone.

Squelching a sarcastic reply, Brad grabbed a glass and poured her a foamy Pabst Blue Ribbon. Not his beer of choice, but PBR had seen a resurgence of popularity that he'd never understand.

After serving the women and topping off a couple of nearly empty pretzel bowls, he moved down the bar to slap down drinks for preoccupied customers. By the time the first note of music rang out, Brad was able to take a breather.

The singer launched into a rather ear-splitting rendition of "Take It on Back." Brad got himself a Coke and a handful of pretzels, hoping that the next act wouldn't sound like someone's cat was caught inside a clothes dryer.

After finishing his soda, he leaned back against a wall, closed his eyes, and tried to dismiss the noise as he chewed on the pretzels. Familiar smells filled his nostrils. Beer. Fried food. The mixture of perfumes and hairsprays with a slight hint of cigarette smoke that seemed to be the essence of a large group of people gathered together.

The smell of Words & Music.

God, he was proud of himself—a pride that had been a long time coming. It had taken him so long to accept he'd made more than a few mistakes and was ready to change his life.

Opening his eyes, he let his gaze float around the cavernous bar and restaurant. He took in the tall tables framing the stage and the dance floor. They were all full of people who clapped, whooped, or swayed despite the rather dissonant cover of a good song. The large dining area was packed, and there was a decent line in the waiting area, which looked to extend out the door. Every seat surrounding the wooden bar was occupied.

He let a lazy smile cross his face. Words & Music was prospering under his management—and his partnership. The old Brad was gone.

Hopefully forever.

"Man, my joint is jumpin'," he sang softly.

"What d'ya say?" Ethan Walker, one of his two partners,

cuffed Brad on the shoulder, near to knocking him over since he hadn't expected it.

"I said we're busy tonight."

Ethan nodded, his eyes following a route similar to the one Brad's had just taken. "Yep, we are."

Brad gave Ethan a quick appraisal, taking in his friend's ragged jeans and well-worn shirt. "Did you come right from the farm?" He chuckled. "I guess chicks like the rugged cowboy bullshit."

"Bullshit? I *am* a rugged cowboy. Besides," Ethan said, "since when do you care if I pick up a woman tonight? The way you've been acting lately, I'm amazed Trojan's stock hasn't plummeted."

That comment didn't deserve any kind of reply. Brad made one anyway. "I'm sure you're more than making up for my slack. Besides, I haven't found a woman worth taking a night off for. Not in a long time."

Unfortunately, the first performer was preparing to launch into his second song. Worse, he'd received enough applause that he'd probably be back to perform again next month—applause loud enough that Brad missed whatever smart-ass remark Ethan made in reply. Probably for the best.

Ethan nodded at the stage. "One to ten?"

One to ten. Their typical way of rating the possibility of any Indie Night act moving to the "big time" and finding a place in the cutthroat world of country music. "Two. Tops."

"You'd know," Ethan retorted.

Brad wasn't so sure. Once upon a time, he'd written songs for the stars, but he'd been on the periphery of that world since he'd vowed to get away from the shit and dishonesty that were such integral parts of being famous. As rapidly as Nashville reinvented itself, a few years might as well be a century.

No, Words & Music was his world now. "Hard to believe," he mused aloud as he looked around the place.

"What's hard to believe?" Ethan asked.

"This used to be two buildings instead of one."

"Yep. The Grand Theatre and Cole's Haberdashery, both of which were toast by the 1970s."

"Glad your parents saw the potential," Brad said.

Ethan let out a chuckle. "What they saw was a tax break—two rundown joints in the middle of town they could turn into a bar? Like they could resist that. No, I'm glad *you* saw the potential."

"We," Brad corrected.

"God, you're a pain in my ass. Fine. *We.*"

Why Brad had so much trouble taking credit was a mystery. Maybe he just wanted Ethan to know he valued the ownership trio they had with Russell Green too much to ever let them think this bar was his own one-man show. But once the three pitched their lots into turning the neglected dive into a showplace, Brad *had* been the one who insisted they renovate the old stage of the theater instead of replacing it. That stage had too much character to destroy. Instead, they'd knocked down walls to open up the buildings and make one enormous bar/ restaurant/dance floor/stage. There wasn't another place like it in Nashville, although places like the Black Mustang gave it a shot. Sure, there might be other multipurpose venues, but they didn't have the character of Words & Music.

Instead of commenting, Brad watched a woman preparing for her turn on the stage. Her back was to him as she looped the strap of her acoustic guitar over her head and draped it over her shoulder. She spoke to the two men who were her backup musicians. He'd seen them before, many times. Studio musicians who backed up a lot of different acts, which meant she was probably a solo act and had paid the guys to be her accompaniment.

When she turned to face the crowd, he drank in a deep breath. Damn, she was a pretty thing. Long blond hair—so sun-bleached it was almost white—that held not a hint of wave or curl. She'd tinted some of the strands framing her face a deep blue, something he found oddly attractive in its quirkiness.

Why did she look so familiar?

Brad moved closer to the stage to get a better look, not at all surprised when Ethan followed right behind.

The closer Brad got to her, the prettier she got. Her clothes were more "flower child" than Nashville. Flowing, gauzy skirt in a sky-blue hue. Ivory peasant blouse, secured around her slim waist with a braided leather belt. She wore several silver bracelets on her left wrist and a necklace of silver and turquoise. There was a small tattoo, the outline of a bird, on the inside of her right wrist.

Once she was settled on her stool and had adjusted the microphone stand, she spoke softly. Shyly. "Hi, everyone. Are you ready for a few songs?" She tucked some long blue strands of hair behind her left ear.

The crowd had grown apathetic during the set change, but she seemed undaunted by their listless applause. It had been years since he'd seen a performer who could exude such innocence and timidity yet still show poise, a stage presence, as though her shyness was part of her act rather than who she really was. Most singers would be shaking in their boots at facing an audience who seemed ready to start complaining at any moment.

With a sweet smile, she said, "Once upon a time when I was all of twelve, I got to meet the best singer that has ever lived. Y'all know her. Reba McEntire."

The audience warmed, applauding her choice of idol and punctuating their clapping with a few approving whistles.

"I doubt she'll forget meeting me," the woman said, adjusting her guitar strap. "After all, I tend to make a perfect first impression."

She gently strummed her guitar—a well-tuned mahogany Martin. C chord. Then a D4 before she gave the audience another bewitching smile.

The dimple in her right cheek made Brad's heart skip a beat.

Adjusting the mic one last time, she said, "Of course, my family will never let me live it down. How many people spill a Coke in their idol's lap and still get an autograph and a kiss on the cheek?"

The audience chuckled. With her spell now woven around the crowd, she nodded to her backup musicians and started to make music. Her voice, sweet and clear, was perfect for the old Juice Newton song "Queen of Hearts." The up tempo and her infectious enthusiasm had the audience enraptured. The crowd was eating right out of her hands.

So was he.

A hand waved in front of Brad's face. "Earth to Brad."

He ignored Ethan and kept watching the angel on the stage as she sang a second song—a Chelsea Harris tune—and then once again bantered with the audience. A rarity that the rather persnickety stage manager, Randy, was giving her a chance at a third song. He was notoriously stingy with new acts, but he evidently recognized talent when he saw it.

"Um…hello?" Ethan said, all but slapping Brad.

He smacked Ethan's hand away. "What?"

"Where'd you go?"

"Go?"

"Yeah, you zoned out there," Ethan insisted. "Missed a couple of really dirty jokes I was trying to tell you." His gaze followed Brad's to the stage before a knowing grin spread over his face. "Oh. *Now* I get it."

"As dense as you are, you don't get anything."

Ethan let out a snort. "The hell I don't. She's why you trotted up here. You wanted a better look. Damned pretty, isn't she?"

She was a hell of a lot more than pretty, but it wasn't as though Brad was looking for any feminine companionship. Even if he were, he wasn't going to get mixed up with an up-and-coming singer.

Where had he met her before?

"And that voice?" Ethan hooked his thumbs in his belt loops and rocked on his feet. "Do you see how she's seducing the audience?"

"I see." What the woman didn't realize was that she wasn't only affecting the patrons at Words & Music. She was also seducing one of its owners. "What do you know about her?"

"You mean you don't recognize her?"

"I think I do." He rubbed his forehead. "It's driving me crazy 'cause I just can't place where. You know how bad I am with remembering people."

All Ethan did in reply was laugh—too long and loud for a simple question.

"What's so damn funny?"

"Would it surprise you if I said I know quite a bit about her?"

"Where'd you meet?" Brad asked, not able to hide his curiosity.

"I know her birthday."

"Did you date her or something?" Not likely. Ethan wasn't known for being with the same woman long. He surely wasn't with someone long enough to know her age or when her birthday was.

Just the thought of Ethan having slept with the woman made Brad want to hit something. Hard.

"Or something," Ethan replied with a smirk. "I know her address, too. Might be able to get my hands on her phone number and social security number."

"Spit it out already."

"I can also tell you that she works tomorrow from ten 'til five."

"How the hell could you know all that?"

"You seriously don't recognize her, do you? God, what kind of manager are you?" Ethan asked.

"For shit's sake, can you please stop talking in riddles? And what does me being a manager have to do with anything?"

"She works *here*, Brad. Her name's Savannah Wolf. She's been waitressing for us for the last six months."

"What?" Trying hard to picture the woman on the stage in one of the red T-shirts the waitstaff wore, Brad finally made the connection. "Well, I'll be damned." As her song hit the bridge, he realized that he wanted to hear more from her and decided to do something for her he'd never done for an Indie Night performer. "Ethan, I've got a great idea."

"Don't you always?"

"How about we offer this woman a *new* job?"

A broad grin filled Ethan's face. "As a singer, right?"

Brad nodded. "Think Russ will agree?"

"Absolutely."

"Then let's talk to him."

* * *

Savannah Wolf gently set her favorite guitar inside its velvet-lined case. Her satisfied smile couldn't be contained. While she'd hoped for a warm reception for her first time on this stage, having Randy—Words & Music's rather particular stage manager—tell her to sing a third song meant she'd knocked her performance right out of the park. For that third song, she'd chosen "For My Broken Heart" by her idol, Reba McEntire, knowing most of the people she was singing for would recognize the pain behind the words.

Thanks, Juice, Chelsea, and Reba.

Those women represented the kind of country singer she hoped she was—a singer who took risks, who sang songs that meant something rather than churning out silly tunes that jumped on whatever the trend was. Her tactic had worked well the first time she'd stepped into the country music world. She'd started to build a nice fan base.

And then…

Nope. Not going to feel sorry for myself. Never again.

Her mother's mantra echoed in Savannah's mind, a mantra that had helped her through the last five years of hell.

"Everything happens for a reason."

Perhaps her budding career had died because it simply wasn't her turn. After the warm reception from the audience, she now had hope that her time had finally arrived—she could support herself with her singing and bid waitressing good-bye.

She had no illusions of being the next hot ticket, nor was that what she wanted for herself. Just a modest living singing at small venues, doing commercial jingles, or even backing up big names when they were near Nashville would allow her to provide for her family in a way she could never do waiting tables. That's what she wanted. What she *needed*.

When she'd finally made the decision to try for her dream again, she'd worked up some guts and dove right into the deep end.

And she'd been able to swim just fine.

Randy held up his hand, waiting for her to give him a high five.

Savannah obliged, even as he grinned and raised his hand a little higher as a tacit tease about her height. Or lack thereof.

"You kicked some ass tonight, pretty lady," he said as the next act launched into their first song.

"Thanks. And thanks so much for letting me have a third song. I sure didn't expect it."

Randy nodded toward the bar. "The bosses want to talk to you."

Shifting her gaze to the bar, she found her bosses standing there—Brad Maxwell pouring drinks, Russ Green and Ethan Walker sitting on stools. "About?"

"You'll hafta ask them."

Setting her guitar case out of the way, she said, "Then I should go talk to them."

"You do that." Randy patted her shoulder. "You really did kick some ass out there, and I'm not just blowin' smoke."

"Thanks, Randy," she said before heading to the bar. Practically floating on air, she made her way through Words & Music.

The place was packed, and despite the fact that a new act was performing, several people stopped her as she wove her way through the high-top tables. She smiled with each kind word about her performance. By the time she reached the bar, she had a broad smile on her face.

"Well, well, well," Ethan said when she took the stool next to his. "Aren't you full of surprises tonight, Ms. Wolf?"

"I suppose I am," she replied. Then she shifted her gaze to Brad. "Randy told me you wanted to talk to me."

After setting the beer he'd just poured on one of the empty trays, Brad nodded. His blue eyes found Savannah's.

The color was so vivid that she could only compare them to the ocean surrounding Saint Bart's that she'd seen so very long ago. The intensity of his stare almost made her glance away.

"You were really great up there," he said.

Her face heated as her smile returned. Here was the validation she needed from a man who had once upon a time been a successful songwriter. One day she'd find the nerve to ask why he'd stopped composing and now owned a bar.

"Quite a performance," Ethan said with a pat on the back.

She'd met Ethan at her interview. He'd hired her on the spot when he'd found out she was a single mother. His compassion had amazed her. Most people who came from money couldn't seem to realize exactly how hard it was for other people to earn it. He'd been around the restaurant from time to time to see how things were going for her and the other waitresses, and he always had a kind word for their hard work.

Ethan's hand dropped away. "Funny thing about seeing you onstage..."

She quirked an eyebrow. "Oh? What's that?"

"Brad didn't even recognize you."

Russ barked out a laugh as the scowl Brad leveled at Ethan was hot enough to set the place on fire.

"What?" Ethan's grin could only be described as cheeky. "You didn't, did you?"

Brad held his tongue.

It wasn't as though she was surprised. Ethan had interviewed and hired her. Russ had been in charge of most of her shifts. And the head waitress, Cheyanne, had trained her. The only times she'd seen Brad were on busy weekend nights. There had to be at least twenty-five servers working on Fridays and Saturdays. She was only one among many who wore the same red T-shirts with the Words & Music logo and black shorts. Since Brad requested that the waitresses keep their hair in neat ponytails, they tended to look like Stepford servers.

Plus, she'd only added the blue highlights to her hair three days ago. From his perspective, Savannah was nothing more than another short, skinny blond waitress. As manager of the place, he'd probably seen hundreds.

She tried to put him at ease. Not because he was her boss but because he looked so awfully uncomfortable at Ethan's teasing. "So you didn't recognize me?"

Brad shook his head.

"No wonder. For pity's sake, you must have to supervise more than a hundred people a day to make this place run as well as it does."

His frown eased and then morphed into a crooked smile. "Did you really just say 'for pity's sake'?"

Savannah folded her arms under her breasts, not quite sure of his motives. Sure, it sounded like he was teasing. But he was, after all, the man who signed her paycheck. "I did."

"Who says that?" Since his voice held a bantering lilt, she eased her stance.

"My mom. My grandma. Pretty much *everyone*."

"Not anyone I've ever known," he announced.

If he was open to joking, she could give as good as she got. "At least *I* recognized *you*."

"Touché." With a flourish of his hand, he gave her a corny bow. "I admit it. I didn't recognize you."

"Seriously, though," she continued, "I don't know how you do it, but this restaurant is the best organized one I've ever worked for." Not an idle compliment. She really did enjoy her shifts, although not enough to give up her dream and become a lifelong waitress. But for now, it paid the bills.

"Thanks," he said in an *aw shucks* manner. He pushed a wayward lock of his tawny hair away from his eyes. The man was in desperate need of a proper haircut since his hair was neither short nor long. Just somewhere in between, which gave it an unkempt look.

"You're welcome."

Brad waved to the stage manager, who came to join them. As Randy made his way through the crowd, Brad whispered something to Ethan and then to Russ. Both nodded as smiles broke out on their faces. Then he said something quietly to Randy. His grin was every bit as broad.

Finally turning back to Savannah, Brad put his hand on her shoulder. "Looks like your waitressing here is moot now anyway."

Savannah cocked her head. "It is?"

"Yep, it is."

Since all the men were still smiling, she felt as though she'd missed some joke. There was clearly something they knew that she didn't. "And exactly why is it moot, Brad?" she asked.

"Because you're going to be our new opening act," he replied.

ABOUT THE AUTHOR

Sandy lives in a quiet suburb of Indianapolis and is a high school psychology teacher. She owns a small stable of harness racehorses and enjoys spending time at Hoosier Park racetrack. She has been an Amazon #1 bestseller multiple times and has won numerous awards, including two HOLT Medallions.

Learn more at:

sandyjames.com

Twitter @sandyjamesbooks

Facebook.com/sandyjamesbooks